Sleepless Nights

Sleepless Nights

A NOVEL BY

Andrew Bergman

DONALD I. FINE, INC.

NEW YORK

LIBRARY OF CONGRESS CATALOGUE CARD NUMBER: 93-074485
ISBN: 1-55611-400-1

Manufactured in the United States of America

10   9   8   7   6   5   4   3   2   1

Designed by Irving Perkins Associates

Sleepless Nights

1955 / (1957)

DARKNESS outside the kitchen window. Five o'clock, an iron-cold January afternoon. I lie in my room, reading a Little Lulu comic book, suffering from a slight, almost comforting, flu. There is sudden shouting from the hallway: my mother is addressing the intercom, as frantic as the penultimate passenger on a sinking ocean liner.

"When will it be fixed?" she shouts. *"Liebe Gott."* That is not good, that *"liebe Gott,"* that means the answer is in the negative. The elevator is broken again; my father will have to take the stairs. Although forty-nine years old and in seemingly good health, my father is perceived in our home as damaged goods: fevers he had as a child, a tendency toward palpitations, things that are mentioned and then dropped without explanation. Things We Don't Discuss.

"He'll have to walk. Three flights," my mother informs me. She stands in the doorway of my bedroom, apron tied over housedress. Although no more than five foot three, she seems much, much larger. Her presence, her very shadow, fills a room. Her hair is already showing streaks of gray, although her face is as unlined as mine. "He has to use the stairs."

She waits for the answer.

"Oh."

"Maybe I should call and tell him."

"Then he wouldn't come home?" I ask, mildly panicked. "He still has to come home, doesn't he?"

"I worry so much about him."

I look at Little Lulu. She is worried, too, worried about her dog. The animal is missing, stolen by practical jokers.

"Who is going to worry about him but me?"

"I worry."

"His own mother doesn't worry. She worries about herself."

"I worry."

She leaves and goes into the kitchen. Moments later, I hear her on the phone. Like many German refugees, she doesn't entirely believe that telephonic communication has been perfected; therefore considerable vocal assistance is still necessary.

"It won't be fixed till seven-thirty," she yells. "I didn't ask . . . Maybe I talk to Mr. Sandy . . . So you'll come."

Little Lulu has found her dog. He was locked in her basement all along, a red rope around his neck. I feel slightly nauseous at the sight of the little dog locked in. I am not good with locked doors. Just imagining being outside the door to our apartment, unable to regain entry, with dinners being served, mail being opened, life continuing as smoothly and rapidly as if I had never been born. It is not even that I would wish to return. It is the thought that I would not be missed.

She stands in the doorway once again.

"So he'll come home. Your father. 'Three flights,' he said. 'So what, three flights.' "

"He's right."

" 'I'm not an old man,' he said. Be especially nice when he comes home."

"I will." My mother's eyes fill with tears; I can tell that a certain panic is gripping her. She wipes her hands on her apron. I feel a slight chill.

"Maybe they'll get it fixed," she says. "Maybe there'll be a miracle."

I AM on the floor of my room, studying the new Archie comic. Archie has accidentally dented the fender of Veronica's father's car, her rich father with the graying hair who looks like a character actor on the Jackie Gleason show. I hear voices in the hallway.

Mr. Sandy the super is standing in our foyer, conversing with my mother. Duke, the black handyman, waits out in the hall. He does not enter apartments.

"Maybe seven-thirty," Mr. Sandy is saying. "More likely tomorrow morning. They're not reliable. Sometimes they show up, sometimes they don't."

"It's for my husband. For myself I don't care."

"He looks like he's in good shape," says Mr. Sandy.

"Skinny as a rail," Duke offers from the hall. The door is open to the hallway. I come running out. Mr. Sandy stands with his back propping the door open. Duke marks time in the hallway, a hammer and monkey wrench protruding from the pockets of his baggy overalls like extra bones.

"There he is!" Duke says. I run straight at him. He grabs me, gets me in a loose headlock. A wooden-tipped cigar is clenched in his teeth. He smells of work.

"Where's your pals?"

"I'm home this afternoon. A little sick."

Mr. Sandy is bald and husky. He holds a pipe in his large, knobby hand.

"Young man." He has a certain formality, the way superintendents of apartment buildings did during the 1950s. To her: "He's sick?"

"The change in the weather."

"I'm not sick sick."

"He's fine," my mother says. She hugs me. "We stay on the safe side. He stays home."

AN ox's tongue looks only like a tongue. It does not look like "meat" or a "roast." It is only an enormous warm tongue with steam rising from it, bathed in the fluorescent light of the circular fixture in the dinette ceiling. Tongue and mashed potatoes. My father sits facing south, facing the window; my mother faces north. My older sister Carol, the model, faces east. I face the west. That covers the significant points of the compass. Dinner is largely a matter of silences, punctuated by my sister either kicking me under the table or, more distractingly, placing her foot in my lap.

My father eats methodically. He is a small, trim man with gray hair and a prominent nose. His eyes suggest that he is withholding some alarming news.

"What did you have for lunch?" my mother asks him.

"A sandwich."

"Where?" I ask.

"The Meister Brau," he answers.

She looks at me. It is the look that says I am to be extra nice to him, to this small and quiet man. He turns to me and smiles.

"I'll take you there again, the Meister Brau. When you're off from school.

"Great," I say. It is a man's place, the Meister Brau, noisy and friendly and a little alarming. I look to her, to my mother. She smiles at me. I turn back to food, then sneak a look at her. She is still smiling at me. Her eyes have not moved.

THE pipe and the newspaper. Silence. My mother on the couch, knitting, legs tucked beneath her. There is a mole on her calf; a crescent. I am on the floor, in a robe and underpants, reading Archie. Jughead has an idea to make money. It is quasi-legal.

"Jesus Christ," he says.

She looks at him, then significantly at me. My cue to speak.

"What?" I ask.

He stares at me for a long moment, then looks down at the paper.

"There's still some cases of polio. It's unbelievable."

"What a saint he was, Salk," says my mother. "A saint."

"*Is* a saint," says my father. "He's not dead."

"To do a thing like that," she shakes her head. "For mankind. Robby."

"What?"

She just shakes her head.

"For mankind. To do such a thing."

"It's great."

"Great," my mother says, staring off. "*Unglaublich.* Unbeliev-able." She smiles at me, wets her lips. My stomach begins to cramp. I arise from the floor.

"You're all right?"

My father fills his pipe. "Eight hundred cases in New York State. How people don't have their children inoculated, it's beyond comprehension."

"You're all right?"

"Bathroom."

"Number two?"

"I don't know."

"Tell me."

I am on the toilet, sweat coming through the pores on my forehead like water through a screen, rain through an open window. She wet her lips. Her brown eyes, the crescent mole a moon appearing on her calf. Night comes to the desert. I am in a tent, warm breezes push the flaps open. It is very dark so I cannot possibly see who is entering the tent. The crescent mole. Warm breath. A hard hand.

"What is it?"

"Please. I'm okay."

"Is it like the other times?"

"I'm okay."

"Is there pain?"

"I'll tell you after."

"Is it watery?"

"*Please.*"

"You promise you'll tell me."

"Yes. I promise."

"I won't have to remind you."

She leaves. I am alone with myself, alone in this house of vigilance. I take a powder blue towel from the rack and wipe my face. I long for a desert breeze. Music begins to play. He has put on a record: *Die Zauberflöte* . . . I bite down on the towel as another cramp hits. Small fibers of cotton in my molars. It passes. I arise, pull up my size twelve briefs, examine the criminal's face in the mirror. A smooth and innocent face seen head on; I stare slightly upwards. A different angle; the first traces of blue on the chin, the nostrils a little too wide, almost a mulatto, the curly hair framing my depraved features. I lower my head; the future bar mitzvah boy appears. I raise my head and the face changes once again. Up, down, up, down; innocent, depraved, innocent, depraved. I lower my shorts and stare at it. Undeniable. I touch it; it stirs, hardens, swings upwards. I press it against the cool sink. Undeniable flesh.

"You're finished?"

"Yeah."

"And?"

"I'm okay."

She pushes the door open with surprising force, the bolt slipping easily. I turn to her, still pushed, pushing, against the sink. She observes, the clinician, and then, then—did it really happen, any of it?—she smiles.

"Could you close the door?"

"Yes." Her eyes are bright. She begins to step inside.

"Not behind you! Please. Out."

"Such a little man."

She steps out, leaving the door ajar.

I SHARE a bedroom with my sister, the model. She models brassieres and panties for Girl-Fit, a large Seventh Avenue manufacturer of ladies' undergarments. At night she is usually out. In the morning, she is often still at large, her absence from our common bedroom weighing heavy on my heart. He's a buyer from Mamaroneck, she has informed me; a married man in the process, she insists, of obtaining a divorce from his alcoholic wife of eighteen years. My sister is a beauty and has allowed me for many years to watch as she dresses and undresses. Perhaps it is the modeling; she has no shame. I have held her breasts. She was sixteen. I was seven.

"See?"

"Yes."

"How they feel. They're heavy."

"Yes. I'm tired."

"You're embarrassed. Hold them. They won't bite."

I don't know what to do with them, these two warm mounds. My wrists begin to hurt.

"They're too heavy." I drop them.

"Never drop them," she tells me, arising from the side of the bed. "Let your hands slide away from them." She demonstrates, eyes closed. My eyes remain open. "Like that." She takes my two hands, places them back on her breasts. Her nipples peek through my fingers like little noses. The weight, the heat. I let my hands slide away with the slow caution of a mountain climber.

"That's it." She kisses me. "That's it."

My sister's absence at breakfast causes no stir, no conversation. The radio is tuned to WNYC, the municipal station which plays classical music all morning. My mother is having her tea and her oatmeal. My father is having his eggs. I pick at my corn flakes. My sister's place is set; she might as well be there, so totally is she ignored.

"It's going to be cool," my mother warns my father.

"I'll wear the blue coat."

"I took it to the cleaners."

"The black, then."

"High in the thirties."

I can only think of my sister, in the bed of this married man. Where is his wife? No, they must be in a hotel, one of those hotels in the garment center that look like bus terminals. He has lied to his drunken wife—unexpected trip out of town, commuter trains canceled—and has met my sister in this small and inelegant hotel. She has walked around the room in her underwear, exciting him. Although my sister has described him as "extremely sophisticated-looking," I imagine a man lounging about in striped boxer shorts and black socks, with a two-day growth of beard and a whiskey bottle on the dresser. Like the cover of a paperback book. "That's it," he tells her. "That's the ticket. Now walk back the other way." I am getting excited. My sister promenades around the room. "Now," he tells her. "Now." My sister stops in the center of the hotel room and turns to him. Mute, she slips one hand behind her back, Houdini, and unfastens her brassiere. They begin to slide out, an avalanche of flesh. The whiteness. The buyer can barely speak. "That's the ticket," he croaks. "That's it." He takes a sip of whiskey from a squat hotel glass, his eyes never leaving her. She doesn't even see him. She's thinking of me, me in the kitchen of her home thinking of her, missing her. Soulmates.

HE rises, wiping egg from his lips.

"Six-thirty?" she asks.

"Like usual."

"Don't get yourself too excited."

"I'm worried about Bob Larsen."

She stares at me. It's up to me to say something.

"Don't worry, Dad."

"Listen to him. Bob Larsen. They respect you so much. Bob Larsen, he changed his name. What was his real name, Lazarowitz?"

"He has friends. Stein likes him, Wasserman . . ."

"Not like they like you." She looks to me.

"You're the top guy there, Dad."

He's at the hall closet, selecting a hat.

"You get too upset over these things."

"You don't know a thing about it."

"I know you get too upset." A shake of her head is enough to cue me.

"They couldn't get a single magazine out without you, Dad." He is an editor at Chronicle Publications, publisher of a variety of trade magazines pertaining to the hotel management business.

He is at the door. The telephone rings. She picks up.

"Hello." She falls silent. "If I find it." She hangs up.

"Six-thirty," he says and leaves. Mr. Curiosity.

"Who was that, Sis?"

She doesn't reply. Of course it was my sister, calling from that hotel, looking for something, some article of clothing. And of course there was no reply. I hear the elevator door closing in the hallway.

"I have to go to school."

She steps toward me, puts her hand on my cheek. Her eyes are the darkest of brown. I remember them as black, but I know that is impossible.

"You get more handsome every day," she tells me.

"Mom . . ."

"Every day." Her lips brush mine, shocking in their meatiness. She smells of Ipana and oatmeal.

In my defense, let me say that I never actually touched her with my hands.

* * *

IN her bed at night, my sister speaks to me of her buyer.

"He is very gentle."

"Really."

"Very gentle. He wanted to be a musician, a pianist, but his father died when he was twelve. Can you imagine yourself, if Dad died? Alone with Mom?"

"It would be very tough."

"So he became a buyer of bras and panties. It suits him. He's an intimate man, unafraid to show his feelings, like most guys are. He doesn't put on a big front, a big show. He likes to touch me. Is this embarrassing you?"

"Not at all." My face is flushed, but it is dark, so she can't tell . . . My sister is lying on top of her bed, fully dressed; her lamp is turned off and her radio on. Perry Como sings softly of two lovers. It is a humid September evening.

"Because sex is really a beautiful thing. Has Dad ever . . ."

"No . . ."

"But you understand . . ."

"Oh, yes."

She turns her light on. "You must know about these things."

"I do know."

She stares at me, then smiles and turns her light off again.

"You know what sex is, Robby?"

"What?"

"Time multiplied by flesh. How does that sound?"

"Time multiplied by flesh."

"Yes."

"Interesting."

"Buddy said that. He said it is time multiplied by flesh. That's when I knew he wasn't just a buyer."

"He had feelings."

"Exactly. I can't talk to Mom or Dad about any of this, of course. Thank God I have you." She lies still. Outside in the courtyard a dog is barking. "Robby, when I'm out all night, at breakfast, do Mom and Dad say anything?"

"About you?"

"Yes."

"No. It's like you're not there at all."

"That's how it is when I am there. She hates me. He could care less."

"I'm not sure . . ."

"No. It's so. You're going to have a beautiful body, I can tell already."

"Sis . . ."

"You have a nice chest. You're slim. Just don't be a bully."

"Me?"

"With women. Respect them. Be soft. Listen to them. Hold them. Last night, with Buddy, we didn't even . . . we just lay there talking all night. About what we would do when he leaves Phyllis. Her drinking has gotten worse and worse, did I tell you?"

"No."

"He finds bottles hidden away. If it wasn't for their son . . . but he's going to Georgia Tech next year. He just got in, isn't that wonderful?"

"Why Georgia Tech?"

"He's brilliant in engineering."

"What about MIT?"

"Buddy has connections with Georgia Tech. Also, frankly, it's farther away and Buddy thinks it'll be easier for David if he's not around for all the mess."

"David's the son."

"Of course he knows his mother drinks. And you can imagine what that is for a kid, to see that lack of control in a mother."

"Must be awful."

"Whatever I say about Mom, she doesn't lose control."

"No."

A match is struck. My sister is lighting a Kent. Her side of the room fills with smoke. She turns her lamp on again. She is wearing a sweater and a skirt, and has pulled the skirt up over her knees, exposing her perfect legs. She searches around for an ashtray, brow furrowed. She finds an ashtray lifted from the Stork Club and the pages of another romance, that with Jack Selig, the former treasurer of Girl-Fit. Her hair is tied in a ponytail and her legs are spread apart as she sits up. She drags on her cigarette and suddenly seems very far away, pulled into another life. My heart sinks at the thought of the future approaching like a black, unlit ocean liner.

"Sis."

She reads my thoughts.

"I'll always be here for you, Robby. No matter what happens with Buddy. I've told him all about you. How brilliant you are." She turns her light off again.

"I'm not brilliant."

"Yes you are." In the darkness I can make out her profile, illuminated by a lit window in the courtyard, smoke webbing her hair. My sister, who rejected the opportunity to study at Vassar in order to remain in New York and model underwear.

"MAYBE she's better off," my father said at the time. "There's money in what she's doing."

My mother was insistent. "I never heard of such a thing. To get into a school like that and turn it down."

"Happens every day," my sister told them. "I have no interest in an academic life. I have a beautiful body."

"Please," my mother said, indicating me.

"I have a beautiful body," she repeated for emphasis. "It's not a sin, it's a gift. Jack Selig told me that in terms of modeling for both the standard and the uplift brassiere, that I had the perfect body."

My father began turning the pages of the *World-Telegram*, stopping to read the "Major Hoople" cartoon.

"Just so you don't regret . . ." he said. "With your grades."

"I can always change my mind."

"After modeling bras and panties," she said, "they won't see you in the same way." To him: "Tell her."

"I don't know that for a fact. Either do you."

It was May and the windows were open. Mr. Lander, the Jewish alcoholic, was screaming at his wife Ruby. The only word I could decipher was "raisin cake."

"I know that underwear isn't going to lead back to college. That much I know."

"And so what if it doesn't," said my sister. She was wearing her famous toreador pants, the ones she would don like armament before a battle. They were tomato red and she would complete the ensemble with a white blouse tied at the midriff and a paisley kerchief tied like gift wrapping around her slender neck. The total effect was devastating. To walk down a street beside my sister when she was so clothed was to experience the palpable lust of complete strangers, the yearning of pedestrians jolted out of their daydreams by the walking and breathing real thing.

"I want you to think about this," he said, looking up from the *World-Telegram*. "It's not something you just do."

"I know. I've thought about it."

"You're very young . . ."

"Not so young . . ."

"In future years, you may think, 'I could have waited for modeling . . .'"

"That's not really true . . . The average age of a top model today . . ."

"Listen to your father." She looked to me, shook her head. I folded my arms, then put my head in them to rest.

"In future years, and I know the feeling of regret, because I pooh-poohed"—and here there was a pooh-poohing gesture with his right hand—"the idea of education when I was in Germany and then when I was thrown out, it was of course too late, because I had to come here and make a living. But now I feel that the lack of necessary degrees has hurt me. I could have made more money . . ."

"I'm a woman. It's not the same for women."

"She knows everything," she said to him. "Every answer she has." The phone began to ring. It was eight o'clock, time for my grandmother's phone call. My father's mother.

"What should I tell Oma Herta?" She looked to me. "What do I tell her about the brassiere model? She'll have a heart attack if I tell her the truth." She leaned past me to get to the phone, her breasts pushing against my arm. She leaned harder, harder than was really necessary to get at the phone. Her breasts were now past my arm, digging into my armpit and part of my chest. "Cutie pie," she whispered into my ear, all hot, damp breath. Into the phone: *"Guten abend, Oma Herta."*

He arose and headed for the living room. Time for "The Masterwork Hour" on WQXR.

"So?" my sister called after him. "What's your final opinion? You've sort of taken both sides."

"Do what you think best. Either is probably okay." At this point my sister began to weep.

On the phone to Oma Herta: *"Robby is tser gut. Meine beste, beste bube."* She beamed at me, her hand in my hair.

"I DON'T see myself as brilliant," I tell her.

"You are. You have everything."

I hear rustling. "You getting undressed?"

"You want to watch?"

"Come on."

"I'm not getting undressed. Just writhing a little. Thinking about Buddy." The dog begins barking in the courtyard again, then reconsiders, growls, trots off, nails clicking on the concrete.

"Robby?"

"What?"

"You ever think about killing yourself?"

"Not really. Sometimes."

"How would you do it?"

"I don't know. Jump off the roof. Just such a mess."

"That's terrible, the roof."

"What would you do?"

"Gas."

"No.

"Yeah. I am taking my clothes off now." I hear her rise, then turn to watch the silhouette. My beautiful sister pulls off her sweater, unhooks, then sort of shrugs out of her bra, drops her skirt to the floor, raises one leg and pulls off her panties. She leans toward the window to open it, her breasts dusting the top of the dresser. I watch raptly; like all great performers, she draws strength from my attention.

"Why gas?"

"It's perverse, isn't it? After all the stories about the camps."

"It's awful. It's a terrible way to go. I thought women take pills."

"I think gas is less neurotic than pills somehow. Taking pills implies *having* pills, having them around. Gas is impulsive; it says she reached a sudden point beyond which she simply could not live."

"Which is more romantic."

"Which is more *serious*."

"I think they'd be horrified."

"By gas or by killing myself?"

"Both obviously, but the gas . . ."

"I think that's why it appeals to me." She pulls the window open. The Flushing elevated train can be heard, wending its way toward Elmhurst, Jackson Heights and points west. My sister steps back, runs her fingers through her hair, holds one breast and then the other, examining them. "Breasts," she says.

"Yes."

She gets into her bed. I hear her breathing. I hear a fire engine, far away, Northern Boulevard maybe.

"Robby?"

"What?"

"Come into bed with me."

"Sis . . ."

"I don't like being here alone. I miss Buddy."

"I'm not Buddy."

"I know you're not Buddy. You're you. Just come into bed and hold me, that's all I'm talking about. You're so far away."

"I'm across the room."

"You might as well be in New Jersey. I can't feel you."

"That's okay. You're not supposed to feel me."

"I didn't mean *feel* you. Don't be such a twelve-year-old. I meant in the sense of companionship. We put our arms around each other. I kiss your hair. Closeness. Feeling each other's sweat."

"What about them?"

"They never come in here. They could care less."

"But if they do . . ."

"I locked the door."

"You did?"

"While you were getting undressed under the covers."

I slide out of bed. My bare feet touch the linoleum floor. The floor is warm.

"Robby."

Two cats begin to fight in the courtyard. I sit motionless on my bed.

"Come on," she whispers.

I cross the room, pulling at my baggy New York Yankee pajamas. It is dark but for dim reflected light from neighboring apartments.

"Hi."

My sister tosses open the sheet under which she lies. She is casually naked. I get in, keeping my back to her. I am shivering.

"You're shivering."

"This is weird."

"Not weird at all. Lying in separate beds talking across a room is weird."

She snuggles closer to me, puts her left hand on my hipbone.

"What a bone. So sharp."

"Yeah."

"So here we are."

"I'm tired."

"No, you're not. Let's talk."

"Sis . . ."

"What do you dream about?"

"I don't know . . . all kinds of things."

The cats in the courtyard screech at each other. A trash can lid falls to the ground. I hear him outside the door.

"What was wrong with the other toothpaste?" he asks. Annoyance is in his voice.

"They said this is better," she tells him.

"Like what?" my sister asks directly into my ear.

"I have good dreams about flying."

"You can fly?"

"Yes."

"I had those when I was little," she whispers. "Six, seven . . ."

"I haven't had one for a while."

"Then you probably won't ever again."

"You don't think so?"

"No. It's a little kids' dream."

"I loved it. Over the countryside. Fields below, farm fields plowed like you see in Life magazine. Just by waving my arms."

"Just you, or you and someone?"

"Just me."

"Always?"

"Yeah. And sometimes I know it's a dream while it's happening."

"That's impossible."

"No, it isn't. It's happened. 'I can fly now because it's a dream,' that's what I think *in the dream.*"

"Must be a great feeling of power."

"It doesn't feel like power. It just feels like there's nothing between me and what I want to do."

"And the bad ones, what, the camps?"

"Yeah, Germans. I'm hiding. They're looking for me. 'Robby Weisglass, Robby Weisglass.' Furnaces. Guards in towers."

"I've had those."

"Standing there with searchlights. Sometimes I wonder if it's a dream or just some movie I'm remembering. The furnaces I know are from the dreams. That I never saw in a movie. People are inside."

"Getting burned alive."

"Yeah. When I wake up from one of those I don't want to go back to sleep."

Her hand now drops slightly. Her fingers are resting on the outside of my fly.

"Do they scream?"

"The people in the furnace?"

"Yes."

"No. They can't."

"It's all silent."

"Yeah. And I want to help them but I can't, and then it's not clear if I'm a Jew or a German."

"You're not shoving them in the furnaces . . ."

"No . . . no . . . But it's not clear what I'm doing there."

"You're a growing boy."

"I know."

"You want me to stop this?"

An answer doesn't come immediately to mind. The night is suddenly very still, just her silken hand rubbing the outside of my cotton pajamas, making a sound like soft wind.

"Just tell me and I'll stop."

I turn and lie on my back. I have no words.

"Hi, there, cowpoke. What brings you to Dodge?"

"Don't talk."

"Okay."

I close my eyes. Her breath is in my ear, then on my chest. The wind picks up, and I am lost in its force.

THIS is 1957 we are talking about. This is eight months before my bar mitzvah.

1977

A FTER my father's funeral and interment at the Fern Cliff
cemetery in Westchester, everyone returns to the apartment
of my sister and her husband, Sidney Mann. Sidney is the
president of the Creative Talent Agency, a man of influence in the
Broadway and Hollywood communities, a man who has been very
good to my sister. He has taken to her two children as if they were
his very own and has given her carte blanche in the selection and
decoration of a new apartment. She has chosen well: a ten-room
aerie on Central Park West and Sixty-sixth Street, in which multiple
bedrooms, dining room, library, pantry, kitchen, servants quarters
and massive living room all seem to spill from a bottomless well of
bourgeois good taste. Wherever one turns, there is a place to sit, a
watercolor to stare at, a place to hang one's hat, a window through
which to study drizzly Central Park.

Eunice, my sister's housekeeper, wheels around a silver tea service. A table is laden with cold cuts.

"Mom, you should eat," my sister tells her.

"Where is he?" she asks.

"I'm here."

"Robby's here."

My mother's eyes find mine. She turns to her sister Hilde, gestures for her to slide over. Hilde does so, with some difficulty due to

her hip. My sister puts her hand on my arm, squeezes it, then drifts away.

"Robby, here, sit by your mother," Hilde tells me. She stares at me intently, her eyes radiating curiosity, suspicion and neediness. The classic refugee look. She pats the cushion beside her and I automatically sit down. I attempt to make myself comfortable between Hilde's bulk and my mother's. It is an impossible task.

"How he loved you," my mother says to me, not for the first time.

"Yes."

"How he talked about you, right to the end. 'I'm so proud of Robby and his history.'"

"Yes." In the last four years of his life, my father had stopped speaking almost completely. It was not neurological, nor was it a function of the heart disease that had slowed him first to a crawl and then to a stop. It was simply the logical extension of a lifetime of taciturnity. Never a master of small talk, he had elected to dispense with it entirely. I assumed as a matter of course that conversations referred to by my mother were in fact invented by her in their entirety.

" 'And I'm sure his students respect him so much.' He said that to me on the way to the hospital, in the ambulance."

"I feel so awful that I couldn't get here in time."

"I'm grateful that it was fast for him."

"And I know Sis being here . . ."

"He didn't really know what was happening. It's fine. You had a paper to give, I understand that a hundred percent. It went well?"

"Pretty well, nothing . . ."

"Then that's the important thing. That you have your work." She turns to Hilde. "He had a big paper to give at the convention. In history."

"What?" asks Hilde.

"A paper I did on Wendell Willkie, Hilde."

"And they liked it?"

"It went all right. 'Liked it' is not a term I'd apply in that situation. It's not like going to see *Gypsy*."

"I'm all alone now," my mother says, pulling me from Hilde.

"You're not all alone."

"You'll come live with me?"

"I can't do that."

"Your room is still beautiful. The neighborhood hasn't gotten any worse."

"It has nothing to do with any of that. I'm thirty-two years old and it's just something that I can't see doing."

"What your friends say has nothing to do with it."

"I'm not talking about my friends. I'm talking about me, my judgment."

"What they say. Many of them, if they had their choice, would live with their mothers."

"I can't agree with that, but in any case this is hardly the time . . ."

"The social pressure. They're embarrassed to admit it."

"You're wrong about that."

"Are you afraid?"

Her hand is on my leg.

"Mom."

"I'm not stupid. You can tell me." This is the first time the Event has been acknowledged.

"It's not something I've forgotten."

"What?" She looks past me.

Maybe it is not being acknowledged. Maybe she partially acknowledges, maybe she obliquely acknowledges, maybe she is simply searching for what I remember, what lawyers call "discovery." Or maybe, my darkest thought, she is engaged in a kind of conversational chemotherapy, in which diseased cells of memory are cleaned out.

"You know what," I tell her.

"We were always so close."

"Close is one thing. But, really, this isn't the place . . ."

"When you saw that person, your friend on the West Side . . ."

"Dr. Singer . . ."

"He had his reasons for driving us apart . . ."

"He didn't drive us apart. I'm here, aren't I?"

"They have their reasons, those people. Closeness between parents and children, to them it's like a freak of nature . . ."

Sidney Mann stops by. He is a small and impeccable man of

perhaps forty-five. He wears a blue blazer, gray slacks, and black tassel loafers; his hair is prematurely white, his hands are small and startling in their softness. He kneels down beside us.

"How is everybody doing?"

"You're a saint to do this," she tells him, stroking his hair.

"It's taken for granted." He looks at me. "Right?"

"Of course," I say, I who take nothing for granted.

"Anything you need, Rob, *anything* . . ."

"Thank you."

"I don't think of you as a brother-in-law, not at all. Carol is so special, I always tell her, to me her family is my family."

"I appreciate that." I spot Carol across the room. She is speaking to her children, Jeffrey and Wendy. Her children from Stanley Warshauer, the famed patent attorney. My sister always married dynamos, as well she should have; but they only had her on loan. Hers was a nature, hers was a passion . . . one could not own her entirely. She spots me looking at her, smiles, points me out to her confused kids. Jeffrey, age thirteen, stares at me and I feel, as of course I must, that he knows something. This is a family in which secrets are as copious as termites.

"Carol looks gorgeous," I tell my mother.

"When should I expect you?"

"I'll stay for a couple of weeks only. Don't think I'm giving up my apartment."

"Who said anything about giving up an apartment?"

"You implied . . ."

"That was in your mind. You're a grown man, why would you give up your apartment?"

"I'm a little uncomfortable with your hand on my leg."

Aunt Hilde rises.

"Hilde, where are you going?"

Aunt Hilde doesn't reply. She is above replies. She is walking toward the food. My mother's hand is still on my leg.

"I need you there. I know you want to be there."

"I'm not sure."

"You just said you were coming."

"There's a lot of very strong stuff that happened in that apartment."

"I didn't have strong stuff? I wasn't thrown out of my country when I was just a girl in my twenties? My grandparents . . ."

"I'm not denying that . . ."

". . . weren't murdered in their beds?"

"All I'm saying is that the sexual stuff can't be just avoided."

"Your father was a wonderful lover. Only in the last couple of years . . ."

"I'm not talking about that."

She cries a little now, and that concludes this portion of the conversation. It is not sobbing; it is somewhat more alarming than that; it is a younger, almost girlish sound. After a painful and vacant moment, I take her in my arms, a father, not a lover. She is sixty-six years old, her hair is dyed black, and I don't know who she is. She has changed forms on me, but she has still weight in my arms. I sense all of her in my arms.

''IT'S only for a couple of weeks, until she gets straightened out."

The sky is black outside Dr. Singer's office. The only light comes from his desk lamp. Evening sessions invariably give me the creeps.

"I mean, I didn't know what else to say. I just couldn't find the means to turn her down."

"No."

I wait for more. There is no more.

" 'No,' is it? That's really not helpful."

I hear rustling behind me. Is he taking notes, is he leafing through a magazine, is he tucking his shirt into his slacks?

"No reply to that either?"

"To what?"

"My telling you you're not being helpful." A photograph of Easter Island, sepia-toned, adorns the wall over the couch. Those massive, primitive heads I've looked at a thousand times—inscrutable, dumb. The picture was taken by some famed refugee photographer, Lore or Lotte somebody. One of the hundreds of semi-talented Lores and Lottes who dispensed Art the way this balding putz dispensed Analysis. Why I continued to go, week after week . . .

"I said 'no.' "

"After I said I didn't know what else to tell her."

"I meant, no, don't fall for it."

"Don't fall for it because, what, it's some kind of trick?"

Silence.

"Is that what you're saying, that it's a trick? Listen, here's how I feel: she was married to my father for forty years. Over forty years, forty-two, I think. They met in Germany; there's a tremendous amount of history there—Escape, Renewal, Family. And now he's dead, not a complete shock, but he's dead, and she's obviously suffering. This is just not the time to turn my back on her, no matter what happened. It is not an appropriate gesture. We're talking about basic human decency, the obligations a child has to a mother."

"And you're the child."

"Yes. I am the child. If I was ninety and she was still alive, I'd be the child. Don't let's start with a lot of semantic horseshit, not today."

"When you hugged her . . ."

"I held her. She was sobbing. What would you do, minutes after throwing dirt on your father's coffin, tell her, Mom, go fuck yourself, because when I was twelve . . . Come on. It was a natural response."

"To embrace her?"

"To hold her while she was crying, yes. I didn't whip out my dick. I took a weeping widow and held her while she cried."

"And what did you feel?"

"I'm going to throw up. How can you even say that with a straight face? 'What did I feel?' Jesus H. Christ."

"Suggest another way to say it."

"To say what? The whole concept is so banal—this registering of feelings, one by one, like beads on an abacus. You put them together, they don't add up to shit."

"To shit."

"*Please.*" One of the Easter Island heads reminds me of my Aunt Hilde: that stony certainty, that mindless rectitude, that total absence of physicality. My Aunt Hilde could just as easily be called Uncle Hilde.

"When I say 'don't add up to shit,' I am simply using the vernacular; there is not, trust me, some unconscious doo-doo message lying beneath the surface, if that's what you're implying."

"I'm not implying anything."

"Of course not."

"I am intrigued by your reaction to my even using the word 'feelings,' banal as its use might be in society, the way it's been reduced by the dime-store psychologizing of the popular magazines. I can't help that; I still think it's a legitimate word; it doesn't have to be debased or hooted at."

"You know the song 'Feelings'?"

"No, I don't. But I can imagine it's a song that treats feelings like episodes of a soap opera. Again, that's not the business that I am engaged in."

"The business you are engaged in?"

"That's correct. I get paid for this work. It is what I do to support myself. I am a professional."

"You sound a little defensive."

"Not at all. What I am saying as a professional is that my asking you to describe your feelings about holding your grieving mother in your arms, considering the repeated instances of sexual molestation she engaged in . . ."

"I thought we agreed that it takes two to tango."

"We did, but you keep forgetting that I also pointed out that there is a qualitative difference between a twelve-year-old person and a forty-four-year-old person in terms of culpability. As far as I'm concerned, she took the initiative and to me that's sexual molestation."

"I hate that word."

"I don't love it either, but probably for a different reason than you."

"It makes me feel castrated."

"Castrated."

"Literally. Makes me feel like a young girl."

"Feel."

"Very funny."

"No joke is intended." I hear raindrops begin to pound on Dr. Singer's air conditioner. I turn around to see the rain begin to fall. He is staring straight ahead, a notepad in front of him, the only thing on his bare desk. Despite my fantasies, Dr. Singer is not doing the *Times* crossword puzzle, or scanning Buy-Lines for prices on used cars. He smiles. He has more hair than I remembered.

"Checking on me?"

"No. The rain."

"Yes. It's started to rain."

I turn back. It appears to be late afternoon on Easter Island. A hollow feeling coats my stomach, an atavistic yearning. Easter Island.

"I hate coming here in the evening."

"I have an hour open in the morning. Seven-ten."

"I can't come here at seven-ten. It's barbaric. But this . . . I feel I'm being kept in after school. Being punished."

"Because it's dark."

"Because you punish me. I volunteer to move in with this grieving old lady for a couple of weeks and you're all over me. It's not about anything other than getting her over the hump . . . Great . . . You know what I mean; it's about not simply casting her out there alone with no support."

"And you think only your physical presence can do that."

"Temporarily. Yes, that's what I think."

"What about daytime visits? Going back to your own home at night."

"Obviously, I would have preferred that."

"So you tell her, 'I prefer it this way.' "

"My preferences are not the only things to be considered."

"Obviously."

"You think I don't have the nerve to say that to her."

"I think that?"

"Yes. You think that."

"What do you think?"

"Come on. Stop playing shrink. Answer me."

Nothing. There is thunder from across the river in Jersey. The rain clatters ever louder on the ancient Fedders unit.

"I think you didn't say it," he says.

"I made it clear that I wasn't giving up my apartment."

"She asked you to do that?"

"She doesn't ask things, that's not her style. You say things to forestall the inevitable. It's like putting police barricades in front of a large but slow-moving truck."

"A truck."

"That's correct."

"Police barricades can't stop a truck, you know. The truck would knock them into splinters."

"It was a figure of speech."

"Yes it was."

"So she'll knock me into splinters, that's what you're saying."

"Is it?"

"I've never actually hit you, you know."

"No. You haven't . . . Would you like to?"

"Frequently. Today particularly."

"You're particularly angry today."

"At you. Yes."

"For doubting your resolve in resisting your mother."

"I think that you're sitting there thinking that he really wants to move back with Mom, that this is the moment he's been waiting for, that the memories of sex with her are so intoxicating . . ." My eyes start to burn. Please, God, not more tears. "He died, for crissakes . . . this is my father we're talking about, and for all his lack of feeling, his lack of involvement, his inability or refusal to protect me from her, the fact remains we're talking about my old man."

"We're not talking about your old man, we're talking about your old lady. But"—he clears his throat, I know what's coming—"we're out of time today."

I arise instantly, like a trained animal, and leave Dr. Singer's office without turning around. The waiting room is empty; no one wants to see him. It's a small comfort.

I walk the eight blocks home to West Eighty-third Street in a steady downpour, lacking both umbrella or raincoat. I am still crying, but no one notices, not in this rain. By the time I reach my apartment I feel, emotionally and physically, like The Tin Man. I take my red Samsonite suitcase out of the closet and begin packing; I promised I would try to make it home to Corona for a late supper.

I LIVED with her for two years. But that's another story. And it still doesn't prove that Dr. Singer was right.

1957

I AM very impressed with Lindy's. It is noisy and bright, and the waiters all appear to know about many things so ineffably *adult* that I can't even imagine them. You order the cherry cheesecake and they nod without looking at you; they are looking off, not so much at the future, but at the present, a present you are not a part of, not at twelve years of age. It is their world entirely, a world of waiters with thick eyebrows and yellow jackets, a world of people who consume enormous quantities of dairy products, because they are *experienced*, because they are *worldly*. It's about women in fur coats having their cigarettes lit. It is about what those women know and what I don't.

I am here with Carol and Buddy and *My Fair Lady* has just let out. My sister has sung "Wouldn't It Be Loverly" all the way over here and she is still singing.

"Lots of choco-lates for me to eat."

"She can't get enough of this show," Buddy tells me. "Third time she's dragged me, not that I mind, although it was better with sexy Rexy. This guy Mulhare's very good but he's got a stick up his behind."

"I thought it was great." I mean it entirely. "It was just another world up there."

Buddy smiles. "A better world, but what can you do? That's the beauty of great entertainment, right? Takes you to a better world."

He looks a little like Tony Marvin, Arthur Godfrey's television and radio sidekick. His black hair is combed back, with a strong and attractive wave in the front; liberal amounts of Wildroot give it a bold sheen and a cozy barber shop smell. The suit is sharkskin, the shirt white on white, the green Sulka tie studded with a diamond "BE." It is inconceivable to me that this man could be the father of a college-bound son, but entirely believable that he could have inadvertently married a drunk. He is a true romantic, this Buddy, Buddy Eisenman, and wild for my sister. During the Ascot number, he had slipped his manicured fingers cleanly up her skirt; without missing a beat, she had opened her legs to accommodate him. She was seated between us, and moments after he had taken her with his hand, she put her own soft hand on mine, just to include me. I genuinely appreciated the gesture.

"Thanks," I had whispered and she simply squeezed my hand in reply, never taking her eyes from the prancing lords and ladies on stage.

Now she is staring at a veritable Mont Blanc of plain, unfruited cheesecake. Buddy is sticking to coffee; his arm is on the back of my sister's chair. He watches with a kind of wary pride as the waiter puts a wedge of cherry cheesecake before me.

"Ever seen anything like that?"

"No."

"His first time," he says to the waiter. My sister looks at me and smiles.

"His first time for cheesecake, you mean." She licks some crumbs off her fork.

"Of course that's what I mean.

"Mazel tov," says the waiter. "Many more."

Carol smiles at me. She is wearing a V-necked cashmere sweater, Kelly-green; a small diamond on a gold chain, Buddy's largesse, rests in the hollow between her breasts. I bite into the cheesecake.

"What do you think, son?" asks Buddy, sipping his coffee. "You could go all over the world, I don't care what, you won't eat anything like that."

It doesn't even taste like food; it is some sensual other thing—its slow, soft thickness, its wetness. It is actually overwhelming.

"It's like nothing else, is it?" my sister asks. "There's just something about it."

"She gets started on the cheesecake, I get embarrassed," Buddy says, pecking her on the cheek. "Not that I'm easily embarrassed." Buddy looks to me for something, there is a plaintive expression on his open commercial face. What he wants is for me to like him. Here in Lindy's. "You know, Rob, I have a boy even older than you. He's seventeen, terrific engineering student, good athlete. The athletics he got from me, the engineering, probably from his mother, who was a nursing student when I met her. That's a long time ago, when nursing was, I don't know, not upper-class, but more something for young ladies. You follow?"

"Yes." I don't really know what he is talking about, but there is an aura of declaration about it. It is something of importance to Buddy and my sister senses it also because she puts down her fork and places her arm through his.

"I don't know what you think about a man with a seventeen-year-old son who takes your sister out on dates." Dates. Fucking her till dawn in the Hotel Wallace on West Thirty-fifth Street.

"It's not really . . ."

"Let me finish, please, Rob." He takes a handkerchief from his jacket pocket, dabs daintily at his brow. Carol gazes at me with the serenity of a countess sitting for her portrait. Secure in her sexuality, the owner of my heart and of my twelve-year-old dick. I look down at my cheesecake, not knowing whether it is proper, in this circumstance, to take another bite of it.

"What I'm saying is that my wife Phyllis has a drinking problem. 'Serves him right for marrying a *shiksa*,' I know you're thinking."

"Not at all."

"Robby would never think that."

"Lots of people have," he says to my sister. "Including people you know, to wit, for example, Mr. A. at Girl-Fit, Mr. D. at Contour. They have all said things—sometimes to me directly, sometimes behind my back. I married for love, that's the sum of it, Robby."

"Sure."

"Not for calculation, not for currying favor, God knows. When I told my mother, God rest her soul, who I was marrying, it was some scene, you could have put it on a Broadway stage for the screaming and the carrying on."

"I can imagine."

"Buddy tells me what went on," my sister says, picking a hair from his lapel, "I can hardly believe it. From the Stone Ages."

"Threatening to disown me. This is 1939 we're talking about, a provincial mentality. What I'm saying, Robby, and that's one of the reasons I wanted today to happen, is that I don't hold your sister cheap."

"He knows that, Buddy."

"But he's never heard it from the horse's mouth." He leans toward me. "Rob, with all your sister's beauty and her figure, people can get the idea I'm just some fox hunter, a chaser of trophies."

"I really never thought that, Mr. Eisenman."

"I love your sister." Tears come to his eyes, big glistening tears. My sister appears confused—no one cries in our family, ever.

"Buddy," she says, appalled. "In Lindy's . . . Jesus Christ . . ."

"I can cry anywhere." He attempts to cover the rising sobs with a chuckle, but finally must cover his entire face with a linen napkin. "I love your sister so much."

"I'm sure you do." The people at the next table begin to stare openly. We are an unlikely and photogenic threesome, for sure, but as much as my sister likes to be noticed, she does not like to be observed.

"Buddy," she says to him. "Buddy, please."

"When I think"—he lowers the napkin, his eyes streaming—"when I think of my kid and then I see you at twelve, your whole beautiful life in front of you, and here's this grown man with your big sister, trying to salvage some little raft of decency and romance out of the ship's wreckage of his life . . ."

"Don't get all flowery," my sister warns him, and I can see at that moment that she is a creature made in equal parts of velvet and chrome steel.

"I wanted to be a musician," he tells me. "And then it happens. Bit by bit. From the dreams of being a Josef Hoffman or a Walter Gieseking to the world of commerce, the world of buying underwear for Stern's."

"I certainly don't blame you, sir."

"One has to make a living."

"Yes."

"One has to make one's way. If one door is locked, you try another. That the door which finally opened for me is not an artistic or creative one is a source of regret to me, I don't deny this. But I made my way in this world, I provided for my family, I did what a grown man does. However, I now reach a point in my life where I can't deny my heart." He wipes his eyes, kisses my sister on the cheek. She looks at me.

"Let him finish his cheesecake, Buddy; he's waiting for you to stop."

"You understand what I'm getting at, son?" he asks me.

"I do."

"It must sound . . ."

"No, I do."

"I'm sure your own dad, although from what Carol tells me . . ."

"He doesn't say much."

"Yes. But he must have his regrets." He now looks wildly around the restaurant and calls to the waiter. "Bring me a cheesecake! Plain."

ALONE with my parents on a Saturday night. He is in the living room reading *The Caine Mutiny* and listening to *Fidelio;* she is in their bedroom, "under the weather," making phone call after phone call to relative after relative. My sister is in Vermont, shooting a "layout."

"Ah, die naemenlose freude."

"How's the book, Dad?"

He looks up, nods.

"Helluva writer, Wouk. Helluva writer. You reading something?"

I hold up the latest issue of Mad magazine, which contains a parody of the television show "Maverick." My father stares at the cover—Alfred E. Newman in a Sioux Indian headdress—and shakes his head. "That sells like hotcakes, Abe Weiner told me. Hotcakes. They had a chance to buy in once and turned it down. They're kicking themselves." This is a massive conversation we are having. I am almost breathless—wondering what to ask next, rehearsing questions—as if suddenly granted audience with a celebrity, an Eisenhower, a Stevenson.

"Everybody I know buys it."

"Like hotcakes. They kicked themselves around the block." He stops, puffs on his pipe, listens. " *'Die naemenlose freude.'* The joy without a name."

"What is that?"

"Fidelio."

"No, I meant the 'joy without a name.' What is that?"

" *'Die naemenlose freude.'* The feeling . . ." He stops, turns to the window. It is a February night and the wind outside on Ninety-seventh Street is howling; the shadow of a tree branch moves sideways, reflected by a streetlamp against the icy windowpane. The night. The dark. He turns back, saddened, as if he has just seen something. "The feeling . . . what would be the word? Euphoria? An indescribable joy. Florestan is singing, he's a prisoner, and he has just been reunited, in jail, with his lover Leonore."

"That's why he's singing."

"If he doesn't sing, he gets fired. It's an opera."

"You know what I mean."

"Yes. That is why he is singing. The whole opera is about freedom—political freedom, personal freedom. *'Freiheit.'* 'The nameless joy' is the joy of freedom."

"Did you feel that way when you came to this country?"

"Free?"

"Yes."

"Certainly. Free and frightened. I've told you this story." A million times, but it is the story that sustains me throughout my childhood, the myth of safety, of twinkling harbors. "It was late at night, eleven or twelve, and I was in my room on the *George Washington,* which was basically a tub. I knew we were getting close to New York and so I couldn't sleep."

"You were so excited."

"I stared at the ceiling, imagining what I was about to see, which I had only observed in books . . ."

"In Germany."

"In Germany. We had a book at home, *Fotografieren aus New*

York, which I looked at all the time. So I had an idea about New York."

"The lights."

"The lights, the buildings. And so I was in my bunk, in my room, a little seasick probably, I wasn't the greatest sailor in the world, when I heard footsteps outside, then more footsteps. Then I heard someone say, 'We're there!' "

"You must have felt . . ."

"I leapt up out of bed, and threw my clothes on."

"What were you wearing?" I know the answer, of course; that is what makes it all so wonderful. It is like we are having a conversation, with none of the risk.

"I was in my nightshirt, a red one, I remember, flannel, because it was a cold night. March. I threw off the nightshirt, jumped into my pants . . ."

"Really jumped?"

"Really jumped. I was a young man, remember. I threw on a sweater and my overcoat and hat and I ran outside. People were coming from all directions, running toward the iron stairs that led to the "B" deck. That was our deck, the "B" deck."

"So you started running with them."

"I ran with them and halfway up the stairs, I began to see the lights . . ."

"Of the city."

"Of the city. Then I got to the deck, and the boat was rocking and in my memory I wonder if it was rocking from the ocean or from the emotions of the people."

"They were emotional."

"They were crying, they were shouting. Children were lifted up on shoulders, all to see this unbelievable sight of Lower Manhattan lit up. I couldn't speak."

"You were so excited."

"I saw my cousin Alfred on deck and he was crying."

"Were you crying?" I knew the answer, of course, but I always hoped it would be different.

"No. But I certainly felt this . . . powerful feeling."

"You felt safe."

He is no longer looking at me. "It had been a murderous time with the Nazis—and this was only 1937, before any of the really heavy stuff had started. But it was bad enough. And now here was New York, all lit up, looking, you know, like the photos, but of course the photos couldn't do justice to the size of it all. That was so amazing to me—the size of the buildings."

"And the lights."

"And the lights, the brilliance of the lights, the way they lit up the water, so it was like you were riding on light. And then people started turning their heads, and some began running to the other side of the deck."

"That was for the Statue of Liberty."

"Which was an incredible sight. It was such a cold night, really, but when you saw her there, it could have been twenty below zero, all you would have felt was this warmth, this unbelievable safety. It took another two hours, because the boat was moving slowly, and then of course the tugboats had to come out to guide us, maybe it was more than two hours, who the hell knows anymore, all I know is from that point on no one left the deck."

"So it was two in the morning when you came in."

"At the earliest. Uncle Leopold and Tante Augusta were waiting for me."

"Were you happy they were there?"

"I was hoping Carole Lombard would be there, but since she didn't know I was coming, I settled for them."

"And do you have any regrets?"

"Regrets?"

"In life."

"Nothing major." Does he suspect nothing? Does he know and not care?

She comes out with an ice bag on her head. She is wearing a robe, its belt tied very loosely; underneath she is wearing a black brassiere and black panties.

"Too loud. I could barely hear Tante Laura. Do you mind?" She turns the volume down on *Fidelio* until it is barely audible. "That's better."

"I can barely hear it."

"What were you two talking about?" It does not seem like an entirely friendly question.

"The old days," I tell her.

"He was lucky. He didn't lose anybody."

"Fritz Wallerstein."

"You couldn't stand him. When I think of my grandparents, who were saints. If you had known them, Robby . . ." She goes to the window and looks out onto Ninety-seventh Street. "That this happened to me, with my grandparents, to die like that. With Opa," her father, "that was an accident. Those things happen . . ." Her robe has opened completely. "But this, this horror . . . Whatever happens to you in your life, Robby, thank God, that is one thing you don't have to worry about."

"You never know . . ."

"You can't imagine. To look out your window in the morning and see SS guards outside, telling you they will shoot at you if you leave the house . . ." He has gone back to *The Caine Mutiny*. He has gone back to puffing on his pipe. "This is something you never forget." She turns back from the window, her robe open. Her body is still, at forty-four, trim and firm, not as lush as my sister's but more wicked in some elusive way. Maybe because of who she is, my actual birth mother, or maybe because of her need, which is not for seduction but for something more urgent.

THAT night, at three in the morning, my sister frolicking in remote Vermont, I am alone in my room, asleep beneath my down comforter. But not so deeply asleep that I cannot hear the door across the hall suddenly close and my own door open.

"I can't sleep," she whispers. I don't respond, so she simply climbs into bed, quickly covering me with her own body. I am overwhelmed with terror.

"Mom . . ." She kisses me.

"Little girl friend you call me. Little girl friend. Suzie . . ."

Her body is warm on top of my body and she is really moving, rapidly. Her hand finds me and, yes, I respond. Not fully, God knows, but enough. A hand is a hand.

"And you're my little boy friend."

"Where's Dad?"

"He's tired and he doesn't feel so well, Robby. This is something you do for him."

"And if he wakes up?"

"He doesn't wake up. You talk as if we do something wrong. What is this? This is because we love each other." Her warm hard breast brushes past my lips. It lacks my sister's full rosy newness. This is a European breast, older, more worn. But it has a kind of bristly, no-nonsense sensuality.

"Now, for fun, little boy friend . . ."

And suddenly I am in the place of my very origins, the liquid center of the earth. My eyes are shut tightly, there is a pounding in my ears.

"Little boy friend, little boy friend . . ."

There is a creak in a floorboard. She stops for an instant. I throb, eyes still shut. Another creak; it is upstairs. She resumes—slower, quieter. I put my pillow over my face, then I feel her head resting on the pillow, hear her whispers, growing ever quicker, like The Little Engine That Could.

"Little cute boy friend. Little cute boy friend."

When she leaves, wordlessly, three minutes later, I am unspent.

"It was just for fun," she tells me.

THE next morning, Sunday, I do not want to get up for our traditional eggs-and-salami breakfast. There is much door-knocking. Finally she enters.

"Your father made them special for you. Don't disappoint him."

"Mom."

"What, darling?"

"Last night . . ."

"Hurry. They're getting cold. And we have to pick up Tante Bertha by eleven I told her." She leaves. I arise from bed, open the fly of my pajamas. It is still there, smooth and unmarked. As if nothing had happened. Still mine, after all.

At breakfast, he reads the Sunday *Times* and Sunday *News*. I scan the *News* comics—Dick Tracy, Gasoline Alley, Smokey Stover, Winnie Winkle—and don't look up except to pick at my eggs. The radio is on, a Mozart flute concerto.

"Eisenhower's health isn't so hot," he says at one point, staring into the *Times* as if into the future. "Can you imagine if something happens to him and we get Nixon. *Liebe Gott.*"

I look at him at this point, this wiry silent man with his wire-rimmed glasses and Sunday flannel shirt. This man who I have stabbed in the back without meaning to or wanting to, this man whom I have castrated. My mother notices me looking at him and, amazingly, smiles. Coffee cup in hand, she looks around the table and announces, "It's going to be a wonderful Sunday. A real family day."

I get my coat and put it on, then proceed into our bathroom, where I retch. My face in the mirror is now utterly criminal. My father knocks on the door.

"Hurry, Rob."

I wash my face, hands shaking, and go to join them. My mother puts a hat on my head. I take it off and throw it to the floor. My father doesn't notice. My mother picks the hat up off the floor and puts it back in the closet, then walks out the door.

Despite the fact that it is February and the temperature no more than forty degrees, my parents have elected to drive to Rockaway Beach for the *"frische luft,"* the fresh air. This outing first involves a stop in Woodside to pick up my mother's Tante Bertha, the youngest sister of her late father. My mother's mother, Oma Hedwig, to complete this run of genealogy, is in residence at the St. Clair Home, an asylum for the insane located off the Palisades Parkway, in West Nyack, New York. My mother visits Oma Hedwig once a month and then takes to her bed. I go twice a year with my father, while my mother waits in the car. My maternal grandmother is a majestic woman, nearly six feet tall, with a leonine shock of white hair and frozen blue eyes. Despite her piercing and intelligent gaze, she recognizes no one; and has not since 1944, the year after her husband's death in a traffic accident. My grandfather, Heinrich Kurtz, drove a Bungalow Bar ice-cream truck, despite failing eyesight, and was, according to legend, one of the company's most beloved drivers. Photographs depict the bushy eyebrows and cartoon mustache; a thick accent and tendency toward the ice-cream malaprop—"pinstachio"—complete the aural portrait; he was a figure of Alpine quaintness, by legend irresistible to both young and old. One July afternoon, apparently daydreaming, he looked up on Junction Boulevard to see that he was on a collision course with a trolley car. Swerving to avoid disaster, he lost control of the vehicle and barreled into the window of the Loft's Candy Shop, dying instantly. The Loft's company sued Bungalow Bar, in a court action that made the local papers as "The Chocolate Wars," and made my grandfather's defective vision a matter of public record. It was a very mild form of notoriety, but enough, coupled with the shock of his bizarre and untimely end, to drive Grandma Hedwig insane.

Insane but impeccable. She sits in her room like Queen Victoria, disdaining her bed and radio, always beautifully groomed and dressed. There she sits, serenely eating newspapers and magazines. My father's little joke to me, out of earshot of my mother, is that we should bring Oma Hedwig the Sunday *Times* as a Thanksgiving treat. She eats these publications slowly and methodically, ripping out a page at a time, then tearing each page into quarters, folding them over again and then placing them in her mouth like communion wafers. "All the News That's Fit to Eat" as my father puts it. We do not speak on these visits, just basically sit and watch her eat. My father always brings flowers and is able to spend some time finding a vase for them, going down the hall for water or sending me. That kills a few minutes. And then we leave, for a "report" to my mother, the report always being the same.

"All right," she says calmly. "What can we do. It's God's will." And then we go home and she takes to her bed anyhow. Just proximity to the St. Clair Home is enough to send her into a spell. She eats no dinner, just tea and some zwieback, while my father, my sister and I have quiet sandwiches, keeping some sort of watch, as if a religious holiday was being observed.

The other Sundays are, on the surface at least, more conventional. The wrinkle today, as we pull up in front of Tante Bertha's apartment building, is the young girl standing beside Tante Bertha, who, as always, has elected to wait out front. Tante Bertha is wearing a kerchief and talking animatedly to the young girl.

"Who's the girl?" I ask.

"I have no idea," my mother says.

She looks to be about fifteen, tall and slim, with shoulder-length red hair and horn-rimmed spectacles. She is a little goofy-looking, but I yearn for her at first glance.

Tante Bertha approaches the car. She carries a shopping bag filled with fruit and sandwiches.

"This is a friend of Barbara's," her granddaughter, "down from Boston to look at some colleges. She's only fourteen, but she skipped two grades, a whiz kid. Annelise called me Friday, asked if she could stay." She opens the door. "Get in, darling." The red-haired girl climbs into the back and smiles at me. In the rearview mirror I see a look of utter and guileless horror cross my mother's face. "I said, of course, are you kidding, I love the company, and she's a wonderful girl and her name is Libby."

"Hi," says Libby, her face a few sandalwood-scented inches from mine. "Very nice of you all to take me along." Her voice is deep and smoky.

"What's her last name?" my mother asks suspiciously.

"Kalter." Tante Bertha gets in the back, bumping Libby ever closer to me.

"I'm Robby."

"And this is my niece Liesl Weisglass and her husband Herbert. This is a little cold today, isn't it? *Schon aber kalt.* We are going to Rockaway?"

Libby looks at me. "The beach? It's February."

"It's a thing about fresh air."

"A nutty thing?"

"A nutty thing."

"Herbert, how do you go?" Tante Bertha puts on her sunglasses for the drive, very Garbo.

"Woodhaven, like always."

"I brought some fruit, I brought sandwiches if anyone wants."

"We were going to stop at Weiss's for lunch," my mother says from the front, not turning around.

"Just in case anyone is hungry on the beach. I bring these things just in case." Tante Bertha stares out her window. "*Schon, schon aber kalt . . .*"

Libby's thigh is flush to mine. She is wearing jeans and a blue loden coat. I feel the heat from her body coming through my corduroys. She wiggles her eyebrows like Groucho Marx.

"You really skipped two grades?" I ask her.

"What?"

"I was talking to Libby, Mom." I look at the rearview mirror. She looks disoriented.

"That's not polite, whispering."

"He asked me if I really skipped two grades, Mrs. Weisglass. The answer is yes. I skipped kindergarten and eighth grade. That's why I'm a junior and I won't be fifteen until June." She smiles at me, drops her voice. "She's a ball-buster, huh?"

"Very little traffic," says Tante Bertha, who, like many refugees, fancies herself an expert on road conditions and navigation despite never having been behind the wheel of a car. "Herbert. Very little traffic." My father never speaks while driving. It is serious business, negotiating this Plymouth through an alien world. "In the summer you should see it." Bertha continues her analysis. "Packed. *Liebe Gott* . . . Herbert. Who's hungry?"

I feel Libby's hand tapping mine. I turn. She slips her head behind mine in order to whisper without being observed.

"You have some family."

"You don't know the half of it."

It is, of course, freezing on the beach. My parents and Tante Bertha walk on ahead, Libby and I trail behind. Every few seconds, my mother turns around and looks at us.

"Your mom keeps checking on us, huh?"

"Yeah."

"She jealous? You're her little boy."

"I guess so."

"How old are you?"

"I was twelve in December."

"Really? I thought you were like fourteen."

"No."

"You have a way. You're mature."

She turns around again. This time she waves. Libby and I wave back.

"What's the deal with her?" Libby takes off her glasses, which have gotten fogged up and salty. She tries to clean them off on her loden coat, but it's hopeless. "This is impossible." She sticks the glasses in her pocket. Her eyes are blue, with that slightly unfocused look common to the bespectacled. "What's the deal with her?"

"She sleeps with me. I also sleep with my sister, who's away this weekend. I've never told this to anyone before."

To her credit, Libby believes me from the first moment.

"What do you mean, 'sleeps with you'?"

"Sleeps with me."

"Sexually?"

"Yeah."

"Your mother?"

"Yeah. And my sister. With my sister it's almost normal compared to my mother. My sister's really beautiful."

"But she's your sister."

"I know that."

My mother is looking again.

"And your father . . ."

"He doesn't know, of course."

"He seems a little strange, I hope you don't mind my . . ."

"Not at all. It happened again last night, I had to talk about it."

"Happened with your mom?" Libby takes my arm, guides me toward the ocean. A dozen gulls trot before us like an escort. My mother stops in her tracks, and then Tante Bertha takes her under the arm and pulls her along. "When? When your dad is not around?"

"He's a deep sleeper."

"He's in the house?"

"It's in the middle of the night and she's very quiet."

She stares at me. "You're pretty tall, so you're like . . . mature."

"Yes."

"Does anything happen? What if she got . . ."

"Nothing happens. We stop before. It's 'just for fun' she calls it."

"And with your sister?"

"Something happens."

"Jesus Christ."

"But we do different stuff." I'm turning the colors of a jukebox, even in the cold wind. "She couldn't get pregnant or anything."

" 'Different stuff'?"

"Yeah. You know . . ."

"She blows you, your sister?"

"Yes."

She laughs, but it's a dark and serious laugh. "I'm not sure I can

get back in the car with you guys. Does Mrs. Rosenthal know?"
Meaning Tante Bertha.

"Of course not."

"Of course not. Yikes."

They are all—by which I mean both Bertha and my mother—
now waving at us to join them.

"What should I do?" I ask Libby.

"I'm not sure. Would you mind if I told my dad about it? Not
using your name of course."

"What does your dad do?"

"He's a psychiatrist."

I look over my shoulder. My father has brought his old Rollflex
camera along and is taking photographs of Tante Bertha and my
mother. She looks toward me, waves her arm.

"A psychiatrist?"

"Yes. I mean, you seem like a normal person. How do you feel
about this? I hardly know you, so maybe it's none of my business,
but you did tell me . . ."

"You mean how do I feel when it's happening?"

"For a start."

"Well, I don't like it with my mother. It's scary and at the same
time it's like it's not happening. With my sister . . . it's a little
. . . I don't know . . . If you met her . . ."

"It's sexier. I mean, I'm a virgin, you know, but I can imagine . . ."

"We share a room, when she's there. She's out a lot at night.
She's a model and she has a boy friend, a married guy."

"She's how old?"

"Twenty-one."

"Yikes."

Tante Bertha calls to us.

"Come! For pictures!"

"In a minute!" I yell back. My mother leans toward Tante Bertha
and I know she is asking her what did I just say. When my mother is
agitated, which is a great deal of the time, she has difficulty hearing.

"It can't go on," Libby tells me. She takes my hand, starts tracing
my fingers with hers. "Even with your sister. It's sick."

"I know. I tell my mother, but she doesn't hear."

"She forces you."

"She just does it. It's not even like force. She just comes in and does it and then she's gone."

"You have to refuse, Robby, really. I mean, I'm talking rationally and all"—her blue eyes are tearing, I don't know if it's from emotion or the wind—"but inside I'm churning. I've never heard of anything like this."

Tante Bertha is walking toward us.

"I mean I've heard about it in books, but I always thought it was like toothless men in Kentucky ravishing their teenage daughters. But German Jews, this is really out of left field."

"Don't tell your father."

"Why not? I won't use your name."

"Sooner or later you will."

"I won't."

"What if I start writing to you? He'll put it together."

"You want to write to me?"

"Yeah."

She smiles—a contented and nearsighted smile.

"Okay, then."

"What?"

"I won't tell him, not if you're going to write. But let me know what's happening, although I'll probably be able to tell just from the letters, how you feel—if it's getting worse, if you're falling apart. Because sooner or later you will, you know. Fall apart."

Tante Bertha is on top of us.

"Your mother, Robby, is getting very nervous."

"About what?"

"She wants you with the family."

"We're just talking."

"You can talk with us. You don't have to be shy, right? She just said, tell him this is supposed to be a family day."

"It's my fault, I guess," Libby says.

"It's no fault of anybody," Tante Bertha says. "You're my guest. Just in our family, we're very close and a family day means more than to other people."

"Everything means more to German Jews," I say.

"Don't be so fresh." Tante Bertha smiles. She breathes deeply. "Smell that air. This is better than all the doctors. Come."

WE were all together the rest of the day. Libby never let on, treating my mother with exquisite, though formal, manners. We traded addresses publicly, which set my mother back visibly. Had she seen Libby holding my hand in the back of the car, God only knows what manner of migraine would have been the result. Tante Bertha noticed the hand-holding—lowering her sunglasses, then turning to stare out her window for the rest of the journey.

My darling Libby.

1951 / (1973)

I T IS July and there is no air in our apartment. Valises stand in the hallway, preparatory to our drive to the Hotel Mahopac in Lake Mahopac, a trip that will consume three and a half hours of drive time and end in a free two-week stay at that venerable hostelry. One of the perks—no, the only one—of my father's job at Chronicle Publications is the occasional gratis summer vacation; the trade-off being a major article in Lobby News or American Hotel, two of Chronicle's eleven magazines. My father is out getting the car, no small undertaking given that it is parked, for reasons of economy and safety, in my uncle Kurt's garage in Fresh Meadows. My sister has gone with him, "for company." The heat is unendurable. I am six years old and lie doglike on the kitchen floor, seeking some solace from the cool linoleum.

"Robby," she calls from the back of the apartment.

I stretch my skinny limbs. No breeze comes in, though the kitchen window is thrown wide open.

"Robby! *Wo bist du?*"

I get up and walk through the apartment. She is not in her bedroom, nor in mine. The bathroom door is ajar; I push it. She is in the bathtub, the shower curtain pulled open. In the instant before I turn my eyes away, I see her about to lower a green washrag to the utterly black region between her legs.

"I need a towel, darling."

45

I pick a towel off the ceramic bar beside the toilet and walk backwards, crablike, toward the tub.

"Don't be shy."

I continue to back up and then simply drop the towel on the floor next to the tub.

"Bye."

I begin to walk away when I feel her wet, warm arm around my bare chest. Even on the hottest day of the summer she is taking a scalding bath. Steam rises from her muscled forearm.

"My shy *bubele.*" Her arm is tight on my chest.

"I want to go." Why so dark between her legs?

"You're so *schvitzig.* You could use a bath."

I begin to cry. Her arm drops away from my chest and I dash away.

"WHAT do you think she wanted you to do?"

On a June afternoon nearly as hot as that July day in 1951, I can barely hear Dr. Singer over the din of his air conditioner.

"Do?"

"Yes, do."

"Probably have me take a bath with her."

"Had she fondled you previous to this?"

"She didn't fondle me."

"Okay. Other times."

"I don't remember. That's not the thing. It's that blackness."

"Between her legs?"

"Yes."

"It frightened you."

"Terrified me. I didn't know what it was."

"You had never seen your sister naked?"

"No. I had seen her breasts, but never her . . . her pubic hair. Funny, I find that difficult to say."

"Pubic hair?"

"Yes. Maybe because it's part of this great, terrifying mystery about nakedness. I had never seen my father naked, you understand."

"Not that you remember."

"If I had seen him, I would have remembered, trust me."

"Maybe, maybe not."

The air conditioner's compressor pauses for a long moment, then starts up again with a straining, heavy sound.

"Have you thought of investing in a new air conditioner?"

"You think I should?" The master turns it around.

"Yes. I think you should. How's that? I think you should."

"Are you uncomfortable?"

"Physically?"

"Yes, physically."

"Not particularly. It's not freezing to death in here, I'd say, but I'm not dying from the heat. I just believe your air conditioner is going to croak soon, and then we'll all be very hot, won't we?"

"Then I'll have to get a new one."

"Yeah."

"You said you were very hot in the bathroom in 1951."

"I didn't say that. I said the apartment was hot."

"Ah."

"Ah."

"There's a difference."

Silence.

"I'm not saying that the bathroom wasn't hot. It probably was. It's just that from the moment I walked in the door, my memory no longer seems to be focused on the heat. It's her bush that I remember. My mother's bush."

"Bush?"

"Bush. Her undergrowth. Her jungle."

"And that's a jungle you could get lost in."

"And never find my way out."

The air conditioner sighs once again. Dr. Singer sneezes.

"God bless you."

"Thank you. We're out of time today."

I AM an assistant professor of America history at Columbia at this time, teaching the second half of the freshman survey (Civil War to the present) and my own specialty, Twentieth Century Social and Cultural History, to the increasingly de-politicized and career-oriented upperclassmen. In the faculty lounges, my younger colleagues deplore the decline of activism; I nod and shrug, but am secretly grateful for it. I prefer things quieter, I prefer not having to make the sort of choices forced upon undemonstrative me in the sixties and early seventies. I can make more progress on my book, *Shrinking Violets: German-Jewish Refugees and American Culture*, now in its sixth year of creation.

Several things are interfering with the speedy completion of my work. One is the continual seesaw of point of view between respect and contempt for my subjects; the other is the same process with respect to myself. After fourteen months of cohabitation, my relationship with Dr. Gail Ballenzweig, a second-year resident at NYU Medical Center, is on the verge of collapse. Gail's erratic and nocturnal schedule has made our life together an ill-tempered and bleary-eyed approximation of the sourest of marriages. Our sex life, once flourishing and acrobatic, has dimmed to the obligatory and begrudging. And she no longer finds my family history interesting.

"Isn't Singer helping you at all?" Gail says this over espresso in a Second Avenue coffeehouse, after a rare Saturday date at the movies. It is a wet and windy March night and a strand of her long black hair is stuck to her cheek. I remove it.

"Don't pick at me," she says. She used to have a sense of humor. Her once-lustrous brown eyes have grown dull and black-rimmed from her vampirelike schedule.

I sip silently at my cappuccino.

"What's the answer?" she inquires again.

"That was a real question? Why isn't Singer helping me?"

"I said *isn't he* helping you at all. I thought the object was to find out why you were so obsessed with your family." She didn't know, of course. I had told no girl except for Libby.

"Obsessed?" I say.

"Yes, obsessed. Your conversation constantly refers back to them. This fucking book you're writing. I'm sick of hearing about the goddamn refugees . . ."

"Maybe if we spent a little more time together, it wouldn't seem like so much. But given your schedule . . ."

"My schedule is my schedule. Fuck, we're not going to start that again." She lights a Pall Mall. Her wire-rimmed glasses have fogged up from the heat of her espresso and the humidity in the room, so she removes them. What did I ever see in this girl? I move out a week later and find an apartment on West Eighty-third Street.

"YOU'RE better off, that's my honest opinion," my mother says. My father spoons his soup. I am having my weekly dinner in their apartment. They are now among the last Jews in the building, living with a kind of dour and Malamud-like resignation amidst their explosive and brightly dressed Latin neighbors. The tropical smells of rice and beans and roasting pigmeat suffuse the halls and the lobby. Salsa vibrates in the street.

"I'm better off in that it had turned into an unhappy relationship." I sip at a beer. "I'm not better off in that I don't like being alone."

"A doctor's life"—she shakes her head—"What is that for you? The hours. You're the husband of a doctor . . . Mr. Doctor."

"He has a career." Some soup dribbles down my father's chin. He wipes it daintily with his napkin. He is aging, no question; everything seems to come a beat slower. This is his last year as a wage-earner.

"It's a career, but it's not enough for him. I know him better than he knows himself." She taps my hand. "Am I right?"

"No. You're not."

"I'm right. You're more ambitious than that. An assistant professor, it's wonderful for what it is. But you always wanted more."

"I did?"

"Carol, too," my father says.

"Carol's a different story." That's all for that. "This one was ambitious, too."

"It's not all in the past tense. I'm thirty-one."

"He always tried to hide it, but he had ambitions, too." She turns back to me. "Never lose them."

"What exactly are you saying?"

"Don't sell yourself short."

"By teaching at Columbia?" No, that's not what she's saying. What she's saying is that she didn't sleep with her son for him to grow up to be a college professor. She thought she was doing better than that.

"You're disappointed."

"I've never been disappointed with you, not for two seconds, what are you talking about? Only when you were disappointed in yourself."

"That's a lot of crap. You're disappointed." I lock my eyes into hers. From an upstairs apartment a Latin tune explodes in trumpets.

"Yo soy quiero . . . su corazón."

"I was never disappointed. Not for a half a second."

He puts his soup spoon down. "How could we be disappointed in you? It's not possible."

"You're too hard on yourself." She puts her hand on mine. I get a stomach cramp.

THE manager greets us as we arrive at the Hotel Mahopac. He is standing on the great lawn in front of the white-columned porch that surrounds the ground floor of the hotel. Children and adults are playing croquet on the great lawn, other guests sway in the outsized rockers and swinging chaises on the porch. To the rear of the hotel, sailboats and powerboats make their random journeys across windy Lake Mahopac. Flags on the dock are stiff from the breeze.

"Herb!" shouts the manager, thus clearly identifying himself as a man who has never met my father. "Jim Bushnell."

We are all introduced to the bald and vigorous Mr. Bushnell. His eyes linger on my sister for the briefest of moments. Her white blouse is soaked with the sweat of our hot and dusty drive and she has undone its top three buttons. She is not wearing a brassiere.

"You're going to have a wonderful two weeks," Mr. Bushnell tells us, then turns and shouts, "Kenny!" A blond college student, his khaki shorts revealing the tanned and finely muscled legs of a tennis player, opens the Plymouth's fiery trunk and begins to unload our luggage. "The bags will be taken care of." My mother stares back uncertainly, fearing baggage theft, as Mr. Bushnell ushers us onto the porch, where the other guests barely regard us, and into the lobby of the Hotel Mahopac.

OUR adjoining rooms face the lake; they are large and bright and austere in the manner of gentile summer resorts of the 1950s. The word is *unadorned*.

"*Tser goyische, gel?*" I hear her ask in the next room.

"It's the Hotel Mahopac," he says.

"Which means that it's restricted?"

"It used to be."

My sister, bare-breasted, stands at the open window. She raises her arms, for the wind to cleanse her sweat. In that pose, she could adorn the prow of a clipper ship headed for the Indies. Sixteen years old at that instant in time, a moment of physical perfection caught by the winds off Lake Mahopac.

"But not anymore?" my mother says. "I looked at that porch. *Alles goyim. Alles.*"

"You want to turn around and go home? This is a free vacation."

"I just hope it works out."

"Jim Bushnell knows who we are."

"He does?"

"I'm sure he does. Weisglass."

"Could be German. In this country . . ."

"Isn't it beautiful here?"

"If it's restricted I can't enjoy the beauty. Those faces on the porch."

"Just *Amerikanner*. Doesn't mean they don't want us here. You saw the welcome he gave us. In two seconds, that boy was taking our suitcases. Compare that to the refugee hangouts in the Catskills."

"I just hope it works out. That's all that I hope."

"What do you think is going to happen?"

"Just if they find out . . . if they find out."

I AM on the dock with my sister. She is wearing shorts and sneakers over a white bathing suit. I am in a polo shirt and dungarees and sandals. The lake is blue and noisy with boat traffic. Kenny appears. He is wearing a white tee-shirt with the words "Hotel Mahopac Staff" embroidered over his heart. He smiles at my sister.

"Want to take a boat ride?" He points to a speedboat bobbing in the water. "That's the hotel's boat."

"Sure. Robby? He's my brother." She squeezes my arm. "How about a boat ride? I'll tell Mom and Dad." She gets up from the dock and runs into the hotel, where my mother and father are lingering after lunch. Kenny looks at me.

"How old are you, champ?"

"Six and a half."

"No kidding. And your sis?"

"She was just sixteen."

"Really. I would've thought eighteen, something like that."

"No."

"I'm nineteen." In memory he is a blond Adonis, a person I know I will never grow up to be, a person of easy sexual confidence. To be nineteen and to be this person, this Kenny, to inhabit the world with such serenity, to know this was a world in which you actually *belonged* . . . "I'm at Yale. Sophomore. You play tennis yet, champ?"

"No."

"I teach it here. If you want to have a lesson, just come by the court." He is untying the boat from the dock, completely at ease with boats and docks and lakes. "Your folks are friends of Mr. Bushnell?"

"My father writes about hotels. For magazines."

Kenny smiles.

"That's why he said be specially nice to the Weissmans."

"Weisglass."

"But I'd be specially nice to you anyhow because I really like kids. I think the thing I like best about teaching tennis is teaching kids. You know, six and a half, champ, that's a great time to get started." He hops into the boat, then holds out his arms. For me. He is holding out his arms for me. I step forward and he lifts me into the boat. I have never been in a powerboat. It rocks beneath my feet.

"Why don't you take a seat back there, champ." He points to a bench running along the stern of the boat.

My sister and mother appear from the hotel dining room. My mother puts her hand over her eyes, protecting herself from the glare of the lake.

"Mrs. Weisglass, I was just going to take these guys out for a quick spin around the lake."

"He doesn't swim yet."

"We have life jackets. No problem. If you'd like to come along . . ."

She shakes her head. "Not for me." She smiles, as though she has just said something funny. My mother's fear of all bodies of water, save our porcelain bathtub, is part of the received truth of our family. The Time She Almost Drowned. A Lake Near Stuttgart.

My sister walks upon the dock and holds out her hand. Kenny takes it and guides her onto the boat.

"Not for too long." My mother continues to shield her eyes, even though the sun is behind her.

"We'll just take it out to Pine Island and then back. I have a clinic at two-thirty." He starts the motor.

"Just be careful. Robby, you don't stand up . . ." We are starting to move away from the dock. Hand over her eyes, she points: ". . . life jacket . . . you listen . . ." And that is all I can hear as the boat begins to pick up speed. I hold tightly onto the railing along the stern. Carol sits opposite me, then rises and stands beside Kenny as he steers the craft. The engine is very noisy, so I can't hear what Kenny says to her to make her laugh. Carol looks at me and then laughs again. I close my eyes, and listen to the wind. I hear another boat pass closely by; grownups are laughing, a woman is singing. When I open my eyes, the impact of water-reflected sunlight is almost overpowering. My sister is now steering the boat, with Kenny leaning over her, making adjustments. Both their hands on the wheel. I close my eyes again.

"That's what we call Pine Island, champ," he calls to me. I open my eyes. A few hundred yards away is a small island covered by Canadian spruce. It has a little sand beach on which small craft— rowboats, speedboats—have landed. People swim around it.

"It's beautiful, isn't it, Robby?" My sister sits down beside me. "Just a whole other world people can live in."

"You folks are from New York?" He is slowing our craft down as we near Pine Island.

"Yes," my sister tells him. "From darkest Queens."

"Darkest Queens," he repeats and laughs. I have never heard her say that, "darkest Queens," I wonder when she thought it up. "I'm from New Canaan. Connecticut."

"Oh, yes," my sister says. "New Canaan." She suddenly puts her hands on my shoulders. I reflexively lie back, on her warm thigh. My sister. "Isn't that restricted?"

"Restricted?" asks the tennis pro.

"Restricted. No Jewish people."

"I don't think so."

"Oh, yes it is." She lowers her head to mine, so I can smell her hair, her suntan lotion. She puts her nose on mine, nuzzles me. "Oh, *yes* it is." She laughs, a laugh that can be heard around the lake, as loud as the birds and the powerboats and the prop planes droning overhead. In my memory, every bit as loud.

DINNER at the Hotel Mahopac means jackets for the men. That includes me, so I sit in a state of itchy formality, housed in what my mother insists is a "lightweight" wool jacket. My sister is demure, bordering on the severe, in a dark skirt and cashmere sweater worn over a blouse with a Peter Pan collar. Her hair is pinned up and she looks pristinely beautiful. My mother wears a dress—I can never remember the color or fabric of anything she wore, ever—and my father is sporty in a striped seersucker suit which he has apparently purchased for this trip. An unlit pipe is clenched between his teeth, and it rises up and down as he studies the evening's menu. He suddenly seems uneasy, and I find it vaguely frightening.

She addresses me.

"They have different courses, Robby, but only in the main course is there a choice—Boston scrod or chicken à la king."

"Pfui Teufel," mutters my father. This is an untranslatable expression of disgust, usually reserved for dishes my father finds unpalatable.

"Chicken à la king," I decide. The dining room is vast; perhaps three hundred people are seated here, examining their menus with sober delight. Considering the numbers, the room is surprisingly quiet.

"This is some menu," my father says. "Jellied consommé, *liebe Gott.*" It is a gastronomic nightmare for him—things in aspic, boiled vegetables, puff pastries. Anti-Semitism in edible form.

"Very *goyische,* but that is no surprise."

My sister puts down her menu. "I say we just eat and enjoy it. What's the big deal." She looks around the room and observes the quiet multitude. Extended families, ranging from frail yet formidable matriarchs wearing old jewelry on their thin arms, to their blazered and plaid-skirted sons and daughters, and on to their blond and obedient grandchildren, sit around massive oak tables, tinted water glasses and oyster crackers placed before them like the sacraments of a bloodless communion.

"This is real America," declares my sister.

"And that's so wonderful?" My mother's reply is strident.

"They seem perfectly happy."

My father is still studying the menu, as if attempting to decipher it. Our waiter, Peter, a painfully thin boy of perhaps twenty with an enormous and artistic shock of black hair dangling over his forehead, has placed a Schlitz before my father, an iced tea before my mother and sister, and a Pepsi before me. We fall dead silent at his appearance, as if he is were nothing less than a spy in our midst.

"You folks ready to order?" he asks us.

My father needs another minute, so Peter retreats, long fingers pushing his hair back.

"I don't know why everybody is so tense," my sister says, sipping her tea. "It's not like anybody's been nasty or anything. They're all perfectly pleasant." She taps my hand. "Wasn't Kenny nice?"

I nod.

"There you are," says my sister. "So there's no Jews here. So what."

"Please," my mother says. "This is something you can't understand. I don't even ask you to understand it."

"I understand it, but I think it's stupid. There's no Jews here, but it's not like the room is filled with Nazis. It's just a lot of people actually born in America having their supper."

"You don't understand it." She is turning slightly gray. "You haven't . . ."

"Please. Not again."

"You can talk about this because you don't know it. There's a reason that all these people are here, and nobody looks like anybody we know. This is a restricted hotel. Period."

"I'll have the chicken," he says, finally lowering his menu.

"You think so, too, Dad?" Carol asks him.

"Think what?"

"That this is a restricted hotel."

"By law . . ."

"By law it can't be, right?"

My mother shakes her head and takes a very soft roll from the basket before her. "By law . . ." She takes her napkin and wipes the corner of my mouth. "By law."

Seated there in our summer finery, the feeling was that four quarrelsome paratroopers (three, really; I didn't participate in the debate) had dropped behind enemy lines.

"It's all moot," my father said. "We're here."

"That's what I say," my sister says, patting my father on the arm.

"I like it here," I say. "I liked Kenny."

"And anyhow," my father adds, as if for the first time, "it's all moot."

"It's not moot if I feel this way," my mother says, and begins to cry.

"Jesus Christ," my sister says.

At this opportune moment Mr. Bushnell appears. He is wearing a green madras jacket and white ducks.

"Herb, everybody . . . enjoying yourselves?" My mother has a napkin over her face. When she lowers it, her cheeks are still wet.

"Liesl has allergies."

"Well, this is the season." Can he actually be fooled by this explanation? He smiles at my mother. "Helen, my wife, she's got the same problem. June to September, she's *hors de combat*. You order yet? Scrod's delicious." He puts his hand on my shoulder. "Enjoy the boat ride, junior?"

I nod, then ask my question.

"Is this restricted?"

I am looking at Mr. Bushnell, so I cannot see the reaction of the rest of my family. Mr. Bushnell's smile is fixed; he leans closer to me, as if having trouble with his hearing.

"Is this restricted, this hotel?" I repeat in my small, clear voice.

"Oh, *restricted*, you said. No, it's not. We do have wonderful traditions, though, as I'm sure you can all see. Enjoy your dinners." And he is off like a shot. Like an American gunshot.

In what I believe is the middle of the night, I awaken and sit up. The room is very still; crickets and cicadas are percussive in the starry night outside the window screen. I look over at my sister's bed. It is empty. I bury myself beneath my sheet and pull my pillow over my head.

We leave a week early, and spend the rest of my father's vacation at the Breezy Hill Hotel in Fleischmanns, New York. At the Breezy Hill Hotel, everyone is Jewish and English is spoken as a second language. Refugees, refugees forever.

1962 / (1985)

D R . S INGER asks me if I mind if he lights his pipe. I say that I don't mind, of course I don't mind; twenty minutes later his pipe remains unlit. Lying on the couch, I sniff in vain for a cloud of Blue Boar.

"You keep saying 'refugee,' " he says. "I'm not exactly sure what you mean by the word."

"I mean a lot of things. What's with the pipe?"

"The pipe?"

"You asked me if I minded if you smoked. I said of course not, and then you never smoked. So did you ask me for some other purpose?"

"No, I just wanted to know if you would mind."

"Have I ever minded?"

"No, but perhaps you have a cold, or you simply wished I rather didn't."

"And then you never smoked."

"I actually forgot about it."

"Because what I was talking about was so engrossing?"

Objection. The patient is asking his analyst for approval. Objection sustained.

"I see. Anyhow, by 'refugee' I think I am referring most specifically to the sense of being an outsider, and that is a sense I find I can never escape."

"You feel it now?"

"I feel it most of the time. Sometimes I wonder if it isn't a function of what went on at home in a physical way, rather than the fact of literally being a refugee, or the child of refugees."

"You mean that the incest marked you as an outsider."

"Exactly. Except that I really think this sense of being an outsider began before any of that."

It is the winter of 1985, nearing the end of my first decade with Dr. Singer. His radiator is banging, but it is still pretty chilly in the office. Is he wearing a sweater? I can't recall.

"Do you feel like an outsider when you are here?"

"You mean on the couch?"

"Yes."

"I always feel it."

"Always?"

"Yes. I feel like I am looking through a window. This is not to say that there isn't a door next to the window, and that I do not occasionally walk through that door and take a little stroll in the real world. That happens. But it is to say that I generally feel that I am outside of events. Even the events of my own life."

"And in here?"

"In here, I am still largely unable to walk through that door. In here I am using my intellect to construct a dialogue that is essentially between me and myself. I'm not sure you're involved in it yet. It's only been ten years. What are you saying, that I should call it quits?"

"I don't know if I would phrase it that way. I don't think that we are getting anywhere."

"You don't?"

"Not recently. That's why I'm interested in the notion of the outsider. I think it is true, but I also find myself becoming an outsider in this process."

I turn around, in shock.

"You don't want me here anymore."

Singer blinks. "The issue is not my wanting you. The issue is what are you doing here." He blinks. He begins filling that goddamn pipe. I turn back.

"You won't get me out of here so easily."

"It's not a question of 'getting you out of here.' It's a question of what do you want. That question has to be addressed. What do you want?"

What do I want?

IN August 1962, I visit Libby. She is at the University of Wisconsin, attending summer session, picking up some lost credits preparatory to her senior year. I have completed my first year at Queens College, and have spent June and July as a messenger boy for Trans-Ocean Trading, my uncle Kurt's export-import firm. The job entails conveying bills of lading from Trans-Ocean to various steamship company offices (Norwegian-American, Holland-American, Cunard), then on to the majestic U.S. Customs office on Whitehall Street for stamping, and then back to the home office on West Sixteenth Street. I ascend and descend subway stairs at the most stifling times of day during the most stifling summer anyone can remember. In seven weeks, my weight has dropped from 150 pounds to 138 pounds and I am running a cold brought upon by alternating the volcanic heat of the Lexington Avenue IRT with the Nordic chill of the steamship company lobbies. At night I silently watch television with my parents and am asleep by ten. Even by my standards, it is not much of a life. At the end of July, I inform Uncle Kurt of my intentions to visit a girl in Madison, Wisconsin. I give notice.

"You're quitting?" Uncle Kurt is a sophisticated man, my father's younger brother. He lives in Larchmont, smokes Jamaican cigars, wears custom-tailored suits, and has a new blonde wife, an American. Kurt's divorce of his first wife, Grete, was our family's equivalent of King Edward's renouncing the throne for Wallis Simpson. My father never tired of discussing Kurt's "selfishness."

"When you took the job, you said nothing about quitting, nothing about a girl . . ." His secretary, Miss Nadel, enters the office. Miss Nadel is a plain woman with an enormous bosom and a pageboy hairdo. Uncle Kurt addresses her.

"My nephew's quitting on us. He has a woman."

"It's not that simple," I explain.

"When?" she asks, sensibly. "I have to call Ajax."

"A week and a half," Uncle Kurt tells her. He clips the blunt end of a Macanudo cigar and smiles at Miss Nadel. "Relatives can't be trusted."

"Uncle Kurt, if it really screws you up . . ."

"Do your parents know this?"

"Yeah." This is a lie.

"Bullshit, pardon my English."

"I have to call Ajax."

"This is definite, Robby?"

"Yes."

Miss Nadel bites her lip, then turns and leaves the office. It is an old office, with frosted glass doors and a globe light suspended from the tin ceiling. Uncle Kurt lights his cigar.

"You and this girl"—his eyes narrow—"I assume you're sleeping with her or else you wouldn't leave this fantastic career opportunity."

"I really like her a lot."

"In other words, none of my goddamn business." Like I said, Uncle Kurt was a sophisticated man. "Who can blame you? Do it while you can. Do everything while you can." He arises, puts his hairy arm around me. "Robby, can I tell you something?"

"What?"

"Your mother's a real *mishugenah.*"

"I know."

"You do?"

"Yes."

"That's good. Then maybe she can't hurt you."

"Hurt me?" My knees tremble a little bit. She can't have told him. He would never have hired me, or even shaken my hand.

Uncle Kurt lights his cigar, slowly turning it in his mouth while the rising flame illuminates his face theatrically. "I don't mean hit you . . ."

"No, I understand . . ."

"I mean affect you in some other way. She's very strong. Very strong."

"Yes."

"Strong the way only these refugee broads can be. American women can be tough, but you can get at them, they have weaknesses you can identify, you know?"

"I guess."

He smiles. "I know. I've been through the battles. German women are like armored tanks, and German Jewish women are the worst, because you have to feel sorry for them while they roll over you. That's really the reason I left Grete, with all the scandal. All that self-serving horseshit. I don't like feeling sorry for people. For what? We lost people? Everybody lost people, that's what war is. The Russians lost twenty million people."

"That was different."

"It wasn't genocide, but they're still dead. Dead is dead."

"The camps . . ."

"Please . . ." He starts back to his desk. "What's the point of martyrdom. It was a catastrophe, it's over and done with, here we all are in Nueva York, life goes on. The reason I speak about your mother—and you're not offended by this, are you . . . ?"

"No. Not at all."

"I once had the same discussion with your sister, when she was about thirteen, but she knew everything already, Carol. I think she was born knowing everything; she's a special breed of what I call the International Woman. It doesn't make any difference who the parents are, they are born to be a particular type of person. In the fast lane. She still living with that *schvartze?*"

"No."

"I'm sure your father is relieved."

"He hardly spoke about it."

"What else is new." He sits on the edge of the desk. "She have a new guy, I'm sure?"

"A painter."

"White?"

"Yes."

"So she's out of that phase of her life."

"I liked Clarence. I thought he was a very interesting guy."

"I'm sure he was." He smiles. My uncle Kurt, the cosmopolite. Barely twenty when he came over, thus qualifying him as an American. "I like your sister a lot. I'm sure you do too."

"Yes, very much."

He puffs his cigar and stares at me, nodding a little. Do I betray something in my face or in the way I stand? I look down, to see if my fly is open.

"All I want to say, Robele, is this: go your own way in life. Your mother is close to you, in a way that I don't think is altogether healthy." How can he know all this? We rarely see him, twice a year at most since he married the blonde and moved to Larchmont. "Your father is my brother; obviously, I love him dearly, but he's not the kind of guy who's going to take you aside and talk to you, so it's up to me. Be your own guy, hold your head up and go screw your brains out in Wisconsin.' "

"Thank you, sir."

"You're a little like your old man, guarded, defenses up at all times, battle stations manned, but that's understandable." He takes out his wallet. "Get away from home more often, that's today's advice from Uncle Kurt." He steps forward and presses a bill into my hand. I look down and see that it's a fifty. Uncle Kurt hugs me and whispers: "I always thought your mother would fuck you if she could." He steps back; is that a tear in his eye?

"I had to say it."

LIBBY lives on the ground floor of an aging frame house on South Bassett Street in Madison. She has two roommates—Anne Levin of Brookline, Massachusetts and Anne's boyfriend Steven Gaskin of Portland, Oregon. This taken-for-granted cohabitation is a fact I attempt to acknowledge with a certain easy sophistication. When I meet Anne she is wearing a halter top and panties and is scurrying out of the bathroom, preparing to meet Steven Gaskin for dinner on University Avenue. She is quite stunning, in an overdecorated (hoop earrings, Indian bracelets, headband) sort of way. My un-adorned Libby, in her plaid Bermudas and white cotton tee-shirt, is a veritable Shaker meeting house in comparison.

Libby kisses me demurely on the tip of my nose.

"So you're here."

"I'm here."

I stand in the living room, surrounded by the aging and dun-colored furniture one always finds in student housing. There is a rocker and a nonworking fireplace. A poster on the living room celebrates the picketing of a local and discriminatory Woolworth's;

James Dean smoking a cigarette and Marlon Brando astride his motorcycle complete the artwork.

"Very cozy."

"It's a shithole, I know, but it's home." Her hair is up, horn-rimmed glasses resting on top. Maybe it's the tee-shirt, but her breasts seem fuller than I remembered. I put my hands on her warm shoulders; she puts her hands on my chest.

"I was really surprised when you called," she tells me. "Pleasantly, but surprised."

"It's been a terrible summer."

"Thank you very much."

"You know what I mean."

"Maybe you could try again."

"I really wanted to see you."

"That's a little better." She slides her hands up, squeezes my arm. "Muscles."

"From all the intense physical work I was doing." She feels the muscles again. It thrills me. "I really missed you a lot. I kept thinking of you out here and what you were doing."

"What I was doing?"

"I don't know . . . boyfriends."

"RobbyRobby."

I pull her toward me, none too smoothly. She stumbles a little.

"Princess Grace, that's what they call me."

I kiss her, a summer kiss; her breath is warm and spearminty. I kiss her again. Anne Levin comes speeding by, having thrown on a peasant skirt and sandals.

"We'll be at Lorenzo's if you guys want to meet up with us. Have fun." Such casual recognition of our passion. This must be college. She leaves with a slam of the defective, mousetraplike screen door. We kiss again and I start to walk backwards toward the couch.

"Not here," Libby tells me.

HER bedroom is festooned with posters—Mozart, Marx, Einstein. The air is faintly evocative of incense and Je Reviens perfume. She plops down on the bed and kicks off her clogs. I lie down next to her; we face each other, body to body. I am acutely conscious of the fact that I smell unwashed.

"I don't smell too great."

"Oh, was that you?" Libby laughs.

"That's funny?"

"To me it's funny." Her glasses fall out of her hair. She picks them up, puts them in their case, leaning across me as if our bodies were the oldest of friends. The familiarity is at once frightening and reassuring. My body and Libby's body.

"I'd like to sleep with you."

Libby stares at me. "You just got here."

"So what."

She takes my hand, kisses the palm, then holds it between her hands. She shakes her head, in the negative.

"No?"

"Not now."

"Now meaning on this trip, or now meaning at this instant?"

"Probably meaning now at this instant."

"How come?"

"How come? Well, because we haven't seen each other in eight months. Also, because we have never slept together. And finally, just because."

"Just because."

"Because. I like you and you have flown here, but that doesn't mean that you walk in the door and we make love. That's not my style. It's too . . . weird."

"This has nothing to do with my history?"

"No. Actually, I find your history exciting."

"It gets you hot?"

"Yeah. It gets me hot. Particularly since I met your sister. And then imagining the two of you together. It gets to me."

"But not at this immediate instant."

"Not at this immediate immediate instant, no."

"And that's all of it?"

"That's all of it. Trust me."

I trust her.

DUSK beside Lake Mendota. Beer and dinners are casually consumed, dogs are walked along the terrace behind the Student

Union, fraternity boys sail by on their fathers' boats as if from some Scott Fitzgerald dream of the proud and alcoholic Midwest.

Libby's bare feet are in my lap. Steven Gaskin and Anne Levin are smoking Kents and appear to have had an argumentative supper. Gaskin is a blond and ruddy political scientist whose handlebar mustache and wire-rimmed spectacles appear attached to his nose like a mask. His work shirt and jeans look to be fresh out of the laundry, all starch and sharp creases.

"Kennedy's a hypocritical asshole." Smoke pours out of his nostrils. "Anything he does for Negroes is completely political. You think this guy ever knew a Negro except as a valet or a butler?"

Libby's feet feel like sex organs on my lap. She rubs them together.

"What his experience with Negroes is or isn't is completely beside the point," Anne Levin insists. She looks especially beautiful in the reddish light of late day, patrician, as if her family had arrived in Boston on a Jewish *Mayflower*. "The point is, does he believe in civil rights or not? I believe that he does."

"He could care less about civil rights. He could care less about anything. He's a total opportunist, a charming opportunist, granted, but an opportunist. And his father was an active fascist, completely pro-Nazi until it bordered on treason. That has to make you think."

"What's your opinion?" Anne asks Libby.

"My opinion." Her heels are now resting on my fly.

"You have an opinion?" Steven is clearly eager for confrontation; he thrives on the dialectic. "Despite being a clinical psych major, the world must occasionally intrude into the rat cages."

"I think he's gorgeous," says Libby.

"Great," he says.

Anne nods. "No doubt about that."

"Gorgeous but a little cold. His eyes appear to retreat into his skull sometimes, I don't like that. I have the feeling he's not a great human being."

"That's the ladies' perspective."

"Fuck you," his girl friend tells him.

"What about you?" He directs some smoke in my direction. "What are they saying at Queens?"

His condescension isn't lost on me, but I don't like him anyhow, so it doesn't seem to matter.

"At Queens? They sort of like him."

"They would."

"What is that supposed to mean?" Libby says.

"I know people from Queens. Not the college. The borough," he says.

"And?" I ask.

"And it figures. It figures."

QUEENS. Darkest Queens. It is an ungainly Chicago of a borough, senseless, in light and air, of the raging Atlantic pounding at its shores.

"Hard to imagine," I say to Libby one afternoon at the beach; this is after she has gotten sick. "That this ocean and Rego Park are so close to each other."

She clings to my arm. The sea is in a roil this day, a wintry Sunday in 1969. Gulls are racing along the cold sand like characters in a Swedish cartoon; two black men in earmuffs are fishing, standing hip-booted in the surf. This, too, is Queens.

"It's not so hard to imagine," she tells me.

"No?"

"Not really. I mean, the Atlantic is the Atlantic, like the sky is the sky. Is this completely inane?"

"Not yet."

"It was here first. Rego Park is an afterthought. Worse. A nonthought. A construction."

"So?"

"So they aren't really close together. They coexist, but one has no influence on the other. If you walk around Rego Park, you have no sense that the Atlantic Ocean is anywhere in the vicinity."

"That was exactly my point."

"It was?" She laughs.

"Yes."

"I thought you said it was hard to imagine."

"That's what you just said."

"No, I said it was irrelevant. Their only relationship is in their proximity to each other."

It is very windy. Libby wears a purple knit cap pulled down to just above her eyebrows. I kiss her, my sick Libby.

"Thank you," she says.

"Don't say that."

"I have to. It just comes out."

"Kissing you is still kissing you."

She shakes her head.

"It is," I insist.

"It can't be."

I kiss her again, and hold her close to me. She has lost about fifteen pounds already.

"Miss Bones." She stares at me, not looking for a denial, just studying my panicky face. Then she bites my nose.

"Aren't you glad we didn't get married?"

"No."

"Me neither." She ducks her head, a most familiar gesture, that began when she became, as she put it, "a giraffe" at thirteen.

"Then why don't we?"

"Please."

"I want to."

"After it's over, Bubba." She has taken to calling me that. "Then we'll talk about it." She looks around. The two black fishermen stand motionless. "God, it's cold here."

LIBBY'S house on South Bassett Street has a porch out front. A couch and an upholstered chair, mildewed and cat-wrecked, are the porch furniture. We are on the couch, my head on Libby's lap as she licks the remains of a butter pecan cone.

"Anything new with your mom?" she asks.

"Nothing unusual."

Libby laughs. "Well, that could mean anything, given the definition of 'usual' in your household."

"Nothing unusual."

"And your sister?"

"She's got a painter now. White guy. Clarence is over."

"What did your folks say about that?"

"Nothing."

"Not a *thing?*"

"Not that I know of. What they might say at night, in the privacy of their room . . . is probably still nothing."

"I find that hard to believe. My parents dissect *everything.*"

"They're shrinks."

"Even given that, they're *huge* talkers. Your parents . . . it's like they're *spies*, or something, you know? The level of secrecy, it's unbearable. Everything is unspoken."

"I can't deny it."

A motorcycle stops at a red light. A blond boy, bare but for cut-off jeans, is driving, and a dark, Peruvian girl embraces his belly, her long brown legs dangling down to the pavement. She laughs and whispers into his ear. The light turns green.

"And she hasn't tried any funny stuff lately?"

"No."

"Promise?"

"Lib, Jesus . . ."

"Just asking." She strokes my forehead with her index finger. "Just asking. I'm trying to look after you, meatball."

I look up at scholarly, skinny Libby. She smiles, rubs some ice cream onto my lips. "A pecan for your thoughts."

"I love you."

"Now, now . . ."

"I love you." Her tee-shirt smells of sweat and detergent and I see her upside-down, her glasses where a mouth would be. I love her in any facial arrangement. Her free hand balls into a fist and she rubs my cheek.

"You ever hear from your aunt Bertha?"

"I don't want to talk about any aspect of my family."

"Fair enough. Let's move on to the next category."

"What's that?"

She leans over so her warm face is an inch from mine.

"Fucking."

She smiles.

"There. I've gone and said it."

I T is probably not surprising at all that after we make love, I begin to cry.

"Oh, Robby . . ."

I have turned around and she is holding me. It is the first time I have slept with someone other than a member of my immediate family.

"It was wonderful . . ." I whisper. "Don't think . . ."

"Okay . . ."

"But besides them, you know . . ."

She sits up. "This was the first time besides them?"

I nod, the pillow pushed against my eyes.

"Oh, God. No wonder."

"No wonder, right?"

"No wonder. No wonder, baby."

I cry for five minutes. When I am done, I turn over. She is staring at me. Naked, nearsighted.

"So?" she says.

"I'm fine."

"Fine as wine." She touches my hair.

"It was so different."

"Than with them?"

"Oh, God. Like a different thing entirely. Just . . . lighter."

"I liked it very much."

"You did?"

"Very much. Particularly knowing about you." Her head is on my shoulder. "Considering everything, I'm flattered that you could even function."

"Are you serious?"

"Very." She snuggles closer; her arm is around my waist, her elbow a tantalizing inch away from my dazed warm cock. "One day, you'll look back at this and you'll be amazed that you just . . . you know, that you just did it without complication."

"Except for crying like a baby."

"You should cry like a baby. How could you not? I mean, when was the last time that you and one of them . . ."

"My sister. With my mother, not since fifty-seven."

"So your sister?"

"Fifty-eight it ended. That was the last time."

"So it's been four years."

"Correct."

"And you were great."

"I wasn't great."

She raises her head.

"I'm saying you were great." All her lipstick is off; she looks rumpled, like a girl in bed. "Not just great considering, but great, and that's all I'm going to say about it, because I don't want you to get all full of yourself about it."

"I just tried . . ."

She covers my mouth.

"I don't want a class report on it."

"No?"

"No."

Her elbow now grazes me, just a nudge of flesh, and the process begins again. The Need.

"See?" She looks at me. "You're all eager." She reaches over me and gets her glasses off the night table, then places them over my blind organ.

"Looks very much like the Dean of Women."

"He's bald?"

"Bald and red-faced. With little veins in his neck." She takes the glasses off my cock and puts them on. "They're all warm."

It excites me enormously, the sight of these dick-warmed glasses on her freckled face.

"Should I keep my glasses on this time?"

"No more talking."

She tosses her glasses off and grabs my hand, then sinks her teeth into my palm. I roll on top of her; her eyes seem to turn a darker blue, as if her blood has thickened.

"Right now," she whispers, "is perfect."

1957 / (1979)

CAROL, Buddy, and I are at Yankee Stadium on a sultry June afternoon to watch the Yankees play the Baltimore Orioles. It is Ladies Day, a Saturday afternoon, and we have arrived early, in time for batting practice. We are seated in the mezzanine, first base side, row C. My sister sits between Buddy and me; she wears a blue sundress, off the shoulder, which clings to her breasts with a stretch material, so that her breasts appear to be the sole support of the dress. This sundress does not go unnoticed in the mezzanine of Yankee Stadium; fathers of baseball-capped sons watch my sister breathlessly as she rises to summon the peanut man. Their wives, good sports on Ladies Day, laugh as if something was funny.

Buddy is smoking a White Owl cigar and wears a panama hat and a blue blazer over a starched white shirt. The look is very Day at the Races. He is not really comfortable with baseball, in the manner of a man who has devoted his life to the search for women. The first time I don't entirely trust Buddy is also the first time that I somehow feel sorry for him and realize that his quest for my sister is utterly doomed. It is the moment when he says, "This Yogi Berra is a real character, isn't he?" and no one answers him.

THE game proceeds by methodical strokes: Berra, a run-scoring double in the second, a solo home run by Jerry Lumpe, a two-run double by a gimpy Mickey Mantle, nursing a sore hamstring. Bob Turley gives up six hits. The final score is 4–1. It is a merely competent outing, all the more reassuring for that very reason: the Yankees arrive, do their chores and go home, unruffled, having won without conquering or vanquishing. That is for later in the season. In these low-blood-pressure days of June, the Yankees need only to win and remain unhurt. So it is an afternoon to calm, rather than excite, the heart, to restate, rather than inspire. It is all that I want from my Yankees—simply to know that these men in pinstripes, arranged across the desert and meadow of the infield and outfield, will always be there for me.

My sister grows edgier as the game proceeds. She starts clutching my arm and biting her nails with her free hand. Buddy seems oblivious to this fact, attempting to communicate with me in an avuncular fashion about the game.

"Mantle is terrific, but you should have seen DiMaggio, Robby. That was a ballplayer, that *paisan*. Not as strong as this guy, but his knowledge of the bat, of the glove . . . I knew a guy who sold to him wholesale, after-hours . . ."

"Robby," my sister whispers to me, "we should cancel Sardi's."

"Nat Fox had a firm, Princess Judy Fashions. That's before your time, sweetheart . . ." He kisses his index and middle fingers, touches them to Carol's lips before she turns away. "He said he was like royalty, DiMaggio. Like a prince. He'd walk into Nat's showroom, everyone would go crazy—girls, boys, grown men—and he wouldn't even notice. Just go about his business. He was seeing a Copa girl, gorgeous, Patty something, and he was buying from Nat. And particular, not just buying any *dreck* with a price tag. Quality goods. Look at that Berra"—he turns his gaze to the field—"What a body on him, like a fire hydrant. Is that a cliché to say? But he does. He has a build like an actual hydrant."

"I don't know, Robby . . ."

Carol is concerned because, following the ballgame, we are all going to have dinner at Sardi's with my parents. It is their first meeting with Buddy, fourteen months after this illicit relationship has begun, and it is a meeting Buddy has insisted on. It is his bid for legitimacy, for being taken seriously, despite his married state.

* * *

"HE'S a married man," my mother says. "We go to meet him
. . . I don't know."

"It's up to you," Carol says. "Dad?"

"Where does he want to eat?"

"I don't know. I don't think that's particularly relevant. Listen,
I'm more than willing to tell him that you don't feel comfortable
doing this."

"WHAT would you do?" she says to me before dinner. We are
lying on her bed. Her head is in my lap, a burning Kent in her hand.

"I don't know. Why not go ahead with it?"

"He's a decent guy, right?" She blows smoke at the ceiling.

"Sure."

"Mom'll sit there and stare at him, with that look, those eyeballs
of death; Dad'll tune out, and then Buddy'll keep trying to engage
him in conversation. That could be awful." Her hand is under my
leg; she pulls it toward her so it rests on her chest. A fire engine
rages on the street below, horns and sirens like the end of the world.
"That could be death, if he keeps pushing Dad."

"MAYBE we do it," my mother finally says. She is eating small
pieces of pot roast—my mother always cut her meat into tiny portions, like someone who was ill. "Maybe we meet him. Herbert?"

He shrugs, but his eyes are not happy.

"We should do it early," he says.

"Early meaning soon?" my sister asks. "Or in the early part of the
day?"

"An early dinner. Where does he like to eat?"

"They go everywhere," my mother says.

"Not *every*where."

"Wherever he wants," my father says. This discussion has already
gone on way too long for his comfort. He is eager for the eight-
columned comfort of his newspaper. "Just not too expensive."

"He's going to pay."

My mother stares at my father.

"No," he says.

"For him, he'll just write it off as a business . . ."

"No," my father repeats.

"When your father says 'no,' Carol, that means 'no.' " She smiles at me, takes my hand. "What do you think, *bubele?*"

"About who should pay?"

"About the whole thing . . . This man . . ."

"Mom, I don't think Robby should be put in this position."

"He's met this Buddy . . ."

" 'Buddy.' Not 'this Buddy.' "

"He's met him. He has an opinion."

My sister is shaking her head at me from across the kitchen table. My father has arisen.

"Herbert?" my mother says to him. "This is not finished." He turns on the radio, to justify getting up, and then resumes his seat.

"He seemed very pleasant." My sister smiles at me, wraps her finger around the gold chain that hangs from her neck. She's wearing a yellow polo shirt two sizes too small for her.

"And?" My mother squeezes my hand tighter.

"And I don't know. If he wants to have dinner with us, what's the harm?"

"I don't understand." My mother stares across the kitchen table toward the window and the windows outside, that geometry of venetian blinds and houseplants and dozing cats. "If he's married, what's the point?"

Carol leans forward, elbows planted on the table. "I've told you before, it's not a real marriage."

My father, in misery, crosses his legs.

"If he's married, it's a real marriage," my mother says. "Herbert."

He begins to fill his pipe.

"All marriages are real," my mother says, and now she stares at me. My stomach begins to cramp. "As long as two people are married, and have not divorced, as long as they live in the same house, Carol, this is a marriage." She kisses my hand and lets it go.

My sister begins to bite her thumbnail. She raises a bare leg, rests her lovely brown knee against the cool formica table.

"So what are you saying?" she asks my mother.

"I don't see the point, but I don't want to be rude. So we'll have a dinner. An early dinner, for your father."

* * *

WE walk into Sardi's at five-thirty. My parents are already there. My father is examining the menu; my mother notices us the instant we arrive; she appears to blanch when she observes Buddy in his panama hat. He takes it off and hands it in to the cloakroom, but the damage has been done. My mother nudges my father; he looks up from the menu and begins to rise. Carol takes my hand as we enter the dining room.

"Did you see her when we came in?" she whispers to me.

"It'll be okay."

"It can't be okay."

"Louis Calhern," my father says. "In the corner."

Buddy turns around. No one has been introduced. In the corner, the actor Louis Calhern is seated with a man in his sixties. Drinks and nuts are on the table before them. Louis Calhern has started to laugh. The older man laughs with him.

"He came in about ten minutes ago," my father says. My mother remains seated, studying Buddy's clothes, his hands, his hair.

"Buddy Eisenman, these are my parents, Herbert and Liesl Weis-glass." My sister's voice is quavering slightly.

"I've heard so much about you," Buddy says. "That I feel we're old friends already."

My parents simply nod and shake his hand. This is not a greeting they can possibly respond to because they have no friends. Friend-ship, American-style friendship, is an alien concept. "Friends" are for people without family.

"We had quite an afternoon at the ballgame," Buddy says. He nods at us and we sit down, like obedient schoolchildren.

My mother stares at me.

"You were warm enough?"

"It wasn't cold."

She touches my arm.

"Your arm is cold."

"Mom."

"It was a beautiful afternoon," Buddy reiterates, then looks around.

"Waiter!"

"I didn't know Carol liked baseball," my mother says. "Since when?"

"It's just a nice afternoon out," my sister says. She puts her foot on top of mine, presses down, then removes it. She is seated between my father and Buddy. I am seated between Buddy and my mother.

"Sardi's." My father looks around the room, gazing at the theatrical caricatures on the walls. "Can't remember the last time I was here. Has to be five years. Minimum."

"I try to come two, three times a year," Buddy says. He appears distracted. "Waiter!"

My mother looks at my sister and then nods vigorously, as if she has asked a question and received a definitive answer.

"The service used to be a little quicker," Buddy says. There is some perspiration below his nose and his beard is beginning to show through. "But then nothing's what it was, am I right, Herb?"

My father half-nods, half-recoils from the easy "Herb." A white-haired waiter arrives—Buddy orders an old-fashioned, my father a beer, iced teas and sodas for the rest of us. The waiter gone, Buddy reclines in his chair, hands in his lap, attempting to appear relaxed.

"There's a magic about the place. Liesl, I always tell your daughter . . . may I call you Leisl?" My mother makes no reply, so Buddy forges ahead like a swimmer of the English Channel, goggles down, coated with Vaseline. "I always tell your daughter that New York, as I know it, as I've experienced it, has always been for me, a magical city. In the thirties, in the forties . . . you were here then, right, Herb?"

"1937."

"In that period of time, when I was a young man, this city had a magnetism that pulled you right in; you couldn't fight it. The streets were crowded day and night, but somehow clean; all those men going to work in their hats, like soldiers." He looks to Carol. "They all wore hats, men. When did that end, Herb? Last couple of years, it seems."

My father takes off his glasses, as if to jog his memory.

"Last couple of years."

"I have friends in the hat business, Liesl, they're crying to me about their volume. It's sinking. Robby, when I was young, to be seen in public without a hat, it was like going outside without your pants! You were naked without a hat."

Naked. My father puts his glasses on. Carol smiles, rises to go "freshen up." Buddy stands with her and remains on his feet until she disappears from view. My mother puts her hand on my leg.

"Mr. Eisenman."

"Please, Liesl, I would hope we're on a first-name basis . . ."

"Your son is how old?"

"David is seventeen. An engineering genius. Next year . . ."

"And you don't mind if I ask how old you are?"

"Not at all." He smiles, professionally. "Forty-two years young."

"A little younger than we are."

"If we're getting to the sixty-four-dollar question, and you think it better while Carol is powdering her nose . . ."

"She's twenty-one, my Carol." This is the first time I have ever heard my mother use a possessive pronoun in connection with my sister. Even my father notices, looking up from the back of the menu, where he is studying "Cocktails and Wines."

"A very mature twenty-one," says Buddy, with feeling. "With a fantastic set of manners, with social graces that girls in their thirties frequently don't have."

"You're married how long?" She squeezes my knee, removes her hand.

"Eighteen years, Liesl." Each enunciation of her name from Buddy's lips appears to hit my mother like a slap across her face. "But, and I don't know how much Carol has told you . . ."

"Almost nothing she tells me."

"The last six-seven years have been a nightmare due to Phyllis's drinking problem." He looks to my father for sympathy. "Marry a *shiksa*. Who would have dreamed the cliché was correct? Something went off after her thirtieth birthday." Our drinks arrive. "This is some timing with the alcohol. I should have ordered a Pepsi-Cola."

"She just started drinking out of the blue?" my mother asks. "Without a warning?"

"Her own parents did a good deal of drinking." He says this so easily that I immediately doubt it. "But I was so eager to impress them that I didn't pay it any mind; I had the illusion, at that time in my life, that they were from a higher class of people than I was. Not exactly wealthy, but he was an insurance company executive. Passed away since." He nods his head solemnly. "I was a poor Jewish kid from Jerome Avenue, they seemed to me like out of *The Philadelphia Story*, so when they had a couple, or maybe a couple couple, of highballs before dinner, I just thought, 'Goyim at play, this is how they do things.'" Buddy smiles at me, then smiles at my parents. I have the sense that he is unsure as to the appropriateness of this discussion in front of me. But my parents' utter lack of reaction encourages him to continue. Drops of sweat have appeared on his brow. "I never thought deeply about it, I have to admit. I was too worried about my own precarious social position."

"So they were real boozers?" my father says.

"Very definitely. But, as I say, I hardly took notice of it, really, until it started with Phyllis. She'd always enjoyed a social drink, but so do I, nothing out of the ordinary, what's wrong with a little *schnapps* before dinner." He smiles desperately at my mother. She squeezes some lemon into her iced tea. "But then she began with a little nip at four o'clock in the afternoon, then with lunch, then before lunch, until obviously we're talking not about social drinking but alcoholism."

My sister returns from the lounge. Buddy rises, mopping his brow.

"The third degree?" she says pleasantly.

"I'm just telling your folks about Phyllis, what a tragedy it is." He holds my sister's chair for her, unable to resist studying her ass before she sits down. He circles back to his chair. "And a tragedy is what I call it, because she's a terribly bright woman, loves to read, used to be up on all the news events . . ."

"Do you take her to Alcohol . . ." She looks to my father. *"Vas ist das?"*

"Alcoholics Anonymous," Carol says.

Buddy nods gravely, The Man Who Has Tried Everything.

"Liesl, a person has to *want* to do it. That's what they all say, every expert, every doctor, every psychologist. First comes the willingness to do it, the willingness to say, 'I have a problem, I need help.' Without the willingness . . ." He shakes his head. "God knows, I've suggested it enough times."

"And your son?" my mother asks.

"My son?"

"How does he react to this?"

Buddy sips at his old-fashioned.

"To her drinking?"

My mother nods.

"He's a quiet boy. An engineer. Not like his bigmouth father . . ." He flashes a smile; Carol takes his hand. My father sinks deeper into the menu.

"So he doesn't say much?" I hear myself say.

Buddy turns to me, as immediately grateful for my contribution as if I was a hired shill in the audience.

"He doesn't say much, Robby. He keeps to himself. When she starts drinking, he's out of there. He goes into his room to study, or out with his pals. At seventeen, of course, he has a life outside the house and for that I say thank God, considering the circumstances."

"I'd probably do the same," I say.

"You would, sure." Buddy smiles, leans toward me. He smells strongly of his old-fashioned. "Kids have their defenses against things."

"Things happen, you screen them out," I say. My sister looks at me, raises an eyebrow, a little hurt. "You still have to live your life. Your kid-life."

"Your son is a philosopher," Buddy tells my parents.

My mother looks at me.

"My son is my son," she says. Her face is suddenly as gray as her dress. My father looks up from his menu.

"Have you had the cannelloni?" he asks Buddy. "That's stuffed with meat, isn't it? Like lasagna."

My mother's eyes fill with tears.

"My son is my son," she repeats, this time to me, in almost a whisper. "He says what he feels, like I always have."

"The cannelloni is always excellent, Herb."

She places her hand upon my thigh.

"Mom, what I was talking about . . ."

"You're a hundred percent right." She nods, wipes her eyes. "You know why I get emotional."

Buddy leans forward as if the conversation is aimed at him. My sister appears confused.

"Buddy," she says, "could you get me a pack of Kents?"

"Waiter!"

My mother squeezes my thigh. "You know why?"

"Why you get emotional?"

"Because I know how grateful you are," she whispers, "that I don't have a drinking problem."

"Is that what you think?"

"And you don't know how good that makes me feel, that you have that gratitude, that special feeling for me." It is as if we are the only people at the table. "That you love me that much. What that makes me feel, this is indescribable. *Unglaublich.*"

I turn around. My father has begun ordering, Buddy is finishing his old-fashioned and Carol is winking at me.

B Y dinner's end, Martha Raye is seated at the adjoining table, and has been graciously introduced to us by Buddy, who once bought foundation garments from a first cousin of hers. My mother does not know who Martha Raye is, and keeps staring at her, as if waiting for her to turn into something else—another person, a cloud, a fish. Buddy insists on picking up the check.

"I can't have that," my father says.

My sister turns halfway to Buddy. "We talked about this," she mutters.

"I know we talked about this, but in my business when somebody does the inviting, he picks up the check. Herb, please, it's my honor. For the privilege of knowing your daughter."

"What are you, buying me from my father?" Carol says. There is only the slightest humor in her voice.

Buddy appeals to the table, his palms turned upwards.

"Can't a guy get a break?" He turns to me. "Robby, my best pal in the world, is this fair?"

"Don't put Robby in the middle," my sister says.

My father has taken out his wallet.

"Herb, it would give me so much pleasure to do this . . ."

My father looks at my mother.

"I just have one question, Mr. Eisenman," she says.

"Sure. Guess 'Buddy' is still too familiar. In my field, everything is so first-name, maybe this is better, more honest . . ."

"I just have this question, which is"—my mother lifts her head, straightens her spine—"this is Saturday. Where do your wife and son think you are?"

Buddy nods, as if he expected the question all along.

"Like I said, it hasn't been a real marriage for so long . . ."

"But your son . . ."

"He's staying with friends, Mrs. Weisglass." He begins to unwrap a toothpick, carefully, as if it contained a secret message. "On weekends he likes to stay with friends."

At the next table, Martha Raye begins to howl with laughter. Her head is tossed back, her large mouth thrown open as wide as the exit of a funhouse. We watch her laugh, and then I notice my sister staring at me. I smile at her, a sheepish half-smile. A tear rolls down her left cheek. The waiter comes by and fills her coffee cup.

ONE week later she tells Buddy she never wants to see him again.

"SO what does this mean to you?" Dr. Singer asks.

"That she threw over Buddy?"

"The whole situation, why you tell me this story now."

" 'Now.' You mean today?"

This is the winter of 1979. I have been living with my mother for a year and a half in a kind of half-life, still maintaining my apartment on Eighty-third Street, visiting it weekly after my Wednesday seminar on "The Great Depression." The apartment is dark and musty, but not unclean; a cleaning woman still comes in every other week to dust. My books are there, my prints, there are unimportant and rarely-worn clothes in the closet, but the apartment, like a deserted lover, seems to resent my intrusion. I sit down in my favorite chair (shaped like a baseball glove), I lie down on my couch —to warm them, to remind them of my physical presence, but the sense is of singing in an empty theater. It is not so much inappropriate as futile—an apartment must be lived in; I am just a ghostly presence, like in the *Topper* movies, rearranging objects. I pick up my mail and open the windows, just to allow the entrance of contemporary air, then take the train back out to Queens.

Over our quiet suppers, my mother occasionally suggests to me the foolishness of keeping the Manhattan apartment.

"When I think of that expense . . ."

"It's my apartment."

"When I'm gone, you'll have this, for half the rent . . ."

"Please."

The phone rings. I answer. I do a lot of that. Answering calls from her cousins and aunts, my voice on the phone sufficient proof of my vigilance, guarding her from her own pain. As for my pain, it does not exist. I feel, in this time, nothing at all, just vigilance. I am on guard, even in my sleep, going to bed in underwear and sweatpants. The sleep itself is choppy, broken into segments divided by dreams of violence and storms and runaway vehicles which I am unable to steer.

''I GUESS I've been thinking about Buddy and his drunken wife, in connection with my current life. The way in which I am in this relationship which is so false, in a way."

"False for you." I know that Dr. Singer is not wearing yellow slacks, but every time I hear his voice, I can't help but registering that precise image—him seated behind his desk, one canary-trousered leg thrown over the other. Like Buddy?

"You mean it's not false for my mother."

"I don't know what it is for your mother. I wouldn't think false."

"I feel like I died along with my father. My apartment is creepy, my mother's apartment is like a museum . . . The only place in which I feel comfortable is my office, but even that's compromised because Bernie Katz has it on Mondays and Thursdays. It's the Mondays that are so unbearable. After a weekend with her, not to even have my *office* on Monday."

"So why don't you spend Monday in your apartment?"

"Because it doesn't feel like my apartment anymore. It's only a place in which I have a number of my possessions. It's not a refuge, it's a reminder of how utterly fucked my life is. And even when I move back there, I feel there's going to be a residual resentment."

"Resentment by whom?"

"By the apartment."

"The apartment is going to resent you?"

"Obviously, it's a ridiculous statement . . ."

A match is struck; a pipe is lit.

"What I'm really saying is . . . if I was the apartment, here's what I would feel—who is this schmuck who deserted me for a year and a half while he went to live with his mommy?"

"It's an apartment. It's concrete, masonry, glass, plumbing fixtures."

"See, I disagree . . . I feel it's more than that. I feel that there's some connection between physical home and tenant, some deeper thing that occurs. Not unlike the way married persons begin to resemble each other."

"But that's two people. Humans."

"I'm not going to argue this. It's what I feel. I have turned my back on my apartment."

"You've turned your back on your life. You've given it up."

"In the name of grief therapy."

"You've given it up, and willingly."

"Willingly?"

"More than willingly. Almost with alacrity."

"I'm not sure I want to talk about this again."

"Then don't." He sounds exasperated. Is he getting angry at me?

"You're pissed at me. I'm not saying I blame you, but is that a fair assessment?"

Silence.

"Trust me, this is no picnic, living in Corona with her. If you're pissed or disappointed with me because you think this is something I wanted, or this is some role that I always wanted to play, the loyal son, standing beside Mom in her hour of greatest need . . ."

"Is it *her* hour of greatest need? You haven't talked much about that."

"I think it's getting better for her. I see a light at the end of the tunnel, when it'll be much easier for me to move back."

"I thought she wanted you to stay, to take the apartment after she dies."

"She says that, but it's certainly not anything I would consider doing."

"It isn't?"

"Are you serious? Of course not. You actually think I would spend the rest of my life in an apartment where I was molested as a kid?"

"You've been there a year and a half. You speak of being alienated from your own apartment in Manhattan . . ."

"So you believe there's an actual shot of my spending the rest of my life there?"

"I hear an unwillingness to leave."

"An *inability.*"

"No, you clearly have the ability to leave. You're not disabled in any way, you have the physical capacity to return to your own apartment. But you haven't done it."

"I think about it, then something stops me."

"Something with a name?"

"Fear. It's fear. I can call it whatever I want, but it boils down to fear."

"Of your mother?"

"Sure. I leave her, she'll be terribly angry at me."

"And then?"

"I can't get past that point."

"Of imagining the anger."

"That's where it stops for me. I just think of this terrible rage, this sense of betrayal, of my leaving her all alone."

"But it's your father who left her all alone."

"He died and left her alone. This would be different, this would be packing my suitcase and walking out the door."

"What you're describing is a kind of desertion. A divorce."

"I suppose it is. So what?

"It's not either of those things."

"I know it's not. I know all of this rationally. But I can't get past the fear."

"You speak of this terrible rage. You think she'd be angry?"

"She doesn't get openly angry. She would be terribly disappointed. Terribly hurt. I've raised the issue of going back to my apartment time and again and I see how it registers on her face. I feel like I'm stabbing her in the heart."

"You can't only live for her."

"I know that. I know that."

A car alarm goes off on the street outside. We sit and listen to it for the longest time.

* * *

SHE has brought me my dinner, Wiener schnitzel and mashed potatoes, "how you like them," which means a little burned on the bottom, when I inform her that I must move back to my apartment. She hands me my plate, then goes back to the stove and gathers her own dinner.

"It's just time, Mom. I feel you're doing well and obviously I'm just a phone call away."

She sits down.

"You have everything?" she asks me. "Something to drink. You want a beer?"

"No thanks."

She gets up again, fetches me a bottle of Pabst Blue Ribbon, then wanders around to get an opener. Finally, she is seated again. She begins eating.

"If you weren't doing so well, I wouldn't think about this, but it just seems to me that it's time, past time, for this to happen. We have our separate lives and I need to go back to my life, just like Carol, you know, has her life."

My mother simply nods.

"There are all these cycles in everyone's life," I continue, not really encouraged, but feeling the necessity to continue speaking. "And I guess I believe that this particular cycle, of my living here and seeing you through the worst of it, you know, with the adjustment, that this part is now over."

I have yet to eat a bite. She points to my plate, a mute signal I know all too well, indicating that valuable food is getting cold.

"What I was thinking was that by the end of next week, I'd be back in my place."

She is eating steadily. I interpret this as a good sign, meaning that she has not been physically devastated by the news, that her appetite —for food, for life—is unaffected.

"Maybe before the weekend. You have plans for next weekend? With Bertha? Or Hilde?"

She looks calmly up from her food.

"This is your friend's advice?"

"We've talked about it on and off, of course. It's been on my mind."

"And he says of course that you should leave."

" 'Leave' is a strong word." Only to me, of course.

"What do you call it?"

"I just call it going back to a normal life."

"This isn't normal here? Since when? You go to work . . ."

"It's not abnormal here, that isn't the point."

"You come home, we have dinner. You can do what you want at night; I've never said 'Robby, you have to be home tonight . . .' "

"That's not strictly true . . ."

"If you had a family, of course, that would be different . . ."

"But this isn't exactly *accelerating* the process of my having a family."

"I'm the last person to stop you. Nothing would make me happier . . ."

"*Nothing?*" I've begun whining even earlier than I thought.

The phone rings. I pick up, automatically. It's my aunt Hilde.

"Can she call you back?" I ask her. "We're just having a little discussion." My mother shakes her head, as if I had leaked a state secret. "We're still having dinner, Hilde."

"How is she doing?" Hilde asks.

"Fine."

"I think of her all day."

"Hilde, it's been a year and a half. For God's sake . . ."

"If she has the strength, she should call me."

Hilde hangs up. My mother is upset; her cheeks are red.

"It's not her business."

"That we're talking?"

"We're not talking. This is different. This is something she doesn't have to know. You think I tell my sister everything? I don't."

"I'm sure you don't."

"She doesn't tell me everything, either. She never did. I was always the open one in the family. Too open."

"I've never thought that anyone in the family was particularly open, but there's reasons for that, I'm sure. Growing up in Germany, afraid of being found out as Jews. I'm not assessing blame here, believe me."

"What's there to blame? Nobody did anything wrong. Maybe I loved you too much, maybe that was my fault as a mother."

"That's a whole other discussion, Mom."

"Why is that a whole discussion?"

"Whole other."

"Why?" Her eyes are curious. She purses and unpurses her lips. I fiddle with my beer bottle.

"Well, that's something we've never addressed directly. For want of a more polite word: incest."

She gets up and goes to the refrigerator, peering inside with a squinty explorer's gaze before retrieving a bottle of ginger ale and returning to her seat.

"I'm not sure I'm up to talking about it with you face to face," I tell her.

"About what?"

"What happened with us when I was twelve."

She smiles at this point, watches the ginger ale bubble as she pours it into an empty *yahrzeit* glass.

"If you think that was so unusual . . ."

"It was extremely unusual."

She waves dismissively.

"When you have children, you'll see, you love them so much . . ."

"That you sleep with them?"

"I never slept with you. What that was, was just . . . I loved you so much." She smiles again, this time tearily. My heart is pounding. "Now, you're a grown man and I'm an old bag." She shrugs, waits for my compliment, but I am speechless. "So it's all different. If that's why you want to leave, please . . . You've been here a year and a half, has anything happened?"

"No, obviously not. But that's not why I want to go back to my apartment . . ."

"I never even thought about it. There's enough on my mind without that. So I don't know why you bring it up except you're fishing for things . . ."

"I'm not fishing . . ."

"Or maybe your friend started in on it." She shakes her head. "I have no interest in that sort of thing." Can this be a certain disappointment I am feeling? "Why you want to bring this all up now, just for a reason to go back to that little apartment . . ."

"I don't *need* a reason to return to my apartment. I'm thirty-four years old."

"God willing, you'll have children of your own and then you'll see what your feelings are."

"I can't imagine that I'll get up in the middle of the night and go to bed with them."

"There are emotions you have that are indescribable."

"I have a normal range of emotions. What you're talking about is beyond that range."

"You don't know that."

"I know myself well enough, and I remember *so* vividly how I felt when it happened to me, that I can say unequivocally that it is something I would never inflict on one of my own kids. It is inconceivable."

She shrugs. "Okay. We change the subject."

"I don't want to change the subject." My legs are beginning to shake. "I don't think you have a clue as to what it made me feel like."

"When you're young, everything seems like a tragedy."

"It *was* a tragedy. To have my mother sleep with me was a tragedy."

"Maybe you should have me arrested. I've had enough pain in my life. Why not be arrested, make it complete."

"I'm not bringing a criminal action against you. I am simply telling you how I felt."

"Fine. So now I know." She gets up. "You have to go back to your apartment, go back."

"And that's the end of the discussion?"

"The discussion was about how much you had to go back to the city and live in that little apartment. You want to go, you're a big boy, so go."

"I'm talking about the other thing."

She adjusts the straps of the housedress, then bends down and extracts a tub of whipped butter from the refrigerator. When she straightens up, it is with some effort.

"This is an obsession of yours. It was nothing."

"It was *nothing?*"

"Things happen, you accept them, then you go on with your life. To go over and over the past . . ."

"We never discussed this!"

". . . what do you get from it except bitterness? I can't be bitter. That's not me."

It is a familiar feeling, swimming upstream against my mother's view of history.

"All I would like to know is, what did you feel when it happened, when you went creeping into my room."

"All I ever felt was how much I loved my *bubele*. What else could there be? You make such a production about it." She sits back down, rifles through the bread basket for a slice of challah.

"It is a production for me. The biggest production. I have never stopped thinking about it."

She smiles, puts her hand on mine.

"I give you permission to stop. I know your friend, he thinks I'm some sort of monster. I don't care what he thinks, he probably never had children, he never went through the life I did. He can sit there in his office and tell you whatever he wants; I know I loved you and I love you now, no matter what happens. That's all, and all the psychology in the world and the experts can't change that. If it upset you, I'm sorry, but you grew up beautifully, despite having a terrible mother . . ."

"I wasn't saying . . ."

"And that's the beginning and the end of it." She takes her hand off mine. "If you want, I'll pack for you."

How do I feel? Strangely rejected. So I stay for another six months.

1954 / (1988)

M
Y UNCLE Kurt has come to dinner with his wife, Grete. His first wife. She is a wiry and sallow-complexioned woman in steel-rimmed spectacles, a writer of what she calls "thought-poems." She and Uncle Kurt married in 1942, when they were both twenty and living in England. They arrived in America a year later and immediately took up residence in a "garden apartment" in Fresh Meadows, a domicile thought to be above their means. But Uncle Kurt was always ahead of the curve; whereas most refugees progressed by walking slowly backwards, Kurt was unafraid to step into the future. He had no truck with the past; Germany to him was just an evil memory—good riddance to bad rubbish. He arrived in the United States with an open heart and a bourgeois yen for patio furniture and barbecues, for restaurants and musicals and belted raincoats. He confused my father, who thought him "overambitious"; Kurt, in turn, found my father to be at best distant, at worst dysfunctional.

"Herbert, what do you want from life?" he would say. It was a question that deeply offended my father, who thought it inappropriate from a younger sibling.

"*Want?*" my father would say, as if the word itself was absurd.

"Want. As in 'I want that.' "

"We made it out alive. That's all I wanted."

"Bullshit," Uncle Kurt would say. "That can't be enough. Hav-

ing survived. 'What do you want in your life?' 'Not to be slaughtered.' There has to be more."

"Not for me. I'm older, I have a different perspective. What do
you want?"

"I want to be captain of my destiny," Kurt would say. I heard this
more than once. "I want to live a good American life and answer to
no one but myself." Grete would look away or occupy herself when
he spoke like this; sometimes she merely sat with her hands folded,
staring at the ceiling, "using her imagination," as my mother would
say. They were an intriguing couple, Kurt and Grete: theatrical,
vivid, historical, meant to be written about.

THIS October evening, Kurt and Grete are over because "they
haven't been over in a while." Kurt wears an orange shetland
sweater, brown slacks and loafers. Grete is wearing pants and a
sports jacket over an Arrow shirt. This is well before women in
men's wear was a common sight. Kurt hands my father a bottle of
Haig and Haig pinch, and throws his arms around my sister.

"You're too beautiful," he tells her. "You shouldn't be living in
this house." Carol has already begun her modeling career and is on
the way out for the evening, having delayed her leave-taking only to
greet Uncle Kurt, whom she likes but does not entirely trust.
("Sometimes when he hugs me," she had told me, "he gets *very*
close.")

"And this guy." He lifts me up. Uncle Kurt is several inches
shorter than my father, yet he seems to lift me higher. "This guy,
this *momser.*" He is smiling, but there is a cautionary, quizzical look
in his eye, as if he is appraising me for damage. "Getting bigger
every minute." He lowers me and my feet hardly seem to touch the
floor. I feel bigger, bigger than when he entered the door. Uncle
Kurt has that power over me, and I do not know whether it is
because he is larger, or my father smaller, than life.

Aunt Grete has brought my mother a mimeographed edition of
her latest work, a series of "thought-poems" entitled *Blümchen.*
Some of the poems are in English, others in German, and they are
free-association musings based on flowers, hence the title. My
mother nervously looks over the grainy mimeographed sheets, loath

to read them in case she reacts wrong. Grete is known to be extremely sensitive to criticism.

"I don't know where you find the time," she tells Grete. My father is examining the Haig and Haig bottle, squeezing it at the pinched-in part.

"She's got nothing but time," Kurt says breezily. "Herbert, you cheap shit, why don't you open the Haig." He winks at me. "I don't want you to give it to someone else as a present." I laugh. My father grunts and begins the process of laying out glasses and ice, which he does with great deliberation and formality. Grete walks into the living room as if it were a stage, a copy of her *Blümchen* in hand.

"This one is my favorite," she announces, lifting the mimeographed sheet before her eyes. She begins to read, facing the couch, on which no one is seated. My mother and Kurt and I are just entering the room.

> *If it be known,*
> *Little rose*
> *How brief your life,*
> *How short your bloom.*
> *If it be known*
> *In Time.*
> *Would I still tend to you,*
> *Cutting, watering, staring*
> *Out the Window*
> (Aus Dem Fenster)
> *Yes.*
> *If not,*
> *Why do we live?*

Grete asks for some ginger ale and sits down.

"Where you get these ideas, Grete," my mother tells her, before fetching her drink. "This is *unglaublich*. To have such thoughts, such a gift."

Grete crosses her legs and takes a cigarette from a silver Mark Cross case, a birthday present from Kurt. She strikes a match on the sole of her shoe, a gesture which never fails to excite me, then lights up, leans back. She is not a beauty, but in these exotic, eccentric moments, she is desirable. The way Uncle Kurt looks at her in the midst of these gestures—the reading, the match-striking—it is clear that there remains a fascination, an attraction. I watch the two of them closely because I have heard whispers of a troubled marriage. "Sometimes I wonder about them," I hear my mother say one night. She and my father are in their bedroom, the door almost closed. I stop, noiselessly, en route to the bathroom. My father, buttoning his pajamas, is standing beside the bed; my mother is already beneath the covers, her hair down, her hands folded in front of her.

"Wonder?" my father says.

"They're so different. I just get a feeling, an *unglück*, about them."

"They'll stay together," my father says, and shuts off the light. To me outside the door, the implication that a marital breakup was even within the realm of possibility gave Kurt and Grete's union a dark and tragic glamor. They were my Scott Fitzgerald and Zelda.

So this evening I watch their every move for some hint of trouble, as if they were carriers of a disease apt to strike at any moment. Divorce is unknown in my family and my neighborhood. It is something one reads about in the tabloids, a habit of the wealthy, like polo or grouse hunting. It implies choice, and therefore sex. I don't really *know* about the sex part, but I know that Kurt and Grete seem very different from my own parents. They seem to connect in a different way. Perhaps it is the lack of children, whether by choice or not a matter of frequent conjecture in our house.

"She can't," my father says one evening.

"You know this as a fact?" my mother replies.

"Why else?"

"Maybe they just don't want to."

"That's not Kurt."

"It's not Kurt?" My mother shuts off the water. She had been washing dishes. "You think he has such a feeling for children?"

"I love him," I say at this point. I had been pretending to read an Archie Annual.

My mother looks at my father with a glance that says this is not a fit subject for the ears of children. There are hundreds of such subjects. But my father continues.

"Of course," he says, "Kurt has a manner, he's irresponsible, he's a child himself in so many ways. But the feeling for children, this I don't doubt."

She turns the water back on.

"I wouldn't make such a statement."

"Why not?"

"I just wouldn't. He's your brother, so of course I love him, but there is something *shmearisch* about him sometimes." This is to say oily, slippery.

"In business maybe." My father has lit his pipe and is staring at the smoke as it rises to the dinette ceiling. "Not with children."

My mother looks at my father, and shakes her head. It is a nebulous gesture, meant to elicit further comment.

"What?" my father says.

"With Carol sometimes." She begins to scrub a pot. "I don't say anything."

"What do you mean, Mom?" I ask her. My father is gathering up and sorting the *World-Telegram*, preparatory to a visit to the bathroom.

She shrugs.

"I don't say anything."

"He likes Carol."

My father leaves the kitchen, walks quickly toward the hall that leads to the bathroom.

"Yes, he likes her."

"So what's wrong with that?"

She examines the pot she is cleaning, then turns to me.

"Nothing, *bubele*. Nothing wrong with that. If it's from the heart."

THIS evening Kurt is in expansive form. He is talking of a move to the suburbs, of business trips made recently to Larchmont.

"I have a feeling there, of newness. Beauty, yes. Gardens, wonderful homes, many of them built in the twenties, Tudor-style. But that American newness—in the stores, in the school buildings."

"So you would move there? Grete?" my mother asks.

"I haven't been. Kurt is very enthused." She picks at a boiled potato. "I haven't been yet."

"I haven't said we move tomorrow. For us, Fresh Meadows is still good. But I see a day where we outgrow it." He slices a piece of weisswurst, begins to chew it and looks out across the table as if into his future, a future that I could imagine would include no one else at the table, Grete included. "We have to live in this country, Herbert. We're not hiding anymore, right? So we move ahead, we explore. If there are new places, we go to them."

"I don't know," my mother says.

"I have a poem," Grete says, "a poem I work on about Kurt. It is called 'The Explorer.' It is about Sir Francis Drake but it is really about Kurt."

"She doesn't let me see it," he says, smiling at me, and I feel that we are comrades in a secret. An adult secret. "We can only guess, right, Robby? God only knows what she says about me."

"I give a hint." Grete smiles, revealing her irregular, yellowish teeth. Perhaps they are the reason for the infrequency of her smiles.

" 'Sir Francis Drake,' " she begins, " 'picked his boat, and set forth, eye to the future, back to the wind, thinking "If hearts are to be broken, so be it." ' "

My father drinks his beer down. Kurt claps his hands.

"An encouraging start," he exclaims.

"Grete, where you get these ideas . . ." My mother shakes her head in an ambiguous manner.

"I feel," Grete says, "that Kurt's heart contains all the feelings in the world, good and bad."

Kurt is unfazed.

"If one is in the export-import business, then you are dealing with everything in the world. Commerce between countries is like any other relationship. It takes time, it takes care, you have to recognize differences. One country's passion is another country's shame; one country's embarrassment is another country's pride. Every day you learn something; every day you are in the arena of the world, the whole world—the skyscrapers and the dust, the steel and the *schmutz*. Someone comes to work for Trans-Ocean, I tell him, 'Be prepared to engage the entire world.' And this is not a matter of book learning, Robby. This is what they call here street-knowledge."

"Kurt," my mother says, "he loves school."

"Let him speak for himself." He puts his surprisingly small and delicate hand on my head. "Robele, you love school?"

"I like school."

"Like is not love. Trust me."

"He loves it," my mother repeats. "He's just trying to impress his uncle Kurt."

"Are you?" asks Aunt Grete.

I shrug, embarrassed.

Aunt Grete smiles. Uncle Kurt looks at me with curiosity and also a certain discomfit. My love for him is something that he can comfortably accept only as admiration. Admiration for him as a man of the city, a man who has evolved as far into American-ness as is possible for a refugee without voice lessons or cosmetic surgery. His slightly bulbous nose, those pleading eyes, they marked his origins as certainly as a passport. Which is precisely the source of my love for him—his ability to transform himself without losing his refugee's continuous need for approval.

I am excused to go to bed. Uncle Kurt comes in to read to me. What he reads is an article in Sport Magazine concerning Early Wynn, a surly right-handed pitcher for the Cleveland Indians. The magazine features some photographs of Wynn and his children— beside a decorated Christmas tree (Wynn in a plaid shirt, crouching, amiable), fishing in some Michigan lake—but the story, entitled "Burly Early," focuses on a man who would unblinkingly throw a fastball at a cripple's head. Kurt, whose interest in baseball is minimal, reads it to me with his rolling r's and v's for w's, reads it in a kind of monotone. I have my head on his chest and his left arm is around me; I can feel the comfortable sweatered rise and fall of his breathing. "Wynn sat in the dugout seething, quietly furious at Al Lopez for pulling him out of a crucial situation. Lopez walked past him with his head down, but he was clearly aware of Wynn's contained fury. Later, in his managerial office, Lopez said, 'I know Early was angry but that's because he's a competitor. I'd rather have ten guys who get mad when they're yanked than a guy who goes quietly.'" Kurt puts the magazine down and turns his head to me. "What do you think about that?"

"I don't know," I tell him.

"It's no sin to be angry," he tells me.

"No," I say, not believing it. It's not so much a sin to be angry, as an aberration. Anger is as rare in my family as an epileptic fit, and is perceived in roughly the same way—as an attack.

"Your father, I know, he doesn't get angry."

"Not really, no. He gets more quiet than usual."

"But you love him."

"Oh, yes."

"He went through a lot."

"Sure."

"We all did. It's just how you handle it. But Herbert, he doesn't feel sorry for himself, that's the great thing."

"No, he doesn't."

"Does he read to you?"

"Sometimes. Or he tells me a story about when he was small."

"And your mother and he, they get along so well."

"Yeah." I wasn't sure what he was driving at.

"You're a little like Herbert, you know. You don't say so much."

"That's not true."

"Oh, it is. Do you get angry?"

"If there's a reason."

Uncle Kurt hugs me closer to him.

"Sometimes it's very good to get angry when there's no reason at all. Just don't tell your parents I told you so."

He folds the magazine shut.

"So," he says, "back to the world of adults. It's highly overrated, Robele, believe me."

"You get to stay up late."

"Yeah, but look with whom." He is smiling, but I am not convinced that he is joking. He kisses me on my forehead and returns to Grete and my parents in the living room. He closes the door but I reopen it slightly, because I like the low babble of voices; it helps me fall asleep. The knowledge that there is company, the knowledge that there are other people in the house besides my parents. This is very reassuring to me.

IT is still to me the biggest curse of living alone and childless—this haunting sense of unoccupied rooms, of lives unled. Emptiness and quiet. It scares me sometimes and then I must get up and put on the radio, low, tuned to a talk show or the all-night news. Often I turn the radio on in the living room or the kitchen, then retreat back to the bedroom, quickly, on tiptoe, as if afraid of disturbing someone. Then I jump into bed, my head deep in my pillow, and pray for an early sleep, which rarely comes because I am basically an insomniac. I wait for interruptions which never come, and that in itself keeps me up. My empty rooms, my ghost children. I lie there and they enter, one by one, with requests for water, for chaperoning to the bathroom for a midnight pee. I rehearse my answers. I rise and walk around the apartment as if accompanying them. In the distance, the radio speaks of three-alarmers in Brooklyn and the weekend weather. I have been living in this apartment since 1985. It's on 111th Street, six large West Side rooms, with much light and many ghosts.

"I SEE three children," I tell Dr. Singer. "Two boys and a girl. The girl is the youngest, about four, and I have a tendency to favor her. The boys are eleven and eight. Blond children, except for the middle boy, who has curly brown hair, like me."

"And the blond children take their coloring from your wife?"

"I suppose. But I never imagine a wife. Just the children."

"Never?"

"No."

"You like children?"

"I guess. I've always liked Carol's kids, but I'm sort of awkward with them. Not sure of how to touch them. Obviously, my model for how you touch children is not the greatest."

"Yes. How are you with your imaginary children?"

"Very patient."

"I mean physically."

"I touch them. I have my arms around them when I walk them to the bathroom. They lean in toward me when I'm in bed and I can smell their hair. Sweaty. Their breath is warm and sort of chocolatey . . . I feel like I love them." Tears well up in my eyes.

"You want children very much."

I can't answer immediately. The air conditioner turns over with great effort, as do I. An enormous sigh, almost a wail, passes through my body, and then I can speak.

"I would like children. It just seems like the remotest thing. It seems like something that is reserved for other people. Normal people."

"Your sister had children."

"My sister was never molested."

"But her relations with you . . ."

"They didn't seem to mark her in any way."

"Does she acknowledge these relations in any way?"

"In an offhand kind of manner. As in, 'when we were young and crazy.' 'We.' "

"Yes."

"Whatever it meant to her, it didn't prevent her from having children, or from having a series of intense physical relationships from a fairly early age."

"She was always sexually provocative."

"Always."

"And I imagine in your circles, among German refugees, she stood out."

"Well, you were a refugee, you would know, right? Sex was just a void with those people. Except for my uncle Kurt, which is why I keep talking about him. He was like an island of sanity."

"Although, it sounds to me, like he also had difficulty in getting close."

"Compared to my father, he was a figure of enormous intimacy."

I am seeing my kids again. They are seated at the end of the analytic couch. The girl, today her name is Julia, has her hand on my shin, listening raptly. She's a lot like Libby. The boys appear to be bored. Peter and Barney.

"They really are handsome kids, my kids. They have an intelligence in their faces and a trust. And when I see that trust, and think of how my own trust was so completely violated . . . Why can't I get off this? After what, fifteen years? Yammering about being violated. She's dead for two years already, what's the fucking point?"

"It has nothing to do with her being dead. It was never resolved in life."

"So this is a life sentence? Now that she's out of here."

"It doesn't have to be. Not at all."

"How the hell do I get out of it?"

"Libby, when you speak of her, sounds like she represented a way out. We've never satisfactorily resolved why."

"She just was. Had you known her . . . Her whole *persona* radiated mental health. Then, of course, the great irony of her disastrous physical health. Maybe because she was the first person I ever spoke to about the incest, but of course it wasn't an accident that I spoke to her. She was a person you *had* to level with; there was no possibility of hiding with her. When she got sick, it seemed like I was doomed along with her. That I was doomed to live in the past because she represented my future."

"Did you ever feel that you made her sick?"

"That I actually caused her illness?"

"Yes."

"Not consciously. You mean that as a result of what I told her, my vile secret, that she became stricken with leukemia? Or that it was my contaminated, befouled semen . . ." My face feels flushed. "I feel a little dizzy."

"Now?"

I sit up on the analytic couch and put my head between my legs, like a passenger expecting a crash landing. There is a moment in which vomiting seems like a real possibility, then it passes. I lie back down, my forehead, my shirt, soaked.

"Yikes. That's a first."

Silence.

"I said, 'Yikes, that's a first.' "

"You felt dizzy."

"Dizzy and nauseous."

"Out of control?"

"Fine, have it your way: out of control."

"I was asking."

"Then phrase it like a question: 'Did you feel out of control?' "

Of course he does not rephrase the question. He knows that I am stalling. I know that he knows I am stalling, and all of this tender knowledge of each other's intentions is costing me one hundred dollars an hour.

"You were speaking . . ."

"About my semen. I said the magic word and the duck came

down and gave me fifty dollars and instant vertigo. 'Befouled se-men' was the precise phrase."

"Yes."

"Yes. Nice turn of phrase. Like it was contaminated. Toxic waste."

"And you felt a powerful physical sensation."

"Like I was going to puke my guts out. Because I probably feel that way."

"About your semen."

"My semen. My semen lies over the ocean. It's a ridiculous word: semen." The crack in Dr. Singer's ceiling seems a little longer than before. "I feel like I was poisoned. That my fluids were poisoned. That I bear this stain, and that I somehow befouled Libby. That in telling her the secret I somehow killed her. Leukemia is a blood disease, you know . . . all those white cells going berserk. It's a sort of . . . *liquid* disease."

"So you make the connection to your semen."

"You love saying that word, don't you?"

"It's the appropriate word. If you prefer 'sperm.' "

" 'Sperm' I don't like. 'Semen' is fine, wonderful in fact. Yeah, I make the connection: my see-men entered her bloodstream and poisoned her. She became gravely ill. She died. So I never told another woman about it."

"For fear of doing it again, poisoning another woman?"

"Partially."

"And partially what else?"

"Because I wanted the secret to belong to Libby. If she died for it, at least let it be all hers."

"So you feel that Libby was a martyr."

"Yes."

"Like your mother claimed to be."

My children have disappeared from the foot of the couch. I want them back, but can't summon them.

THE little girl reappears at midnight, as I stare at my clock-radio. She wants to get into bed with me.

"You can't, darling," I tell her.

"I'm having a bad dream."

"Then we'll walk you back and sit there until your dream goes away."

"I want to be in bed with you."

She looks a little like my sister: those almond-shaped eyes, her lips already full and seductive at age four.

"You can't be in bed with me. You just can't." I take her small warm hand and lead her (gently but firmly) back to her bed in the study. Then I return to my bed, where I lie awake until dawn.

1970 / (1959)

I AM alone with Libby when she dies. Her parents have gone down to the cafeteria when she slips away from consciousness for the last time. Our final conversation is a search for the name of Mildred Pierce's villainous daughter.

"Velma?" she asks. Libby weighs about sixty-five pounds at this point and has dubbed herself "Miss Turkey Drumstick of 1970."

"Velma?" I repeat. "No. Like that. Verna, Vella . . ."

"Veda," she says and smiles. It's a smile so weak that it looks to hurt. "Veda."

"That's right," I say, and then her eyes close. Her breathing becomes unnaturally and startlingly loud, as if amplified, and I know this is it. I could call the nurse, but I don't. If I leave the room to summon her dazed and frightened parents she might die alone, unobserved. So I witness her death: from one moment to the next. I hold her hand and attempt to speak to her.

"Libby?" Her hand is warm and still. "Libby." The second time I simply state, rather than call, her name. Her face is set in the repose of the sleep I know so well, but I feel that she is spiraling away from me, into history. Receding from me. I sit holding her hand for the longest time, shivering uncontrollably, watching her, attempting to memorize her face. I do this until her parents arrive, with a banana and a white brownie for me, and they see the way I am seated there and then, well, you can imagine. I've sort of blocked it all out, the way I tend to block out scenes of strong emotion. I remember that I left the room before they wrapped Libby up like a leftover and took her to wherever they take the unliving. I remember that her parents offered to call me a cab—one doesn't forget these details, these exercises of manners—and I remember her mother insisting that I take the banana and the white brownie. I also took the book that Libby had been reading at the time, *Portnoy's Complaint*. Dr. Kalter and his wife and I stood outside Mount Sinai for a while until it started to rain, then they went back inside to be in the same building with Libby. Mrs. Kalter kissed me and told me that Libby had loved me so very, very much and I began to cry, and then I started to walk, with my book, my banana and my white brownie, in the rain.

I AM a graduate assistant at Columbia at this time, sharing an apartment on 110th Street with Jerry Raskin, a European History grad student specializing in the Kellogg-Briand Pact. He has a truly scintillating, Algonquin Round Table-style wit but is tortured by his appearance—round-shouldered and ravaged by pockmarks. I hope he will not be in the apartment, but there he is, hunched over the dining room table, eating a sandwich. It is June and river light still streams in through the windows at seven-thirty in the evening. I have lost all sense of time or season: snow would not surprise me, or volcanic heat. I still can't stop shivering. Jerry looks at me and knows.

"I'm really sorry, guy. I mean . . ." His mouth is half-filled with tuna.

"I appreciate it."

"If you want to talk or not talk. Just tell me and I'll lie low . . ."

"For now that's probably the best, not that . . ."

"Hey, I understand. This is not a situation in which you need me to play the role of the Deeply Compassionate Roommate." Jerry is wearing a bright red Columbia tee-shirt. Red does not flatter him. "You need me to be a genuine mensch. This I will endeavor to do." He rises. "I can't imagine that you're hungry, but there is sufficient tuna to feed the Afrika Corps, if they, the Afrika Corps, were so inclined. I'll make you a sandwich, or a casserole, or . . ."

"I'm really not hungry."

"Of course not." He stares at me. "I won't ask . . ."

"Don't. Not yet. In time, I'll probably want to talk, but now . . ."

"Sure." He sits down again. "If you want anything, just holler. Or whisper. Or bleat. I'm going to be in all night working. If you'd prefer absolute solitude, I could go over to Low, I suppose . . ."

"That's really not necessary. I'm just going to lie down for a while." Which is what I do. I close the double doors behind me— my room was a dining room in this apartment's previous, more elegant incarnation, and these doors once paneled in glass have long since been painted over in a kind of gaseous and mustardy yellow-beige, less a color than a suggestion of previous color. I lie down, placing Libby's copy of *Portnoy* on the bed beside me, along with the white brownie and the banana, and immediately begin to sink. It is a measured descent, a sense of weightless fall, as if I am slowly tumbling out of my body. Probably a wish—although I am too numb even to be aware of wanting to die and join Libby. I don't feel alive enough to wish death. I am a survivor, a physical survivor—a wall left after a house has been knocked over. Nothing more.

"Veda," she said. "Veda." Ann Blyth played Veda, and Libby, seated beside me at the Wisconsin Film Society, grabbed my arm every time she lied to poor Joan Crawford.

"Veda," I say aloud, when the phone rings. There can be no doubt about who is calling, or how I dread anything she might have to say on the subject of Libby's death.

I pick up the phone, holding it a little away from my face.

"Hello."

"We heard," she says. "I thought you would call but when you didn't Dad called the hospital. They told us. A beautiful way to find out."

"I just got home."

"Some switchboard they have there. I don't know how many rings until someone answered. Finally we got through. What time did it happen; that they didn't tell us."

"Three-twenty-seven."

"It's almost eight now."

"That's right. It's almost eight now."

"Were you sleeping? You sound tired." This means that she has perhaps detected some anger in my tone.

"I was resting."

"You must be exhausted."

"Yeah."

"These things are always hard. When I heard what happened to my cousin Trude, how she died, in Belgium, what those bastards did to her, and she was only thirty-two . . ."

"*This* has never happened to you, this precise thing, that the love of your life wastes away . . ."

"Don't upset yourself. I worry enough about you."

I put the telephone on my chest and stare at the ceiling. "Veda," Libby was saying, "Veda." Pleased with herself. That last painful smile. Her phone number is 362-8814. My stomach turns over at the thought of dialing that number and hearing it ring. A black telephone in a dark apartment. Her lamp, her bed, her quilt. Our quilt.

"Are you there?"

I pick the phone up.

"Yes."

"You want to come out?"

"No."

"Do you good. Stay here for a while."

"I can't . . . I have work."

"Bring the work with you. We'll leave you alone."

"No."

"Did you have dinner?"

"I'm not hungry."

"You have to eat something. The funeral is tomorrow?"

"Thursday."

"Not tomorrow?"

"Thursday."

"How come?"

"It's Thursday. I don't know why particularly. But it's Thursday."

"You'll tell me the time when you call tomorrow."

"It's at ten-fifteen, at Riverside."

"I don't have a pencil. We'll talk in the morning, you'll tell me. Dad sends his best. You know how he feels."

THEY go to the cemetery, of course. My mother wouldn't miss a burial, although, in truth, this is one she would probably have liked to avoid. I am dry-eyed throughout the stunned proceedings, and even the sight of the pine box being lowered into the damp soil of the Kalter family plot in New Jersey doesn't bring me to tears. I just shiver continually, even though the temperature on this day of interment is near eighty. I shiver and feel nauseated, loose of bowel, liquid, motile. Libby's grandmother is hysterical, close to hurling herself into the earth after the coffin; she serves as a sponge for everyone's emotion, soaking it all up, not allowing a drop to spare. I see it as a deranged and piggish performance, and my strongest emotion of the afternoon, the only one I allow myself to feel, is a wish to stab Libby's grandmother through the heart. She makes grief impossible, only anger. And of course my mother, seated in her kitchen sipping post-burial tea, defends her.

"You can't understand what she felt. That loss."

"What are you talking about? She can't understand what I'm feeling."

"To lose a grandchild."

"Libby's parents weren't carrying on like that."

"They're psychiatrists . . ."

"They're wonderful people." I'm defending them!

". . . so they have this all figured out in some way. 'You don't lose control at your child's funeral. You hold it in.' The old lady couldn't do that. She was too honest."

"She's too self-absorbed."

My father lights up his pipe.

"How old is she?" he asks.

"Eighty, ninety, I have no idea." She's seventy-six, I know exactly, but I'll be goddamned if I'm going to admit it. "She was carrying on so that everyone would feel sorry for her, rather than for her granddaughter. Period. It turned my stomach. There's Lib being buried, and can I even concentrate on it? No! I have to worry about whether or not this miserable old bitch is going to jump into the grave or not." I absently eat a grape, at which point my mother places the entire bunch of grapes on my plate. I pick them up and put them back into the fruit bowl.

"You know everything," my mother says. "You have the whole world figured out."

"If you carried on like that at my funeral," I tell her, "I'd jump out of the box and strangle you."

My mother smiles and takes my hand.

"If you came out of the box, I'd be the happiest person in the world."

"Then it would be worth it," adds my father, happy the conversation has turned lighter. They are both smiling at me, for all their reasons. I feel dizzy and drink some water.

"Give me a minute." I get up and walk into the hallway, then into their room, closing the door behind me. I lie down on their bed. An ice-cream truck parked on the street below endlessly plays a mechanical jingle. My mother knocks.

"Robby?"

"I'll be out in a second."

"If you want anything . . ."

"Just give me a second." She walks away. "He wants a second alone," I hear her say, "and who can blame him." I am intensely grateful for this momentary recognition of my pain. I lean over on their bed, reach for the telephone, and dial Libby's number. It begins to ring, and I listen with a kind of deranged hope. She is still listed in the white pages, is she not? "Kalter, L." immediately beneath "Kalter, Kenneth, DDS." I looked it up last night, gazing for ten minutes at the spot on page 623, my smudged finger pink and corporeal beneath her name, her name like a ghost in this registry of Manhattan's living, of the phoned and the phoning. I called then, last night, just for a minute. Three rings, then I hung up. Now I let it ring and ring, a kind of signal, a call to the beyond awaiting an answering gesture of some sort. Even interference on the line would be sufficient. Static: an indication of the potential for life at the other end. It rings on. I drift into semi-consciousness amidst thoughts of picnics and sex and balcony kisses until the phone is suddenly, heart-stoppingly, picked up.

"Hello?" It is a Slovakian accent. Her super, Josef.

"What are you doing in her apartment?"

"Who is this? Phone ring and ring. Neighbor call. Half-hour phone ringing. Dead, Kalter. Cancer. You are friend?"

I hold the phone away from my ear but I cannot bear to hang it up. I feel violated. This man in her apartment, this bulky, mustached man in his stone-washed jeans and University of Arizona Sun Devils sweatshirts. A neighbor complained. I can't ring a phone for a few minutes? It's a way of praying for me; it is my gift of hope for the world.

"Two days ago die. Cancer. Phone out tomorrow. You are friend? Why you ring so long?"

"I thought she was in the shower."

"Half-hour ringing until neighbor call. Am sorry. Two days die. Very young. Okay? Phone take out tomorrow. You call parents if you are friend. In Boston live. Doctors. But no more this number. Am very sorry if you are friend, okay?"

Josef hangs up the phone and I have to say, all in all, that Libby would have been proud of his performance. A super's eulogy: practical but not without feeling. I would not be displeased to have him perform similar duty for me in the event of my death. And perhaps it should come as no surprise: who better than a super to understand both the aging process and the element of surprise—the decay of pipes, the sudden failure of a young boiler. Both Libby and I felt that supers in New York City buildings were not unlike captains of ships. On stormy nights we would wonder whether Josef might not have the authority to perform our wedding ceremony. Supers understand the life cycle; they await with resignation the signaling of the next Event: the frantic clanging of a stuck elevator, the becalmed and fetid waters of a stopped-up toilet, the bright, unsteady entrance of a drunken doorman. No rabbi or priest is as equipped to deal with the infinite variety of a day's disasters. Libby would have been very, very happy with this conversation. I am curiously elated and tempted to redial her number, simply to identify myself and congratulate Josef, but I am aware that I am not in my right mind.

"I SPOKE to the super," I tell my parents. They are seated in the living room. My father is reading the *Post;* my mother is, inevitably, sewing. I remember a great deal of sewing, but very little in the way of finished products. Perhaps she only repaired things.

"What super?" she asks.

"Libby's super."

"About what?"

"I called her apartment, just to hear her phone ring."

My mother looks up from her sewing; she is wearing reading glasses, her hair is up in a kind of sausage roll across the top of her head.

"I don't understand."

My father, maybe not so surprisingly, does.

"He just wanted to hear the old ring, right? The old ring." Perhaps because he is an expert at the Unspoken, at the Implied, my father recognizes the secret magic of my act.

"Exactly," I tell him. He nods, sucks on his pipe.

"The old ring. I understand that. For reassurance. One last call."

"I don't know why you would do that," my mother says, perhaps baffled. "Just to upset yourself."

"The super answered . . ."

"What's he doing in that apartment? Cleaning it out?"

"He was, in his way, deeply compassionate."

"The super," my father says. "It's not so surprising."

"I think your calling like that is unhealthy." She continues her sewing, while staring at me. "Maybe it's none of my business. But the day of the funeral, to start calling the house just to torture yourself . . ."

"The purpose was not to torture myself, but, as Dad said, just to hear the ring, just to feel the potential of her answering. In a way, it's no different than looking at a photograph."

"Robele, don't do it anymore."

"Tomorrow it'll be disconnected." I look at my father. He has tears in his eyes. It is the only time that I have ever seen this, the only time in my life. His eyes are welling up.

"They do it so quickly," he says. "So quickly they pull the phone out of the wall. What are they afraid of?"

"They need the phone," my mother says with authority.

"They don't need the phone," my father says. Is this an argument? "The line maybe. The number. But why would they be in such a hurry to give this poor girl's number to someone?"

"Maybe it's just a matter of economy," I say, suddenly a voice of practicality. "Her parents don't want the line to be open. They're responsible for the bill."

"Who's going to make calls?" My father won't get off this. "The super? He has nothing better to do than go up to her apartment and place phone calls?"

"They're going to show the apartment, I suppose." Life proceeds. Locks are changed, phones taken out, phones brought in, television cables installed, painters summoned. The world continues; it is not unpleasing to think of this, that we are not actually missing anything; just cycles of repetition. So what is living and dying, then? It is all a series of accidents from beginning to end: who your parents are, what is between your legs, your height, your beauty or ugliness. We are just manifestations of a floating genetic crap game. It is all a kind of comfort. The comfort of helplessness, of fate.

"I die," my father says, "and what am I in this country? An occupant. In Germany you died, the house continued: your children lived there, you had built something. The thought that phones would be removed, that there would be repainting, to me this is like a desecration. But it is like everything else here."

"Herbert, why get excited about this?" My mother looks a trifle alarmed; she looks to me as if there is something I could do to turn the conversation around.

"It's not a question of getting excited," he says. His pipe has gone out and he doesn't bother to relight it. "It's a question of dignity, of what distinguishes us from house plants. Apparently, nothing. This super had nothing better to do than hang around her apartment . . ."

"He had gone up because someone had called downstairs about the phone ringing. Complaining."

"Why do they think it's ringing?" My father is not completely rational at this moment.

"Herbert, it was bothering them."

"Someone is trying to reach the girl. Maybe it's someone who is frantic, maybe it is someone grieving, like Robby. The phone is so loud it's like a fire alarm? It's a phone; let it ring. If someone wants to hear Libby's phone ring for the last time, let them do it in peace.

Instead this man has to rush up there and grab the phone off the hook."

"It was a shock to hear it picked up, I must say."

"Why you had to call . . ." My mother shakes her head as if I have been arrested for indecent exposure.

"My point remains," my father continues, "that there is a level of decency after a death, otherwise death is just the flushing of a toilet. One moment to the next. Monuments must be left. Remains. That's not possible for us in this country. Here we rent; here we borrow. We're a name on a door. The door is made of steel; our name is on a piece of cardboard. Those who were slaughtered in Europe left more behind."

"You don't mean that, Herbert."

My father runs a hand through his hair; it stands straight up on his head, as if he were a Man of Science. He has escaped into pure thought; his eyes seem curiously unfocused. I am a little fearful.

"We are tenants here, we are names on a sheet of paper." It is like a speech from a play. "Everything is temporary. Maybe we should all drive around in trailers and live in parks."

My mother is aghast.

"I don't know where this comes from," she says.

"You miss Germany?" I ask him.

"You would drive into a town, Robby, and you knew who lived there. In each building: mother, father, grandfather, idiot nephew. You knew. Successive lifetimes were lived in each place. That's what I miss. The order." He stares at my mother with a curiously lost look, as if he has misplaced and then found her, and then forgot why he had been looking in the first place. I feel somewhat faint. "Things happen here . . ." he trails off.

"Things," I say, in a hollow, false voice.

"To our generation. Because this adjustment is difficult, this adjustment to being temporary. We pretend to be comfortable with it, but basically we can't understand it. It is like some sort of experiment." He relights his pipe.

"We do our best," my mother says. She's in neutral gear here. "What else can we do?"

"We never adapted. None of us."

"Uncle Kurt seemed to," I say.

"Kurt is the best actor among us. I am probably the worst." He looks at me. He must know. My legs are trembling.

"You're just a different type of person."

"Kurt was younger, he could throw himself into this country with more enthusiasm. The continuity didn't mean that much to him because when the Nazis showed up he was just a boy. But still there are scars. A lot with him is show, a kind of bullshit."

My mother arises to answer the ringing telephone. She leaves the room.

"You had it hard, Robele," he says to me. "I know that."

Tears flood my eyes. Is he forgiving me for fucking his wife? He can't be.

"What you went through today, the last few weeks . . ."

"Yes . . ."

"You had it hard always. What the experience was for us, our discomfort, this was handed down to you; and you, you and Carol, didn't even have the excuse of being refugees. You were semi-refugees. And your mother is very intense. Very intense. So I know this was not an easy thing for you. Growing up."

"No."

"In no respect was it easy. I know this. And I apologize for not understanding this earlier. We were all very caught up with ourselves." Am I dreaming this conversation? "Our complaining, our being so wounded. You had to pity us, right?"

"In a way."

"In a big way. 'My poor parents, what they went through.' It wasn't fair to you; I didn't realize it until recently and then, today, when I saw you burying this sweet girl, again I realize you have your own suffering; it doesn't have to be measured against anyone else's. Whatever the life is in this country, it is your life, let it be yours. The good and the pain. I don't think your mother gets this the same way, but you should know that I do. I felt so bad for you today, Robele."

"Thank you." I can barely speak.

"I thought, 'This is my son and he has suffered. Like everyone else in the world has to suffer, he is now suffering. And it is his separate sorrow. It's not connected to mine, or Liesl's, or the Nazis or any of that self-serving *scheissdreck*. It is all his, this moment of pain.' You looked to me like my little boy, maybe more so than when you actually were little, because then we were all so caught up in being refugees we didn't see your pain. So forgive me for my selfishness."

"You weren't so selfish."

"We were all selfish. We had permission to be selfish. We had a free pass. You kids didn't."

"I sometimes think," I speak very gingerly, "that you must have resented me . . ."

"For what?" He waves a dismissive hand. Okay, he has no idea of what happened. None. Successive waves of relief and guilt wash over me. He will never know; I will forever have this over him.

"I'm very sorry," I tell him.

"For what?"

I am out of words. I go to him and put my arms around him, and then I cry into his shoulder. He smells of pipe tobacco and soup. It is an old and reassuring smell. He puts his arms around me, pats me on the back.

"Okay," he says. "Okay."

My mother reenters the room, sees us this way.

"That was Aunt Hilde. She's so upset about Libby she doesn't think she can sleep."

My father and I, still entwined, ignore her.

"I told her take a sleeping pill."

I T ' S Easter week and school is out, so my father invites me to come into town and have lunch. He is no more a commanding presence in the shabbily genteel offices of Chronicle Publications than he is at home, but the absence of my mother gives him a certain solitary strength nonetheless. It is like seeing Costello without Abbott or Burns without Allen; just the fact of doing a solo act, without being cued, interrupted or contradicted, metamorphoses him. He looks taller, in his suit and cordovan shoes, almost Lincolnesque (if Lincoln had been five foot nine). He introduces me to people with American nicknames: "Tom" Harris, "Bob" Larsen, and to his boss, Mr. Charles Stein.

Mr. Stein is a small man with dense eyebrows and scary rimless glasses. He wears a dark brown suit and a starched white shirt with

French cuffs. I stand in front of his desk like a prisoner brought before the warden.

"You're grown a lot this year."

"Yes, sir." My father stands silently in back of me. While relatively chatty with his co-workers, the presence of Mr. Charles Stein instantly reduces him to hoarse, mumbled monosyllables.

"We all grow up, right, Herbie?"

"Oh, yes," croaks my father. Herbie.

"You should come in more often, Rob. I ask your father about you all the time."

"I'm busy at school."

Mr. Stein takes off his glasses and cleans them with a Kleenex. Without his glasses, he looks younger and oddly mouselike.

"It goes by too quickly, right, Herbie?"

"Oh, yes," says my father. "Like the wind it goes."

Mr. Stein puts his scary glasses back on. "You'll have the story on the new wing of Brickman's this afternoon?"

"Absolutely," says my father.

Mr. Stein nods. My father taps me on the shoulder. Our audience with Mr. Stein is over.

WE eat at Prexy's on Fifty-ninth Street, where they serve "the hamburger with the college education." Banners from Ivy League and other colleges festoon the walls; they make me feel as if I am going to be leaving home soon.

"Does he like you?" I ask my father.

"Who?"

"Mr. Stein."

"Oh, yes. We get along."

"He doesn't seem like the easiest person . . ."

"He's not so bad. A certain manner he has which isn't always very charming . . ."

"He's cold."

"His wife is not so well. She's a little"—my father touches his temple—"a little *mishugah*."

"Like really crazy?"

"She's very nervous." In my family "very nervous" could mean anything from simple insomnia to schizophrenia. "It's difficult for him at home." He cuts a french fry with his knife and fork.

"You're not afraid of him?"

My father looks at me, weighing whether I am asking him or telling him.

"What do you think?"

"What do I think? I guess if he were my boss I'd be afraid of him. He could scream at me, he could fire me . . ."

"Any boss can do that, Robele, not just Mr. Stein."

"So the answer is yes, you are afraid of him?"

"The answer is I find my work pleasant, and do not wish to look for new work. I like my hours. My pay is not for Rockefeller, but it isn't so bad for a *schlemiel* refugee who came here with thirty-five dollars in his pocket. That is my answer. Do you want another burger?"

"No, thank you."

"I take some coffee."

I watch him sip his coffee as the plates are cleared away. The waitress asks "No dessert for the young man?" but no, I do not wish to impose dessert on him. I can't bear to see that extra fifty cents added to the check.

He reflexively checks his watch—"We still have a couple of minutes"—then returns to his coffee, sipping it with slow quiet pleasure. He's getting older: there are lines around his eyes, his hair is turning silver and he's developed a nervous blink. I look at him and I see a photograph, as if he is already dead and looking at me from a mantelpiece. I know that I have betrayed him, yet feel that he has somehow been an accessory to the crime, a silent accomplice. Maybe he wanted it to happen. Maybe it happens in lots of families. Maybe it is normal.

SHE is seated at the kitchen table with a cup of tea, wearing a robe and smoking a cigarette. I have never seen her smoke.

"You had a good time with your father?"

"It was fine. How come you're smoking?"

"It's a Kool. Not like a regular cigarette."

"I've never seen you smoke."

"Before you were born, sometimes. You can ask your sister."

I am standing in the foyer, my jacket still on. She crosses her legs, picks a strand of tobacco from her lip.

"But how come now?"

She shrugs, girlish, fixes her hair.

"I was nervous."

"About what?"

"Things."

She looks at me, then looks away, waiting for evidence of my concern.

"What things?" I say, of course.

She draws deeply on her cigarette; smoke comes billowing from her nostrils. She is like a road-company Barbara Stanwyck, but more frightening. "I worry that you don't love me anymore."

She sips her tea. My legs begin trembling.

"Mom."

"I guess I should expect it."

"I don't know exactly what you mean . . ."

"It's good that you and your father get close. You know how much he loves you. I'm happy for him that you two have lunch. Maybe you and I have lunch sometime."

"I certainly see you a lot more than I do Dad. I mean, Dad and I hardly ever do this."

"That's my fault?"

"I'm not saying it's your fault or anything like that . . ."

"Maybe we have lunch sometime. That's all. Not fancy, in the neighborhood. You're grown so much." Her robe comes loose. She's just wearing a brassiere on top. "I have my memories."

"Mom, what happened with us . . ."

"Nothing happened. Nothing happened that isn't good."

1989 / (1958)

D R. S I N G E R ' S air conditioner has broken down. A window fan pushes warm, sooty air across the room.

"It occurs to me that I may have never really loved anyone or anything in my life."

"Not Libby?"

"It's so long ago. Did I love her, or did I love the fact that she was the only one who knew about me."

"I knew about you."

"But she loved me. You do this for money. She took in that information and then she loved me."

"Yes."

" 'Yes.' You do this for money, let me say it again. For *money*. You're not going to react, of course, but the fact is that two people have known about it—Libby, who loved me, and you, who take my money. Who not only doesn't love me, but who basically doesn't care if I live or die. If I go home and bump myself off, my hour will be filled by somebody else, and that'll be that."

He doesn't go for the bait. I turn around. His hands are folded in his lap. He's wearing that pathetic green sports jacket with the suede patches on it. When I think of him staring into his closet in the morning, deciding which of his awful shrink ensembles he's going to wear . . . He blinks at me.

"So much seems imaginary to you. These children you invent, you turn around to make sure I'm still here . . ."

I turn back and put my hands behind my head, like someone resting in a hammock, like someone enjoying himself. "I know you're there."

"The one thing, however, that you never doubt, that you never feel is imaginary, is the incest."

I let that one sit for a minute or two.

"You're doubting it?"

"I'm not saying I doubt it. I'm saying you never seem to."

Dr. Singer has a rotating fan. It has turned away; now it rotates back, blows across my hair.

"I find that fan extraordinarily distracting."

"Would you like me to turn it off?"

"No."

"It gets very hot in here without it. I realize it can be distracting, but I find that the buildup of heat is equally distracting."

"All right. Enough with the fan. I know I brought it up; I wasn't asking for a fucking onslaught of rationality about it."

Silence. I've hurt his feelings. I don't care.

"Perhaps you're angry with me because I questioned the in-cest . . ."

"Fuck you."

". . . so you raise the issue of the electric fan."

"Fuck you. You're not questioning the incest, you're saying I've invented everything else, so I invented that, too, and I find it the most extraordinary thing for you to say, because it's been the whole raison d'être for my treatment."

"You clearly have a need for it. It's the one thing you cling to through thick and thin."

"Thick and thin. That's a neat turn of phrase."

No response.

"Thick and thin, I said; that's a neat turn of phrase."

"The last time we spoke, you were discussing your father's re-markable forgiveness of you, the night of Libby's burial. It seemed totally out of character with everything you have ever described about him."

"I never said he was a monster."

"No, you never said that. He has been someone, however, who stayed out of your life. Remote. Behind a newspaper. Suddenly, he asks for a kind of forgiveness. He understands the nature of your childhood. Rather than this cipher you've been dismissing for twenty years, he seems to be a wise and compassionate man."

"It was a kind of outburst from him. Spontaneous."

"So what?"

"It was completely out of the ordinary for him to speak like that."

"It would be, I think, completely out of the ordinary for any parent."

"You say that out of your vast experience."

"I say that out of my experience, yes. Vast or otherwise. It sounds like something that people dream their parents would say, taking them off whatever hook they have either been placed on or placed themselves on."

"So maybe I invented that, too. I invented the incest, I invented this . . . Maybe I grew up in an orphanage, maybe I was raised by the Sisters of Mercy. Everything I say is, according to you, bullshit. Maybe I should lie back and have you describe my actual childhood to me. Start wherever you want."

"Our time is up."

"I'll bet it is."

M Y bar mitzvah takes place on January 18, 1958, a gray, arctic and unforgiving Saturday. The service is held in Corona's one shul, a small brick edifice with a blue awning on National Avenue. It is today an *iglesia* honoring that Jesus partial to Columbians; in 1958, it is still Congregation Shearith Sholom, a "reform" temple that pleases no one in my family, but offends the fewest. In January, forgotten Christmas bulbs still sway in the icy wind on National Avenue, a narrow thoroughfare considered off the beaten track even by Corona's standards; discount clothiers, barren "superettes" and Army-Navy stores set its bleak and forgotten tone.

The bar mitzvah is conducted largely in English and seems to be for someone else; I stand outside the entire event. There are several German-Jewish congregations that would have had far more cultural appropriateness to my family history, but they have all been rejected on various grounds: geographical distance, rabbis considered by my mother to be "showboats." Rabbi Shulman, my spiritual mentor, is by no definition a showboat. A stout man in his mid-fifties, his bearing is less rabbinical than low-rent commercial: he would be perfectly at home on the selling floor of a hat or shoe store. But this is in no way inappropriate to the congregation he leads, which is at once poor and curiously undevout. There is a begrudging and obligatory nature to the services, as if the congregants are present less to praise God than to serve out their parole obligations. They are neither proud nor ashamed to be Jews; it is simply a fact of life, like baldness or poverty. They wear their religion not on their sleeves, but sewn into the linings of their Bonds sports jackets. Come the pogrom, they know they will be shot down like the rest of their co-religionists, through no fault of their own; for now, however, they are "Americans," free to stand in front of the candy store and wait for the arrival of the *Daily News* like everyone else.

Rabbi Shulman himself is a *Daily News* reader. On more than one occasion I have arrived for Hebrew lessons on a darkening after-school afternoon to find him hunched over the *News*, studying race results, a Lucky Strike burning in his fingers.

"My high-class German is here," he would say.

I knew nobody like him; he was a social rung below even my sister's former lover Buddy. But what I admired about Rabbi Shulman is that he had persisted in being a rabbi. He had taken the definition of what a rabbi was into new territory; a rogue, outlaw rabbi, hiding out from a theological posse, from real rabbis, the ones who were quoted in the New York *Times* or had their signatures on boxes of matzoh.

"Here." He turns the pages of the *News*, points to the daily aphorism of Ching Chow, the beloved pigtailed Oriental. " 'Man who gambles loses face more than money.' There's something in that." He crushes out his Lucky Strike into a large cut-glass ashtray already littered with butts. "So how's my high-class German today?"

"He's fine."

"Counting your bar mitzvah *gelt* already?"

"No, sir."

He is almost handsome when he smiles. His teeth are yellow

from nicotine, but there is a seductive intelligence in his eyes. His nose looks to have been broken on more than one occasion. The rabbi claims he played amateur ice hockey; other students have passed the word that an enraged husband did the damage with his fists.

"You're not doing this for the money, that's good." He lights another Lucky, starts coughing for such a prolonged period that he can barely wave out the flame of his match. Steam hisses on the radiator. We are in the rabbinical "study" of Shearith Sholom, a dingy ground-floor office directly off the drafty tabernacle itself. "German Jews, the money's not that big a deal, am I right?"

"You're probably right. I haven't thought that much about money."

"It's not discussed at home?"

"Almost never." This was the truth. Money in our family was like the water supply. It simply existed. One didn't save water; one simply used it. That was all; it had no other importance, symbolic or otherwise.

"I get kids in here, they could care less about the Torah; to them this is like a one-shot payoff, like a quiz show. But that reflects the family." He closes the *Daily News*, stares sightlessly at a front page photo of Eisenhower and Anthony Eden. "That reflects the family values. This is a breath of fresh air, a German Jew. My father, may his soul rest in peace, he told me, 'German Jews, they don't talk about their money; they just sock it away quietly.' " He smiles, pulls a strand of tobacco from his tongue. "Your father, he's in the magazine game? Some kind of big shot. Shmule told me." Shmule was the *shamus*, the synagogue functionary—folder of chairs, stacker of prayer books.

"He's not a big shot. He's an editor."

The Rabbi smiles. "An editor is a big shot, my friend."

"He's not the only editor there . . ."

"An editor is a person of authority, he's someone who, when he walks into an office, people stop whispering and sit up straight."

"He's not really that type of man."

"He doesn't make noise? So what. That's not what authority comes from." He taps the newspaper. "Eisenhower, is he a noise-maker? Not at all. The power, the strength comes from inside, comes from knowing who he is. He's also a German, Eisenhower. Not a Jew, of course." Ashes dribble onto the newspaper; he sweeps them onto the floor with his hand. "The Torah is not noisemaking. It doesn't scream, 'I am the law.' It *is* the law. Am I right?"

"Yes, Rabbi."

"Yes, Rabbi." He smiles. "Respect for your elders, this is a vanishing thing."

"I don't know . . ."

"A vanishing thing. Your parents, they never come to shul."

"Not often."

"No." Rabbi Shulman rises, puts his hand on the radiator. He is wearing a green cardigan with knobby buttons under a mud-brown suit. "Starting to get warm. You're cold, Robby? Your hands are in your pockets."

"I'm okay."

"This is not Temple Emanu-El, am I right? This is not the fancy shul. This is a workingman's shul. Workingmen and one German Jew, the child of editors."

"Yes, Rabbi."

"Your mother came to pick you up once. That was her, wasn't it, with the fur collar?"

"Yes."

"She looked like a woman who needs a great deal." Smoke billows from his hairy nostrils. "She saw things, yes? The Nazis."

"She's a refugee. They all saw things."

"And she has many stories."

"Yes, she does."

"Many stories of that terrible time." Rabbi Shulman opens the *News* to the racing pages again, smiles, taps his finger.

"Here's a coincidence. At Hollywood Park in Los Angeles, in the third race, 'Refugee,' Shoemaker up. You know Shoemaker?"

"A jockey."

"A very great jockey. You think this is peculiar, a rabbi who follows horse racing? Tell me, we are friends." He puts out his cigarette, then folds his hands in his lap. Outside, the wind is picking up; bare branches wave under the street lamps. I don't know how to answer this rabbi. It is five weeks before my bar mitzvah and he is asking me to judge his credentials for the task.

"I don't know any other rabbis."

Rabbi Shulman begins to laugh; the laugh turns easily into a coughing fit. His face turns purplish. Tears run from the corners of his eyes. The coughing subsides, he rubs his eyes. "An excellent and diplomatic answer, Mr. Weisglass. I am proud to bar mitzvah you." He lights yet another cigarette, wiping his nose on his thumb. "You didn't know that was a verb, did you? 'Bar mitzvah.'"

THE inelegant translation of the haftorah that I am obliged to read on the freezing Saturday morning of my ascension to formal Jewish manhood is the work of The Jewish Theological Seminary of Akron, Ohio; the tale of Abraham and Isaac is described in a language so stilted and inexpressive that I can barely comprehend what I am reading, even though it is technically in English. I read quickly and without looking up. The audience consists of the usual stoic congregants, plus fifty or so members of my family, who sit with the quiet agitation of hostages.

The Torah is unrolled and rolled, portions are read. My father and Uncle Kurt read, inaudibly; Aunt Hilde's husband, Uncle Poldy, booms out his portion like Richard Tucker. I sing mine with a thirteen-year-old's cracking tenor. The proceedings seem to be occurring at a great distance from me. The one time that I look down and observe my mother, she is staring off into the middle distance; when she remembers where she is, she looks not at me but at my sister, who sits beside her in a scarlet wool knit.

Rabbi Shulman rises to speak of me, "a modest boy from a family of dignity, with a distinguished father and a mother who has known great suffering." He seems to leer at me when he pronounces me "old beyond his years." I am standing before the rabbi at this moment, my back to the congregation, but I can feel my sister crossing and uncrossing her legs; I am thinking of her in the tight knit dress. "A boy of unusual maturity for this stage of his journey through life," he continues. Even in his rabbinical robes, there is the sharpie in him; his eyes glint wickedly beneath the black skullcap, his pinkie ring shines in the reflected Kandy-Korn orange of the candelabra. "I have often said to Robbie, 'laugh a little, the world is not so serious.'" He chuckles when he says this, and there are answering chuckles from the regulars in the audience; I know the laughs are not coming from my family. "But of course, Robbie is right, as the young are so often right. The world *is* serious, with its terrible temptations of power, greed, and naked lust. With its Holocaust, its injustices against Jews since the beginning of time. And it is up to our young generation to make this world *their* place, a better place than we were able to give them. Robbie"—he opens his arms wide, like an evangelical preacher at a mass baptism—"I know how close, how very close you are to your family, a family that was tested in the fires of the brutal recent history of the world. Never lose that closeness, because love of family relates to love of self, and love of God." I want so much to look over my shoulder. At my sister in the scarlet knit.

LAST night. One o'clock in the morning, after a gala "family dinner" honoring the bar mitzvah boy. Kurt and Grete are there, Poldy and Hilde, Tante Bertha; Uncle Max has flown in all the way from Atlanta, where he sells children's clothes, with Friedel, his jolly and obese wife. A transatlantic phone call from widowed Tante Irene in London. Quite a party. Pot roast and spaetzle, red cabbage, apple cake. My mother toasts "the best boy in the world." My father proclaims that I am "everything I could have asked for in a boy." Uncle Kurt, attempting to inject a light touch into the proceedings, says "Robby was a *momser* before; now he'll be a bar mitzvahed *momser*." Laughter here, followed by more toasting with glasses of Moselle wine. My sister drinks throughout dinner. This is post-Buddy, pre-Clarence. She has been dating a man named Fabio Tognazzi, the owner of several Greenwich Village espresso houses. I met him on a sunny Sunday afternoon, accompanying my sister to the Village. While he wore the black turtleneck sweater of a bohemian, Fabio seemed like a lighthearted mafioso, his arm always curled around my sister. He was, Carol had told me, "strictly for fun."

I am asleep at one o'clock—a restless, agitated kind of sleep, but sleep nonetheless—when Carol wakes me by getting into bed with me.

"I'm freezing, Rob. Warm me up."

"Carol, tonight . . ."

"What better night?" She kisses my cheek, pulls her nightgown over her head. "Your last as a boy. Once you're a man, this won't be the same anymore." She flattens herself against me, her breasts warm and heavy against my pajama top. Even in the semi-dark, I can see that she has freshly made up her eyes. This is somehow wildly arousing.

"See?" Her hand is on me. "You're not tired, sweetie."

"Mom and Dad . . ."

"Fast asleep. I checked. Just keep your voice down." She turns around, presses her ass against me.

"Special night," she whispers. "Special, special night." I hear a jar being unscrewed.

"What's that?" I whisper. Carol rotates her rear end, to keep me from going anywhere, and then her right hand, glistening in the moonlight, reaches back and finds me. She begins to cover me with Vaseline, rubbing it in slowly and expertly, top to bottom, as thorough as a house painter.

"No."

"Shh . . ."

"It's cold."

"It is not." She's right, it's not, but I have to say something to fight the almost unendurable pleasure. She rubs it in, spinning a final dollop on the head of my dick, her palm applying the gentlest of pressures.

"Now . . ." She applies the rest of her handful to her ass.

"You can't be serious."

"Please, Robby." She is moving against me, straining like a cat. "Please." Her voice is a whisper; not her speaking voice at all, just the voice of a pure need. "*Please* . . . God . . ." Her hand is on me, stroking, guiding. "*Please*. Now, Robby . . . don't wait . . . *please* . . ."

Gingerly but urgently, I comply, a voyager into a stranger, tense, waiting place. The blood is pounding in my ears; I am deaf with anxiety and pleasure. We proceed in slow motion until she buries her head in my pillow, biting into it, shaking her head back and forth, pushing herself backwards. I shut my eyes.

THERE is a party after the bar mitzvah, held in Kurt and Grete's spacious garden apartment in Fresh Meadows. A pianist has been hired for the occasion; he confines himself to standards and show tunes. The fifty family members who attended the service are there, plus my father's boss, Mr. Charles Stein, and his wife Estelle, a redhead whose face has the slightly lopsided aspect of a stroke victim. All in all, it's a pretty quiet afternoon. I dance with my mother, then I dance with my sister. The pianist is playing "I've Grown Accustomed to Her Face."

"What we did last night . . ."

"You're a man now," my sister says, "a Jewish man, and I made up my mind, last night was the last time, okay? That's why it was so special."

"I don't know."

I step back and stare at her. Her hair is up in a French knot; she looks like Natalie Wood.

"I was so proud of you today," she says.

"Last time forever?"

"You're on your own now." She resumes dancing with me. "I was just a little practice. You'll be fine. Girls are going to love you."

"I don't know . . ."

"Sure they will."

"Never again?"

"From here on in, it would really be unnatural, that's what I feel . . ." She kisses my cheek. "Consider it a bonus of sharing a room with your crazy romantic sister, okay? A little wild love." She looks off. "God, Gary turned into a gorgeous guy, didn't he?" Gary is Poldy and Hilde's son, a sophomore at Columbia. I turn around. He is about six two, with a square jaw and tight curls. He already has an Ivy League aura about him, the look of a young man headed seriously and responsibly toward his future.

"You like him?"

"I like them older, you know that. Except for you."

"But that's over."

The band stops. Carol has never looked more beautiful than she does in this scarlet dress.

"That's over. Time to find your own girl." She walks away and begins talking to Cousin Gary. I am relieved and I am bereft, and when Gary starts talking to Carol and she listens intently, putting one hand over her breast as she leans toward him, I am hurt.

Uncle Kurt spots me and waltzes over in little dance steps, his tasseled loafers gliding over the wall-to-wall carpeting. The pianist is playing "The Shadow of Your Smile." Kurt has a highball glass in one hand and a sandwich in the other.

"You look a little lost, *bubele.*"

"I'm fine."

"This means shit, you know, your bar mitzvah."

"If you say so."

"I say so. I was never bar mitzvahed, of course; in the rush from Germany and then when we got here a bar mitzvah, that was the last thing you thought of, right? So maybe I'm not an expert. But I know that at thirteen the only part of you that's becoming a man is between your legs."

"Okay."

" 'Okay.' Robby, the diplomat. That's what I predict for you, a role in the world of diplomacy." I nod, very much the young adult, clutching a Coca-Cola in my hand like a guest at a cocktail party.

"This is the worst age. Teen-age. The notion that when a boy starts having wet dreams, that this is the correct time to be called upon to read from the Torah, only the Jews could dream this up. With pleasure comes responsibility, is this what the rabbis thought?" Kurt shakes his head. "The pleasure isn't pleasure yet, am I right? You don't have to blush."

"I'm not blushing. It's a little warm in here."

"It's not that warm. What I'm saying is, it ain't enough pleasure to justify the responsibility. Why not have a chance to beat your meat for a while without being called to the Torah? That's all I'm saying. Wait until you're fifteen. When you have a little more perspective. But that's not how Jews think. If you attain perspective then you won't feel guilty; you may actually like and respect yourself. So we do it this way—the minute a hair sprouts on your balls, we throw a tallis on you, just in case you don't feel bad enough about all these needs you have all of a sudden." He looks across the room. "Here comes the rabbi. Maybe I ask him."

Rabbi Shulman has entered the party, accompanied by a thirtyish redhead in a seal coat, a corktip cigarette held between her gloved fingers. Although the rabbi was said to be a widower, a portion of the student body believed that he had abandoned a wife in Toronto in the late 1940s. The rabbi introduces the red-haired woman as Mrs. Augenbraun. He helps her with her coat. Beneath the seal pelt, she is wearing a green silk dress.

"Mrs. Augenbraun is originally from Prague," the rabbi is saying to my parents.

"My favorite city," my father tells her. "Would you like a drink?"

"I would like very much a sherry," Mrs. Augenbraun says in thickly accented English. She is quite beautiful, in an expressionistic, Lotte Lenya sort of way. Her skin is very white and unlined, her eyes blue and full of secrets. I can see instantly that my mother doesn't like her.

"You were at the service?" she asks Mrs. Augenbraun.

"The service I could not be at this morning. My sister in Long Island, I am staying with her. She is ill." She touches my shoulder. "I hear you did very well."

"He was a champion bar mitzvah," the rabbi says.

"Very well," she repeats. "Is good you make your parents proud, yes?" She is really quite dazzling. She smells strongly of perfume and of the cold. My father hands her a glass of sherry.

"The rabbi," my mother reminds him.

"A scotch and water, thank you," the rabbi tells my father. "If you have Johnnie Walker Black, I'll be the happiest rebbe in New York. How are you?" he says to Uncle Kurt, who shakes his hand. "Mazel tov."

"Mazel tov," my uncle repeats. "Robby and I were just having a theological discussion."

"I'm sure," my mother says.

I start to wander off, but Kurt grabs my jacket and holds me up. The rabbi notices.

"One of those discussions." His eyes twinkle.

"I maintain that bar mitzvahs are held prematurely."

"You do. You were bar mitzvah?"

"I wasn't." He looks to Mrs. Augenbraun. "I turned thirteen in Glasgow, Scotland. This is a few months before we moved to London, and it seemed to my family in 1935 that God had taken some kind of extended vacation. He certainly wasn't answering calls."

"That's if you see God as some sort of an office manager," the rabbi replies.

"Not as a force. As a mystery," Mrs. Augenbraun adds.

"Whatever. I had no bar mitzvah." My father returns with the rabbi's scotch. The rabbi thanks him. My mother stares at Mrs. Augenbraun, then declares "I have to talk to Hilde. No one talks to her," and drifts off.

"My feeling," Kurt continues, "is that the coincidence of the bar mitzvah ceremony with the time of puberty and emerging sexual feelings is a conspiracy to instill guilt in young Jewish boys."

"Kurt . . ." my father mutters.

"Just a discussion, Herbert. Relax."

Rabbi Shulman sips none-too-delicately at his scotch and wipes his nose.

"With manhood comes responsibility," he says. Mrs. Augenbraun smiles at me. My face flushes; I can feel my ears begin to burn and can only assume that they are turning as pink as seashells.

"My point is that simply ejaculating at midnight does not constitute manhood."

The rabbi smiles.

"I couldn't agree more. But the Talmudists would disagree. And I make another point: what is to define manhood. I have met persons in their sixties who still didn't qualify as men. Are they to be denied bar mitzvah?"

"Some men are never men," Mrs. Augenbraun adds. She looks around the room as if searching for examples.

"You have to pick some date," my father says.

"Why not fifteen?" Uncle Kurt says. "I say allow a two-year grace period of adolescence. I think Robby agrees with me."

"I didn't say that," I say, looking down at the carpeting.

"I think you embarrass the bar mitzvah boy," Mrs. Augenbraun says. When I look up, I see her beaming at me.

"In any case, it is moot," declares the rabbi, "because young Mr. Weisglass has already gone and done the deed."

"Which one?" asks Kurt and there is a roar of laughter, from all but my father.

"Kurt," he says. "Enough."

"My brother is the serious one in the family."

"Well, every family needs a serious one," says the rabbi, finishing his scotch and turning toward the bar. "I help myself this time," he says, and walks away with his empty glass.

My father and I eye each other. We seem at this moment like cellmates of a sort. Confined by our mutual social misery. Kurt smiles at Mrs. Augenbraun as if he has been waiting for her his entire life.

"Augenbraun," he muses.

"My husband was German." She nods toward my father. "From Frankfurt."

I clear my throat and attempt to speak.

"How long have you known the rabbi?" I know this is probably inaudible—the sound barely escapes my lips.

"Excuse me?" She puts her hand on my arm. It is a large hand with a strong, pianist's fingers.

"I said how long have you known the rabbi?"

"I met him two weeks ago. Quite a rabbi." She smiles at me, then at Kurt. My father excuses himself and slips away.

"In what sense do you mean that?" I ask.

"Oh." Mrs. Augenbraun sips at her sherry. "I just mean that he is not taking himself quite so seriously. That his sense of life is not so tragic as other rabbis I have known."

I look around the room. My sister is dancing with Cousin Gary. Her head is on his shoulder, her eyes are shut. My cousin looks around the room as he dances, as earnestly debonair as if he were gliding across the floor of the Rainbow Room. He spots me and nods solemnly. He is a serious lad, but not too serious to probably have a hard-on at this very moment. Across the room, there is the sound of wood cracking. I hear my mother shout and when I turn around I see that she is lying on the floor and, of course, she has broken her leg.

1989 / (1981)

"THERE is a possibility, of course, that she simply had an accident and broke her leg."

It is a breezy October afternoon during an unusually warm patch of fall weather. Dr. Singer has his windows open. Workmen are yelling at one another in Spanish. A brownstone is being renovated across the way; the building fronts Seventy-sixth Street, and much debris is being funneled into the bordering backyard. A pile of bricks crashes into a metal dumpster.

"I can't hear you!" My analyst arises to close the window. I turn to watch him. He has acquired a potbelly; his blue shirt rides out of his pants. How old is he now? Mid-sixties? I have watched his hair whiten and thin; seen his step slow. What happens if he dies? I can't even imagine. He sits back down.

"I was saying that your mother could simply have fallen down and broken her leg."

I turn back around and snuggle into the couch, the safest place in all the seven continents of this terrifying world. This is my twentieth year of treatment.

"Yes, she could have just fallen down and broken her leg accidentally on the day of my bar mitzvah, while I was speaking with this beautiful Czech refugee."

No reply.

"You think it's a coincidence."

"You think that she willed herself to break her leg?"

"She fell down on thick wall-to-wall carpeting; it's not like a throw rug went skidding out from beneath her."

"You think she threw herself against a chair?"

"I still don't know how she did it."

"But her leg was broken."

"In two places."

"Well, that's that. She had a broken leg."

"And you think it was a coincidence."

"What I think is not important."

"Oh, please . . ."

"I'm not being disingenuous. It is not important. I'm trying to figure out how you see this event. Do you think she set out to sabotage your bar mitzvah because this attractive woman . . ."

"Miss Augenbraun . . . *Mrs.* Augenbraun, excuse me. Marta."

"Marta?"

"Her first name."

"She made quite an impression."

"Yes, she did."

"And she was a redhead."

"Like Libby. Correct again, doc; you're on a roll."

"Approximately your mother's age."

"Younger, I would say by at least six years . . ."

"And your mother observed you speaking with Mrs. Augenbraun . . ."

"Mrs. Augenbraun had her hand on my arm. Very long fingers; I recall the moment as if it happened . . ."

"And then you heard . . ."

"A cracking noise, and then I saw my mother on the floor. She had fallen awkwardly across a chair, and then I suppose landed funny. Oddly, not ha-ha . . ."

"Obviously."

"Obviously. And she cried out in some pain and everyone ran to her and that was that."

"The bar mitzvah was over."

"Absolutely finished, over, and *kaput* . . . Even in her pain, of course, she expressed a wish for the party to continue. My father and Kurt were going to take her to the hospital—Booth Hospital in

Flushing—and everyone else should just continue to have a wonderful time, or words to that effect. Her dress was sort of up."

"Up?"

"Up above her knees. My father pulled it down."

"How soon did he pull it down?"

"How soon?"

"Yes. Immediately. Or . . ."

"It was up long enough for me to notice, and then he pulled it down. She was in a lot of pain and I felt bad for her. I feel bad just telling the story and implying that she had faked it."

"You didn't imply that. Her leg was broken."

"I implied that she manufactured the event."

"Well, it is possible that she saw you speaking with this woman and didn't see where she was going and fell over the chair. That is possible."

"So the roots of the accident are still jealousy."

"Possibly."

"It certainly ended the party."

"Which according to you, wasn't a terribly exciting event to begin with."

"Mrs. Augenbraun had made it interesting."

"Fun?"

"I said 'interesting.' 'Fun' was out of the realm of the possible. How can you even use the word?"

"Well, it seems that there was a certain flirtation between you and this woman. That sounds like fun."

"I suppose . . . I never saw her after that afternoon. I hardly saw the rabbi for that matter."

"You stopped going to synagogue after the bar mitzvah."

"Oh, yes. If I had continued, my family would have viewed me as a religious fanatic. They would have thought that something was wrong."

"They?"

"My mother, primarily."

"She would have disapproved."

"She would have thought that something was the matter. My continuing to attend synagogue would have been perceived as a reproach to her. She always throught she was a sufficient object of worship. So I stopped going, and except for one or two occasions when I ran into the rabbi on the streets of Corona, that was that. I received a note from Mrs. Augenbraun a few days after the bar mitzvah, expressing her regret at my mother's accident, and thanking me for inviting her to the party, which of course I hadn't done. She had just showed up as the rabbi's moll. I also remember that she signed the note, 'Love, Marta Augenbraun.' To me, that has always been significant. You don't sign 'love' unless there's something behind it."

"Did you write back?"

"I did. But it was a very formal kind of 'thank you for thanking me' note. No hint that she had really struck my fancy. I signed it 'cordially,' and sent it to her at 301 West 22nd Street, in Manhattan."

"You remember the address."

"I still have her letter and the envelope. And she still lives on West Twenty-second Street. I check every time the new phone book comes out. The rabbi died in 1980. I have his obituary in a drawer in my apartment. Emphysema. No mention of Marta."

"So you presume that nothing came of their relationship."

"That's right. So I still have a chance with the rabbi's girl friend. Not that I would ever have dared to pursue her." I check my watch. Ten minutes to go. "That's a lie."

"What is? About pursuing Mrs. Augenbraun?"

"Yes."

"You looked at your watch."

Another pile of debris crashes into the dumpster outside.

"Yeah. This is a long story and we don't have much time left today."

"You could start it next time."

"Yeah." I stare at the ceiling. "This happened about nine years ago and I never told you because I was just so mortified about it."

Silence.

"I take your silence to mean that you're anxious to hear this story."

THE truth was that whenever I was downtown, I made it my business to walk past 301 West 22nd Street. I sometimes dawdled across the street and in fact—this *is* mortifying—had made it a habit to bring my dry cleaning to the Allerton Cleaners, which was located just west of Eighth Avenue and gave me a venue to stake a certain claim in the area. I would take the Ninth Avenue bus down from the Upper West Side, reading the *Times* or the *Post*, my stale and rumpled slacks in a shopping bag between my feet, then disembark at Twenty-third Street and walk the block and a half to the Allerton Cleaners. The proprietor of the cleaners, Sol Rubin, a pale and mustached man in his sixties, wore thick glasses and had an unlit corona jammed between his teeth. He never gave me a slip.

"You know which is mine?" I would ask him, glancing over my shoulder in the direction of 301.

"Yeah." He scribbled the word "prof" on a piece of paper. "You're the professor."

"And that's all you need?"

"I have a terrific memory." He would then fetch my cleaned slacks and jackets, and I would return home, ever watchful for activity at 301. The expedition took roughly one hour up and back, but it was time that I never felt was wasted. There was always the potential that I would see her, and there was that other feeling, of visiting another town, that I enjoyed. Each neighborhood in New York, with its separate candy store, liquor store, hardware store and cleaners, is another town. The light is different, there are different people on the street corners, different schoolyards. In point of fact, the pleasure I had come to receive in making this weekly sojourn to Chelsea and having my simple commercial exchange with Sol had almost superseded the original purpose of this trip. And yet a moment in history finally pushed Marta and I together.

ON a cloudy afternoon in April, I walk into the Allerton Cleaners with three pairs of corduroy slacks and dump them on the Formica counter. Sol looks up.

"What do you think?" Sol's cigar barely moved when he spoke.

"About what?"

"Reagan."

"What about him?" Dead, of course.

"Shot."

"Fatal?"

Sol shakes his head, inspects my slacks, front and back. "Wounded. He'll live. Some kid did it. Some *meshugenah*. Twenty, twenty-five. He'll live, though. Tough guy."

"Like John Wayne."

Sol smiles. "John Wayne was tougher. This guy is more of a schmuck, but you gotta like him somehow. He'll live. CBS just said. You want these next Tuesday?"

"There's really no rush."

OUT on the street I stand as if paralyzed. I walk a dozen yards, so Sol won't observe me through the window and wonder why I am standing with no apparent place to go, and then stop, staring at 301. It begins to rain, forcing my hand. I race across the street and up the front stairs of Marta's building, a five-story brownstone.

I enter the vestibule; flyers from Chinese restaurants and lock-smiths litter the ground. There are a half-dozen mailboxes: two of them are nameless, the others are for Epstein, Walker, Costanzo and Augenbraun. She is 3-A. I push the buzzer next to her name and wait. There is no response. A truck backfires on the street, racing my heart. I begin to perspire. I am pushing her buzzer once again when I hear footsteps from inside the house and turn to see Marta Augenbraun walking slowly down the stairs.

She is wearing a green print dress and pearls, as if she has been expecting me. Her face remains unlined and is lightly rouged; her hair appears to be slightly thinner, but is still defiantly red. She reaches the bottom landing and stares in my direction; her look is vague. I wave and point to myself. She squints and walks closer to the door, making no move to open it. Well-versed in the dangers of the city. To make her inspection easier, I step closer, almost flush to the glass, like a man getting a chest X-ray. She appears curious, not alarmed, not really *there*. Glasses hang around her neck on a gold chain, but she does not reach for them.

"My name is Robby Weisglass" I call out. "You attended my bar mitzvah in 1958, with Rabbi Shulman." She continues to stare, raising her eyebrows questioningly. "There was a party and you came with the rabbi. You were very beautiful then. You are *still* very beautiful." She smiles. "My mother fell down at the party and broke her leg while you and I were talking. You and I and my Uncle Kurt, who is still alive." Why do I tell her about Uncle Kurt? "I happened to be in the neighborhood . . ." It is too lame; what can I tell her to justify my appearance? "Actually, I knew that you lived here and I just found out that President Reagan was shot. I wasn't sure if you'd heard . . ."

She opens the door.

"Robby Weisglass," she says, her voice *exactly* as I remember it, a musical memory of Prague, of castles and bread dumplings. She is wearing the same perfume, which I now recognize to be the famous Chanel No. 5. "You grew up to be a very handsome boy."

"I'm sure you have no memory of the bar mitzvah. To me, obviously, it was a major event, so I have a vivid . . ."

"I remember it *quite* well," she says, and puts her glasses on, as if to confirm her initial astigmatic inspection of me. "Yes." She quickly takes them off again; I am flattered, excited. "Yes, your mother, she had an accident."

"Turned out to be a broken leg."

"Tch. Tch."

"Had a cast for weeks and weeks . . ."

"Of course." Behind me the door opens and a middle-aged black man enters, holding two bags from Grand Union.

"Hello, Fred," says Mrs. Augenbraun.

"How are you, darling?" the black man says. "Heard about the president? Shot."

"He's apparently all right," I tell him.

"Fred, this young boy"—Mrs. Augenbraun puts her hand on my arm, as she had done so bewitchingly in Uncle Kurt's living room moments before my mother's famous tumble—"I was at his bar mitzvah quite a long time ago, yes?" She looks into my eyes. My heart is pounding.

"1958," I tell her neighbor Fred.

"No kidding," he says. "That's a long time ago. Even I was young then." He laughs. Marta simply smiles.

"We are having a little reunion. Come," she says to me. "You have time for a cup of coffee and a little piece of danish? I bought this morning."

I actually look at my watch, coy to the end, as if I have not thought of this moment for twenty-three years, and then I hear myself say, "Why not."

HER apartment is more *moderne* than I had anticipated, a fact I find somehow alarming. There are a pair of suede Barcelona chairs, a Villency couch, a teak coffee table, and lamps from George Kovacs. The place could have been furnished by a woman in her thirties; there is no question but that Mrs. Augenbraun has had a lively and varied post-rabbi history. She stands in the kitchen preparing coffee while I inspect the walls. Except for a pair of prints of Prague's Old Town, her artwork is distressingly generic.

"A modern apartment, yes?" She emerges from the kitchen.

"Very."

She sits down on the couch.

"I had old furniture, some of it quite valuable, and then I sold it, to a man on the East Side. He gave me almost ten thousand dollars for it and of course when I thought about it later, I realized he probably made a robbery, but he was a reputable dealer and so"—she extends her hands—"what can I do."

"You were tired of it?"

"I was tired of it; it was tired of me. I needed a change in my life. I had lost my second husband; everything it seemed like it had stopped, you know?"

"Very well." I sit down in a Barcelona chair.

"Yes. When he passed away, he had been quite ill for years, first a stroke, then with the circulation until he wasn't the same man, old in his fifties already, sixty-two when he died . . ." She waves her hand. "And here I was, alone, no children, so I sold the furniture and in one afternoon, I buy everything you see here. For a change. To say, this is a new life. It is nice, yes?"

"Very nice. Cheery."

"Yes." She smiles at me, straightens her dress. "Let me look at the coffee."

She refuses my obligatory offer to help and goes into the kitchen. Her body is still trim, her legs those of a much younger woman. I hear drawers being opened, silverware and plates being arranged, then there is an intriguing silence. When she reappears bearing coffee and danish on a tray, it is evident that she has freshened her makeup. Just a touch. Just enough to make me notice.

"Here we are. It is not the Russian Tea Room, but on short notice I hope you will like."

"It looks lovely."

I walk over to pick up my coffee and apple danish; the odor of perfume is even more pentrating; she has added a splash to her neck and bosom. When she hands me the coffee, her hair brushes against my cheek and I get a little dizzy. I concentrate on walking a straight line back to my chair.

"The rabbi died some time ago, I believe," I say after I settle back in. "1980."

"Yes?" She seems at a pleasant remove from the event. I don't know whether to press the issue.

"I saw the clipping in the newspaper. He was in his seventies."

"Was years since I saw him. We were just together for a short time, Robby." Robby. "I am not even sure he had actually ever been divorced, you know?" She smiles. "There was a wife, I think, in Montreal; sort of a mystery." She sips her coffee, and looks to mine, untouched at my side. "It will get cold." I take a sip. It is extremely potent, laced with cinnamon.

"The kids . . ." I feel tongue-tied. "The other students had various stories about him, I remember. An abandoned wife, his various affairs, his broken nose . . ."

"He had, I think, many secrets. But he had a sense of humor, and, you know, a way about him." She smiles again; I can only imagine the slide show in her mind. "For a few months it was a kind of fun, the racetracks and all that. But not for a life. He was not a responsible person. He was, you know, a vacation. I've had better vacations and worse vacations."

"Yes," I said. Like I knew. "No regrets."

"No." She takes a delicate forkful of danish. "And you, bar mitzvah boy?"

"I teach history at Columbia."

"Yes? This is not a surprise. You have a serious face."

Hope begins to drain out of me. Hope of what?

"I have a sense of humor."

"I am sure that you do. I don't mean that. I just mean that you have the face of a man in a serious line of work."

"I'm not sure that college teaching is as serious as everyone thinks. At times it seems like one of the lower rungs of show business."

"No."

"Oh, yes. Like a kind of vaudeville. Everybody wants to be at the top of the bill and there's all this awful infighting among the opening acts. You know what I'm referring to?"

She nods, sips delicately at her coffee. "When my first husband was alive—and that's a very long time ago, of course—he and I used to go to the Palace Theatre. Once there we saw Eddie Cantor, whom I did not like so much, even though he was the most important one, the topliner . . ."

"The headliner, the last to go on."

"Yes, but there was a fat man, Leonard something, with a white hat . . ."

"Jack E. Leonard."

She smiles in memory. "He was so very funny. Common in a way, made the jokes about his wife and so forth, but there was something, I don't know . . . You *liked* him. . . ."

"I remember him from television. He's dead now."

"Yes?"

"I believe so."

"So." She stares off into the middle distance, traveling toward the community of the dead. Back to the 1940s, seated next to her lucky husband in the Palace Theatre, in that era when grownups were grownups.

"This danish is terrific."

"There are very good bakeries in this neighborhood." She smiles, this time somewhat tentatively. "So you knew that I lived here? That is interesting to me."

"I always thought you were one of the most beautiful women I had ever seen." It just comes out; I have no other response.

"Yes? You are very sweet." She crosses her legs, takes another sip of coffee. "You had a very beautiful and sexy sister, I remember."

"Yes. She's been married a few times. Her husband now is a big agent. Hollywood agent."

"She lives in Hollywood? I could see that."

"No, she lives here. Central Park West. With two children from her previous marriage to a lawyer."

"A very striking girl. I remember asking the rabbi who she was. He said she was a wild one. That's what he said. 'A wild one.' And you are not married?"

"No."

"Never?"

I shake my head. "There was a girl for a number of years, who I met even before my bar mitzvah, when I was twelve, and then we were together, but she died. Ten years ago."

"Oh, no."

"Libby."

"Libby. And since her, no one?"

"Oh, sure. Girl friends, you know. But there are things that are hard to shake."

"You have to, though. Ten years is too long to cry."

"It's not like I haven't looked, and she's not the only thing I'm talking about, when I say 'hard to shake.' "

"But still, you are too young to hang on to things. And you are very handsome. There are so many girls in the world."

"Girls, yes. Not so many women. Libby was a woman."

"There are lots of others." She looks alarmed. "You don't like the strudel?"

I raise my plate, eat another piece of the strudel, but I have no hunger, except for Marta Augenbraun.

"You don't live around here?"

"I live on the Upper West Side. I come down here sometimes. The dry cleaners across the street, he does very good work and it gives me a reason to travel downtown."

"Across the street."

"I have been hoping"—I hear my voice quaver—"to see you."

"Yes." No surprise. "You are how old, now?"

"Thirty-five."

"I am sixty-four."

"Yes. You look gorgeous."

"I'm an old bag."

"That's not true."

She smiles.

"You think that I still look like something good?"

"You have a certain something. It is something I find difficult to find easily."

"High blood pressure?" She laughs.

"You don't think that I am serious."

She shrugs, stares at her danish, adjusts the cake fork on her plate. "I know that you are serious. If you were not serious, I would not have to make a joke."

"You made an enormous impression on me."

"You were a little boy."

"But I never forgot about it. At some point I had to see you. And now that I see you, the impression, the first one, is not really replaced. It's just slightly retouched."

"Yes." She looks at me. "You have been with older women?"

"A long time ago."

"I do not make love like a teenager."

"I understand that."

"It is more . . ." She looks to the window.

"You don't have to explain . . ."

"Is not to *explain*, Professor." She brushes some hair away from her eye. "It is just for knowledge. I don't make love in order to get someplace, yes? It is just for me, like a swim in the pool. Not in the lake. Not in the lake for a number of years. Yes?"

"By which you mean . . ." I don't have a clear grasp of what she is saying, but simply watching her say it, arranging her hair, adjusting her skirt . . .

"The lake is maybe more the unknown. It is more that you start one place to arrive at the other side. The pool"—she laughs—"it is just for the swimming. But I still enjoy, and I enjoy with the young boy."

"I am not the first?"

"This is modern apartment, and I am still modern, too. Maybe my whole life I am modern." She rises. "This would be nice for a whole life, yes?"

"Very. I think I have never been modern. I was old very early."

"Yes?" She walks toward me. Closer up, her age registers with more definition, the delicate lines that run across her cheeks. "This is quite sad." She runs her hand through my hair. "Beautiful hair you have. You had then, too. I remember. So black." She laughs. It doesn't seem, at least to me, to be a quite appropriate laugh.

"Something's funny?"

"Sometimes I see my life is a very small party. Here you are after so many years . . ." Her hands on my shoulders . . .

"Twenty-three."

"Twenty-three years and the president is shot and so you walk into my apartment and we make love." She kisses me, closing her eyes. It is the softest of kisses; her lips are like some sort of steamed vegetable. She kisses me again, her hand on the back of my neck, my hands crossed against the small of her back. I exert the slightest of pressures and she presses herself against me.

"So you are kissing an old lady."

"It doesn't seem like that." Her face is flushed. Her breathing is a little harder.

"No?" she asks. "You are honest?"

"Yes." I am not honest. The breathing alarms me a little. She nuzzles her head against my neck; one hand flattens itself against my ass. I am beginning to regret this.

"WE are out of time today."

I get up off the couch. "I didn't make love to her."

Dr. Singer stares at me. I wonder if he is beginning to be afflicted by cataracts; his left eye doesn't seem clearly focused.

"I just couldn't go through with it. It seemed so sick, even for me. The moment it started, I felt like I had fallen out of a window."

"We'll discuss this next time, if you'd like."

"We couldn't extend the session?"

"No."

SEATED in his waiting room are an eight-year-old girl and her haggard mother. They look at me expectantly, as if I were bringing news from the front.

"He awaits you," I tell them, relieved, and leave the office.

1989 / (1953)

IN THE autumn of 1989 I am conducting my seminar on "The 1920s: Myth and Meaning." It is extremely popular with graduate students because the reading list includes many books *(The Sun Also Rises, Gatsby, U.S.A.)* which are not only immensely entertaining, but which they have read already. I also teach the course very well, and it has become my calling card at Columbia, as well as the vein out of which most of my scholarly articles have been mined. "Calling card" and "vein" do not mix very well, but I find that in discussing my academic career, I get tongue-tied. My career has always seemed temporary to me, a natural outgrowth of my schooling but also a symptom of arrested development, a calling I followed because I never saw the moment, the opening, to leave school. So standing before my closet mirror at age forty-five, I stare at myself in a tweed suit from Wallach's and feel that I am dressing for Halloween.

The way I enter a classroom, peering through the window first, as if reluctant to enter, has become the target of various student and faculty japes; I have been dubbed "Professor Maybe" and "Dr. No." Good-naturedly; no one questions my academic bona fides. It is all a question of style. This is not to say that I am a dull fellow in front of the blackboard; far from it. In a recent discussion of Warren Gamaliel Harding, in which I compared him favorably to Ronald Wilson Reagan, I began ranting at such volume that Professor Dell, conducting his seminar on John Locke in the adjacent room, had to rap on my door and signal me to calm down.

It is after this raucous class that a second-year grad student named Rebecca Rosengarten knocks on my office door and asks for ten minutes of my time.

Rebecca is one of only three women in the seminar. She is a stunning, buxom, quick-witted Barnard grad with long mahogony-brown hair that she usually wears up. Her wardrobe runs to cashmere sweaters and speaks of family money. Anyone in his or her right mind would be in love with her. That, obviously, excludes me. I had once believed that she was having an affair with a Senegalese political scientist named Thomas Ibutu and, despite my seeming lack of sexual ambition, I had been greatly alarmed at the thought of Rebecca becoming a conduit for various aggressive and fatal African viruses. The rumor of her affair proved false and I was surprised at the degree of my relief.

She sits across from me on this dull winter Monday, wearing a thousand-dollar Ralph Lauren sweater, blue with an elk embroidered across her chest.

"You got pretty worked up about Reagan, huh?"

"Was I actually screaming?"

"No."

"I didn't think so. Yelling."

"Almost yelling. Very loud. We all enjoyed it."

"The class?"

"The ones I spoke to. A rare show of emotion."

"From me."

"From anyone here." She smiles. Her teeth must be capped; outside of motion pictures and television, one does not encounter smiles like this. "So." She hesitates, clears her throat. "This is a little awkward, but I think I'll get over it."

"Okay." Can she be coming on to me? Impossible. I have historically not been an object of student lust; the coeds have usually gravitated to two of my married colleagues, Dick Dennis and Harvey Rosen.

"I've just been observing you and"—she takes a deep breath—"something just clicked somewhere and it's probably—not probably, definitely—none of my business, but by any chance were you like abused as a child?"

"Abused," I say in my most neutral tone.

"Sexually abused. God, why am I asking you this? I mean, I *know* why, but now that I'm here . . ."

I stare at her. She is slightly flushed and sits hunched forward over her books, in the manner of many girls self-conscious about the abundance of their bosoms.

"Yes."

"You were."

"Yes. Obviously I am telling you this only for your information . . ."

"Hey, I'll give you the reason . . ."

"Outside of the immediate participants, only one living person, my analyst in point of fact, knows about it."

"I would never tell a soul, Dr. Weisglass."

"I would have to have you killed, I suppose," I say with a forced smile. "It is obviously the central fact of my life . . ."

"Mine, too." She puts the books down on the floor. "Can I shut the door?"

I point to the door. Rebecca rises and closes it, returns demurely to her chair. She is wearing baggy jeans that cannot conceal the beauty of her figure.

"You're like a first generation American, right?" she asks.

"Right."

"I'm a second. My father's parents were Austrian. He was born here in like 1942, and he abused me. That's how I could tell about you. Something about the way you hold yourself."

"My posture?"

"Not just that. You're sort of surrounded by barbed wire and guard dogs. Some girls were talking about that one day, that you were really attractive and not married and we decided not gay, so what was the story, really? Then I started thinking and I came to my not-so-startling conclusion."

"How long did your father abuse you?"

"Three years. From when I was eleven to when I was fourteen."

"And then what happened?"

"He killed himself."

"Really?"

"Really."

"Because, what, he was afraid . . ."

"That I was going to tell on him?"

"Yes."

"I don't think so. If I had told my mom, she wouldn't have believed me anyhow. I never even threatened to. He was my father. It was unthinkable."

"And he abused you on a regular basis?"

"No. Very occasionally. I think it happened when he was depressed about money, even though we had quite a bit. Maybe he felt unmanned when he had a bad day in the market. He worked for the Rothschilds." Rebecca had begun chewing on her thumbnail. "It's amazing though, isn't it? That I could tell that about you."

"He killed himself." I can't get over it.

"When I was fourteen. 1980."

A ray of sunlight pierces my filthy window and then disappears. I feel myself filling with rage, that this man had the decency to kill himself and attempt to take his daughter off the hook, to say to her, in the secret language of suicide, that what he did to her was deserving of death. My mother never even *threatened* suicide. Over what? All she ever did was love me too much. *Is that a crime?*

"You must have felt a certain amount of fury." I have trouble controlling my voice.

"I felt a lot of things," Rebecca says. "First, just the physical fact of his suicide. He had hung himself in our bathroom."

"Oh, for crissakes . . ." Maybe my mother wasn't all bad.

"My mom tried to keep me out, but I caught a glimpse of him and *that* . . ."

"I can imagine. It's such a hostile . . ." I sound like a fucking shrink. "I mean . . ."

"He was just completely screwed up. My mom is from Minnesota, a Lutheran, and she just sort of understood it somehow. Like it was this dark prairie thing to do, you know? Out of a book by Karl Rölvaag."

"So she never had a clue about the incest . . ."

"No. She's always maintained that he died because he was worried about money, and why didn't he talk more about it . . ." Rebecca sighs, shakes her lovely head.

"And you feel, I'm sure, that what's the point of telling her now."

"Exactly." She kicks off her shoes and puts her feet up under her on the chair. "What was the story in your family?"

I look for a moment at my right sock; there is a hole near the ankle. "Well, it's a delightful, colorful tale: I had my mother *and* my sister. My father was the only one in the dark; he was like a panelist on 'I've Got A Secret,' except he didn't even know there *was* a secret. And unlike your father, the women in my household never acknowledged that any of these carryings-on was out of the ordinary."

"So if anybody was going to feel guilt . . ."

"*C'est moi.* At least your old man admitted something was up." She shrugs. "I suppose. Still . . ."

"You feel it was somehow your fault, that you led him on."

She looks at her lap, sniffles. When she raises her head, her brown eyes glitter with tears.

"Don't you ever feel that?"

"Of course. Then I feel like even more of a leper. Statistically, I should have become a child molester myself. It's some sort of tribute to my mental health that I haven't. Of course, I never had children. Never came close."

"I want children." She tucks a stray hair behind her ear. God, she's gorgeous. "Desperately."

"At one point I thought I did, with this girl I was with, the only other girl who knew about me. But I lost her along the way." I shrug, not wanting to do my usual aria about brave Libby. The hell with her. The hell with everybody.

"The relationship didn't work out?"

"It didn't work out." I rip open a brown bag containing sample books from the University of Iowa Press. "What else should we talk about?"

"You don't really want to discuss this."

"That's right."

"I thought once I found a fellow victim . . ."

"I'm the first? Come on, there's thousands of daughters brutalized by their fathers. The most respectable fathers."

"You're not the first, no. But given your background, and given that you're an authority figure to me and that you made something of your life . . ."

"I did?"

"You don't think you did? Everyone around here . . ."

"I'm well-respected."

"More than that. This seminar . . ."

"Very well-respected. Revered."

"You're too young to be revered." She smiles.

"That's true. I'm too young to be revered, and too old to be a wunderkind. I'm like a piece of Danish Modern furniture; like a teak coffee table or a modular couch."

"You don't like yourself."

"*Please.* This is just not something I can discuss any further."

She gets up. Her hair has gotten progressively loosened from her barrette and now partially flows down one shoulder.

"I'm sorry."

"Not at all. I enjoy having visitors."

"I meant bringing up that stuff."

"I didn't have to tell you what I told you. Obviously, you inspire a certain trust."

"If I was a guy, or if I looked different, you think you would have told me?"

"I think that's besides the point, or are you fishing for a compliment."

She smiles. "I'm probably fishing."

"You're an exquisite creature; you're poised, you're cunning . . ."

"Cunning?"

"Cunning, female, intelligent. I am happy that you came here."

"I wanted you to know about me. A fellow victim."

"I don't date my students."

She looks me straight in the eye.

"It's early in the semester. I can drop out." She walks to the door. "Think about it." She opens the door. In the hall, Harvey Rosen smiles at her. She walks away. He winks at me.

* * *

IT'S August 1953 and we have rented a house in Fleischmanns, New York, a refugee hangout in the Catskills. The house is shared with the Nagys, Karel and Magda, Hungarian neighbors of ours from Corona. They have a painfully thin, near-mute daughter named Linda, age ten, whom my mother has proclaimed to be "a genius." Linda spends her afternoons painting in the backyard, rendering robins in watercolor. My sister is working at a local day camp, Camp Ashokan, and is rarely seen around the house. For reasons that I, at age eight, cannot begin to fathom, she has been given the use of the camp director's Hudson Hornet and drives back and forth each day like a movie star going on location.

My father comes up on weekends with Karel Nagy, who is in the artificial limb business. He customizes legs and feet. Samples of his works-in-progress are scattered throughout the house like battlefield relics, and it is nothing to see a dozen legs stacked up like cordwood beneath the bathroom sink. Over my objections, Karel has given me a defective limb, a "second," as a toy.

"You know what that leg costs, new?" he asks me. "Two-hundred-fifty dollars. So that is a special toy, yes?"

I reluctantly agree to keep it in my room, where it leans against the wall. At night, I lie in bed and stare at the lonely limb, expecting that at any moment, it might begin dancing, *Fantasia*-like, across the floor. One morning I awake to see Karel Nagy placing another limb beside it. He smiles at me. "Now it has a little brother." He lifts the new leg, points to a toe. "You see this has a chip. I cannot smooth out." He is a burly man, built along the lines of the actor Lee J. Cobb, with a jutting, prowlike jaw and a head of thick black hair that he works over each morning with twin military brushes. He eats, in my mother's description, "like a stevedore," and goes through bottle after bottle of Prior Double Dark beer with no discernible effect on his bearing or powers of speech. His wife Magda is a short, stout woman whose accent and malapropisms are almost vaudevillian in magnitude. She has never fathomed the distinction between the pronouns "he" and "she," and her attempts to pronounce the solemn Indian place names of the Catskills could serve as set pieces on the "Burns and Allen" program. Magda does most of the cooking in the Fleischmanns house, making no concessions to the summer season. During the long days of July and August, her steaming goulashes and stews constitute the table d'hôte. I can barely get them down, but my mother insists that it is "an insult" not to try. So on my fatherless weekday nights, I sit for seeming hours at the dinner table, sweating as I force noodles and thick, flour-filled sauces into my fifty pound system.

My principal companion and playmate in the Fleischmanns house is the mysterious Linda Nagy, which means that I am alone a good deal of the time. Linda is occupied with her painting and her poetry; long poems about Arthurian knights and women in distress alternate with shorter ones evocative of nature. She generally does not wish to be bothered with me, so my alternate activity is to accompany my mother into town to do the wash. I sit in the Fleischmanns laundromat with my head in my mother's lap, feeling the most intense longing, a central emptiness I carry with me like an ulcer. It is a feeling that washes over at me at odd moments even today, with no mother and no lap to hide in.

"What's with you, *bubele?*" my mother asks. The temperature in the laundromat is close to one hundred, what with the row of dryers churning continuously, and yet I am buried in her lap as though seeking further warmth.

"I don't know."

"You need your mother, is that it?"

"I don't know."

She touches my head.

"No fever. Just *schvitzy.*"

"I'm lonely."

"Lonely?"

"Yeah."

"I'm here."

"I know. I miss something. I don't know."

"Your father?"

"No. Maybe I miss home."

"We're all together here." She kisses my face, wetly. The feeling goes away, dissolves at the feeling of her lips. I snuggle against her bosom. "You feel better?"

I nod.

"So who knows you better than mama?"

No one. It's as simple as that. No one. And this haunts me forever. She knows me better than anyone ever could; she walks
through the physical barrier between us as effortlessly as a clown
through a paper wall. She takes me as if I were a kitten. Because she
knows me. She knows me "better than you know myself." How
many times did she tell me that? How could I not believe it? She
anticipated needs I didn't even know I had, walked soundlessly into
my room with sandwiches and drinks before I even realized that I
was hungry, adjusted my blankets at midnight before I ever felt a
chill. She was godlike, bigger than God actually, because God never
cooked for me. When I looked down upon the ground, her shadow
was perpetually behind me, like Fate itself. So if she claimed to
know me better than I knew myself, who was I to deny it? My only
defense would be to have my own children whom I could know
better than they knew themselves. I just can't bring myself to do it:
to have them, to inflict myself upon them.

''You're afraid you'll molest them." Dr. Singer is wearing a scarf
on this wintry day, although his office is adequately heated.
    "Is that it?"
    "What do you think?"
    "I don't think I would ever molest them."
    "So why don't you have any?"
    "None of your fucking business."
    He sneezes.
    "You're sick?"
    "A little cold."
    "You don't look so hot."
    I hear him blow his nose.
    "This glorious girl in my seminar, she was molested as a teenager
by her father. He was decent enough to bump himself off. She sort
of came on to me." I stare at the Easter Island photos over the
couch. The corners of them are beginning to bend. They look
untended. "I felt drawn to her despite myself."
    "Despite yourself?"
    "Despite telling myself that I wasn't. But I can't stop thinking
about her. She's twenty-four years old. It's ridiculous."
    "What is?"

"The age gap. The everything gap. But we do share this incest thing, however. I never met a gorgeous incest victim before. Not that I knew of."

"She knows about you."

"She had suspected it. That's why she came into my office in the first place. Like a dowser searching for water. But she had figured it out already; she was simply looking for confirmation."

"And you told her."

"Yes. She just went right to it, and I looked at her and said 'yes.' It came out very easily. I mean, it's really been—not counting you—thirty years since I told anyone . . ." Now I'm weeping, big baby that I am. "And it was so *easy* to say it."

"And that upsets you, that it was so easy."

I just nod, wailing into my hands. Dr. Singer sneezes again, inappropriately. It goes on like this for a few minutes—my sobbing, his sneezing. Finally we blow our noses together, like a pair of widows.

"It feels like a betrayal of Libby somehow," I tell him.

"A betrayal or a closure?"

"If you're going to start with the fucking semantics . . ." I reach for a tissue and wipe my eyes. "I guess so . . . A closure."

"Which you don't want to make."

"Apparently not. She still fills some sort of need for me . . . I can't believe I'm *talking* like this, like some putz in a group session . . ."

"It's not terrible to use the word 'need.' She fills a need. Does it sound terrible when I say it?"

"Yes. But she does. She was my ticket to martyrdom. I hate to say it, but it's true. She took me off some kind of hook when she got sick and then when she died. I had given at the office. No reason to follow through on relationships."

"Because look what happened."

"Exactly. But that's not all. I deserved it."

"You had caused it. You've often said that."

"That I made her sick?"

"Yes."

"I don't think I really believed that."

"I don't either."

"You've been letting me say it for twenty years."

Silence.

"I didn't make her sick. She *got* sick. But I deserved it. And it meant I could retire from the field. I'd had a relationship, the girl died, I never got over it."

"I think it served your purpose not to get over it."

"Yeah. I suppose it did. And now here's this twenty-four-year-old girl, just three years younger than Libby was when she died, and I'm thinking about her. A lot. I've never dated students, although she said she'd happily drop out of the seminar."

"She said that?"

"Yes. It's clear that she wants an involvement. And I'm frightened of it. I can say that I'm afraid I'll lose her, afraid she'll get sick, but that's not really it. What I *am* afraid of is that the relationship will fail and then I'll have no future. The question, 'Is there love after Libby?', will have been answered and the answer will be 'no.' And I don't think I can live with that knowledge. I mean, I've been living off the potential for love . . ."

"The fantasy."

"The fantasy. Correct, Doctor. The fantasy of children, the fantasy of women. It has been easier for me than if I actually took the risk."

"Of failure."

"Of failure. I can imagine impotence on all levels besides the sexual—impotence of brain, of imagination, of feeling. I can see myself being entirely wanting, and her looking at me and realizing that this wasn't what she had figured on at all. She had figured on a man and she got this other thing, this almost-man. This partially formed, emotionally crippled creature with the interesting history and the blank present."

"Can you imagine a successful relationship with this girl? Romance, courtship, sex, laughter."

"You sound like a dating service."

"I'm quite serious. Can you imagine any of that?"

"No. No, I can't. I'm not even sure what it would feel like. Would it feel like what it felt like with Libby? I was so young and she was so sick . . . it was an entirely different set of circumstances. She heard my confession and from then on, she was my life preserver. And now you are. This girl, this gorgeous fellow-victim, I don't know what she would be to me."

"Your lover."

"I'm too old to have a lover. I'm forty-five years old. I need something else."

"No, I think a lover is exactly what you need. You don't need another life raft. You need a woman."

"You're putting the screws on."

"I'm not putting the screws on. I think you need a lover. I think you need an Event, something to get you off the dime."

"And out of here."

He sneezes again and I am seized with panic. Is he *sick?*

"Are you all right?"

"All right?"

"You're not sick, are you? You're not telling me something here, about getting me off the dime."

"Do you want to be in therapy forever?"

"Maybe. Why not? It's a process."

"I believe in termination. I believe there is a reason to go and then ultimately a reason to stop going."

"You never answered my question about being sick. And don't duck it, because I won't stop thinking about it. Just give me some warning. If you die on me, I don't know what I'll do."

"You'll go on."

"Are you sick? Come on."

"I'm not sick . . . I have a flu."

"You've been looking lousy."

"I have a flu." He starts to cough, and the coughing goes on for over a minute. A few years ago, I would have joked about getting a rebate on my time. Now I just listen to him cough and feel like I am dying along with him. Because he must be dying.

I AM up half the night, worrying about Dr. Singer, inching along like a man in a boat without oars. I sit in the boys' room for a half-hour. Peter has his sheets wound tightly around his legs; Barney lies as motionless beneath his blanket as a prince who has swallowed a potion. Julia is not at home; she's out spending the night with a friend. At five o'clock, I brew coffee and turn on CNN. I keep the sound lowered, and then, as the sun rises and my children cease to exist, I turn it up. At six-thirty I hear the *Times* land outside my door. At precisely seven o'clock, I call Rebecca Rosengarten. She has also been up half the night and is not at all surprised to hear from me.

IN August, my father takes his two weeks off. He has joined us in Fleischmanns and participates in summer life, in his fashion. He takes photographs of the surrounding Catskills, of the creeks, of the blackberry bushes. At noon he and my mother take me swimming at the pool of the Breezy Hill Hotel, at which Uncle Poldy and Aunt Hilde are staying. I stay in the shallow end, a rubber float around my waist, while my mother speaks with Hilde and my father reads the newspaper. At four o'clock each day, my father takes his nap, which lasts until we have our dinner. I remember this as a good time.

Mr. Nagy is up for these same two weeks and proves to be a physical culturist. In a pair of black shorts, he sits in the garden and assumes a lotus position for a half-hour, then arises and disappears into the garage, emerging moments later with a set of barbells, which he proceeds to lift vigorously. He then invites me to throw around an ancient, much-scuffed medicine ball, brought over from Hungary.

"In this country, no such medicine ball as this," he tells me. I know no better and am deeply impressed, never having seen one in my life. I find its very name, "medicine ball," to be somehow intimidating, hinting at a kind of black magic. And the physical fact of it —this heavy leather sphere smelling of old Hungarian liniment, of steamer trunks, of Nazi-fleeing—is daunting. He throws it directly at me; I catch it and fall right over. Mr. Nagy laughs.

"Is for the muscle," he tells me.

"I didn't know it was so heavy."

"Sure. Is medicine ball."

I pick it up, attempt to throw it back.

"With both hands," he informs me. I throw it about a foot and a half.

"We work on muscle." And so we proceed to lift barbells each afternoon, until my little biceps begin to harden. After each session,

we drink lemonade and eat Mrs. Nagy's lard-laced "butter cook-
ies." I warm to Mr. Nagy; the summer begins to seem less creepy,
the artificial limbs less obtrusive. This serenity is shattered, however, when my father's uncle Siegfried drops dead and my parents
must return to the city immediately in order to attend the funeral
service. I am to be left alone with the Nagys. My sister is spending
the night with a friend from Camp Ashokan, and although I plead
with her over the phone to come be with me, she flatly refuses. I am
to be left alone with the Nagys. Period.

At five o'clock, my parents take a taxi into town, where a bus will
convey them to the city. The dust is still rising from the road when
the Nagys announce that as a special treat we will go to the movies
after supper, and see *Show Boat*.

The movie theater is in Phoenicia, perhaps eight miles away, and
my stomach is churning at the very thought of the car ride. I want
simply to go to bed and awake the next morning with the knowledge that my parents are returning. The night that lies before me—
dinner, the movie, returning in the darkness—is a horror to me.

The sky is still light as we eat on the screened-in porch. I drink
ginger ale and stare at my pot roast and bread dumplings.

"You are not hungry, darling?" Mrs. Nagy asks me.

"Not so much."

"You need food. Too skinny," says Mr. Nagy.

Mrs. Nagy just shrugs.

"If she's not hungry, she's not hungry. Maybe some dessert later,
something sweet?"

I nod and look across at the table at Linda. She is seated with her
legs tucked beneath her, reading *Black Beauty* and drinking Kool-
Aid. She looks at me as blankly as if I were seated across from her on
the subway, and returns to her reading.

"Is not polite to read at dinner," Mr. Nagy tells her.

"I'm almost finished . . ."

"Karel . . ." Mrs. Nagy says to him, and the rest of the sentence
is an elaborate pantomime of rolling shoulders and eyes. I cannot
adequately describe the awe in which the Nagys, particularly
Magda, regard their only child. With her jutting Eastern European
chin, long brown hair and beady eyes, Linda is both stunning and
unapproachable. Her attitude toward her parents is not so much

contempt as disinterest; she wanders through the house like a fellow in an arts colony, books or paints in hand. I am terrified of her; she is neither child nor adult. She is a creature.

Linda pops half a dumpling in her mouth and chews while she turns the pages of her book; she reads with great speed, scanning the pages with those pale, judgmental eyes. I keep watching her.

"Boy," Mr. Nagy says to me, pointing to my crowded plate. "At least a dumpling."

"I have a stomach ache."

"Karel, she has a stomach ache. So." Mrs. Nagy smiles at me. I am grateful for her forbearance but also slightly resentful, because there is pity in the glance, a knowledge—not entirely smug—that not all children can turn out like her scary Linda.

AFTER dinner, we drive off to Phoenicia. My propensity for car sickness is a matter of common knowledge, so I am allowed, as a "privilege," to sit in the front seat of the station wagon. The car has no radio, so we drive in relative silence, except for Magda's random observations about road signs and billboards. Despite the front seat, despite my window being open and the mountain breezes blowing into my face, I am sick to my stomach for the entire trip. My mother and father are in a bus at this very moment, hurtling down Route 17, each minute taking them that much farther from me. I am in a dark, radio-less wagon, heading toward an unfamiliar movie theater. My parents almost never go to the movies, so a movie house is an alien and noisy place to me. My infrequent visits have been alarming; I find the sound too loud and too harsh and the theaters somehow menacing, with their rows and rows of plush seats. The smell of the popcorn makes me ill, the music emanating from the speakers is threatening and vaguely foreign. It does not sound like music from a radio or a phonograph and worse, it can't be controlled. It will be as loud as *they* want it to be. And so it is, finally, an out of control situation for me. Which means that I will be nauseous.

The Phoenicia Theater is a country movie house, which means simply that it is smaller, but no less intimidating than the urban picture palaces. I sit down next to Linda, who has her hand deep into a bag of popcorn; the smell of melted butter makes me turn my head away. A cold sweat beads my forehead; my hands are clammy. Mr. Nagy returns from the candy counter with Raisinets, Dots and Bon-Bons, for communal snacking. I stick a green Dot in my mouth, in a hopeless attempt at being sociable, and the rubbery candy turns instantly to bile in my mouth. Our neighbors, front and back, smell of sweat and shampoo; each new odor, fair or foul, is an assault on my teetering senses. I am grateful for the darkening of the houselights, which permits me to spit my shrunken Dot onto the floor. A deafening roar washes over me as I look up from the floor: the newsreels have begun. In booming, bass-heavy cadences, the newsreel narrator prepares us for the first lurid pictorial: a man named Peterson is about to go over Niagara Falls in a barrel.

"Onlookers line the shores." The narrator's voice shakes my very bones. My stomach turns over as I watch the foolhardy, bearded Peterson get into his "specially-reinforced" barrel. To my left, Linda Nagy methodically munches her popcorn; to my right her parents hold hands and eat Bon-Bons. The smell of ice-cold vanilla hits me between the eyes. I put my head down and breath deeply. This makes me dizzier. Waves lap against the walls of my stomach.

"Peterson waves at the crowd, the first man in over six years to attempt the almost impossible feat! Good luck!" I steal a look at the screen from between my fingers. There is a wide shot of the falls. Peterson is about to go over. I feel myself begin to retch, stranded in the middle of the row. My mother is probably nearing the city at this very moment. How could she have done this to me?

"And there he goes!" The deranged Mr. Peterson begins his rapid descent.

"I have to throw up," I whisper to Mrs. Nagy.

"What?"

"I have to throw up. Please . . ." I arise and climb over her legs, then over Mr. Nagy. The aisles are very tight. I keep my hand pressed over my mouth, attempting to stem what is now inevitable, unstoppable.

"Down and down he goes, nearly crushed by the force of mighty Niagara!" I make it to the aisle, falling over the legs of the last person in the row, a high-schooler in a football jersey. I pick myself off the carpet and head toward the rear of the theater. I am trickling vomit into my hand. The bathroom is nowhere in sight, but I can't ask for

it, because I cannot open my mouth. My stomach convulses and I am now vomiting copiously in front of the concession stand. The remaining customers clear the area. I fall down in a heap, hoping that I might die, or at very least faint and regain consciousness somewhere, anywhere, else.

No doctors emerge to help, however; only the diminutive theater manager, Mr. Brower, and a sneering teenager with a mop and a pail.

"Where you parents are?" Mr. Brower asks, but at this point, Mrs. Nagy has already emerged from the darkness of the theater.

"President Eisenhower goes to the ball game!" I don't even know what happened to the barrel-jumper. Mrs. Nagy kneels down next to me.

"Poor nervous boy, huh?" She pats my head. "Miss the mama too much. He comes back tomorrow." I get to my feet. Except for the disgruntled teenager and his pail, Mrs. Nagy and I are the only occupants of the rear of the theater. Even the concessionaire has rushed outside. He is lighting up a cigarette and laughing.

"We go back to movie, yes?" says Mrs. Nagy. "Can't get no worse." She lifts her eyebrows hopefully. I get to my feet and she walks me toward, and into, the men's room, not even knocking. Inside, she washes me up, dries me. I am terribly grateful but I cannot speak, so deep is my shame. We emerge from the men's room.

"From Paris comes the latest collection of Coco Chanel!" In the darkness I resume my seat, keeping my eyes to the screen as I step over a row of feet. When I sit down, I steal a glance at Linda Nagy. Her eyes are riveted to the screen still, her hand dipping smoothly and mechanically into her popcorn. She never acknowledges that I have returned, or that I even left. I feel utterly invisible, not for the first time in my life and not for the last.

1990 / (1959)

REBECCA Rosengarten and I do not actually begin sleeping together until June, after the seminar has concluded. It is as if a sly sort of arrangement has been made; there is much eye contact and she comes into my office frequently enough so that Harvey Rosen has asked me if something "untoward" is going on.

"No," I tell him. Harvey is approaching fifty, twice married, the second time to a student he is now cheating on regularly.

"Why not?" he asks.

"She's in my seminar and I don't feel it is ethical."

He rolls his eyes to the ceiling, begins unwrapping a cigarillo.

"Please."

"Listen, we're different people. I don't pass judgment on you . . ."

"But you do. Mind if I light this?"

"No."

"You do pass judgment. You think my behavior with students is repellent and unprofessional. The fact is you're a prude."

"I admit it."

Harvey smiles with yellowish teeth. He is not an attractive man, suffering from a kind of elephantiasis; his features are doughy and inflated. And yet he has an ease to him; that must be it. An ease and a confidence that draws women to him with the inevitability of the semesters.

"She's off the charts."

"Rebecca?"

"Off the charts. That body, those eyes. How can you even think of not fucking her."

"I repeat . . ."

"So she drops out of the seminar."

"And then everybody knows . . ."

"So what? You're single, for crissakes. She's, what, twenty-five?"

"Four."

"It's not cradle-robbing. She's a big girl, a great big beautiful girl, and it's an act of insanity not to sleep with her."

"I appreciate the advice."

"No you don't, but that's okay." The smoke of his ten-cent Robert Burns fills my tiny office. "And even if she stays in your seminar, you grade her according to her work. Period. I've done it lots of times."

"I repeat: we're different people."

"I'm aware of that. You're a good person and I'm an evil person."

"I don't think anything remotely like that. I happen to be a prisoner of my inhibitions."

"So she just comes into your office and you stare at each other?"

"We talk."

"About what?" He flings his legs over the side of the chair. He's obviously settling in for a while.

"This and that."

"Why be coy with me? Why?"

"We just talk, you know."

"So you'll fuck her once the semester's over and that'll conform to your complex and admirable ethical system."

"I don't want to talk about this anymore."

"I'm wildly jealous, obviously, which is why I'm jabbering on in this hostile manner. The ass on that girl—it's worth a book of sonnets, really. Somebody told me she was an abused child. Father diddled her, then bumped himself off."

"I don't know about that."

"And if you do you're not going to tell me, but that's all right, really." Cigar in hand, he rubs his bulbous nose. "Makes her even more irresistible, says I. You're going to have a great time when you finally get her in the sack, no question about it."

"How's Emily?"

He waves his hand dismissively, as if I have asked him about an old automobile.

"Fat and sullen."

"She's not *fat.*"

"She's put on weight. My kids were with us last weekend up in Putnam Valley, and they noticed. She never stopped eating. Or drinking. The Stoly hour commences at four-thirty now on weekends. And you can tell that she's checking the clock, too, you know, the old countdown. I said to her, 'It'd be nice if maybe you didn't booze it up when the kids are around,' because of course they run right back to Beth and report *everything*, and what they don't report immediately, she grills out of them on cross-examination."

"But Beth is happily married, yes?"

"Doesn't mean she can't derive *extreme* pleasure from any reports of my discomfort. I'd be the same way."

He takes a long drag on his cigar. What a life he leads.

"The kids are great, though. David loves Dartmouth, surprisingly. I thought *such* a goyische place, but it's really very strong. And he's a semi-jock, anyhow. Alexandra's finishing up at Hunter; she'll get in anywhere she wants. I did something right, didn't I? I mean, Jesus, to have kids like that?"

"I'm sure you did."

"I mean, they'll never forgive me for dumping their nice little mommy for a fucking *graduate student*, nor should they. My only hope is that as they grow older, they'll reach their own strange junctures in life where they'll be able to say, 'Oh, *that's* why he did it.' Forgiveness I do not expect, but understanding would be nice." He leans forward, taps his cigar ashes into the ashtray on my desk. "Why I smoke these awful things; suppose it brings back the Harvard days. Weinberg smoked them." He yawns cavernously. "Life, eh, Rob? What? Dons at Oxford. I should do another year at Oxford; the English understand my adulterous nature."

"Are you and Cynthia . . ."

He shakes his head.

"Negative." Cynthia Thomas was a Visiting Lecturer in American Cultural History, an import from the University of Texas. Within three weeks of her arrival, her romance with Harvey was all over the department. "She was great. *Great.* A kind of Texan generosity and desire to please. And *nothing* made her blush. I mean, she's what, twenty-nine, and there was *nothing* I was going to show her. But she's got some reporter now, some pretty boy from ABC she's hanging around with. He's not married, has his weekends free." Harvey swings his legs back down from the arms of the chair. "What is it all, Rob? What's the fucking point, I ask you?"

"You're asking the wrong guy."

"I'm really not making idle conversation. I worry about you, in my unpleasant, wheedling fashion. You're all closed up."

"This is not untrue."

"I see this golden, libidinous opportunity for you, with this utterly *magnificent* Rosengarten, and you're talking about grad school *ethics* and I think to myself, 'Turn the lights on for this guy. He's living in the dark.' "

"I'm very attracted to her."

"Then fuck her! Take your pants off and fuck her. What are you waiting for?"

THE end of the semester, that's what. For permission. I take her to the movies at the end of June, a Schwarzenegger film, extremely violent, set in the future. His memory is manipulated and he takes a mental voyage to a terrifying and murderous Mars. Deformed faces, three-breasted women, smoke blowing across every bleak frame of the picture. In the last half-hour of the film, hundreds of people are killed. It is appalling and, I'm afraid, very entertaining.

We have dinner afterwards, across the street from the movie theater, at a Chinese noodle parlor called Ollie's.

"That was awful," she says.

"I loved it."

"I know." She smiles. "I kept looking over and you were like": she simulates an open-mouthed, glazed happiness.

"You kept looking over?"

"I was more interested in you than the movie."

"That's sweet."

"You looked very happy."

"I was. I was happy that the bad guys were getting killed and mutilated. My blood was racing."

"You guys." She cuts her noodles with a knife and fork, like my father used to.

"I have this violent streak."

"It's in all of us."

"I walk down the street and imagine some man accosting me, and my immediate reaction: I turn and shove a broken beer bottle into his eyes. He backs up, blood pouring from behind his hands, then I punch him in the stomach—*oof!*—and he doubles over and then I kick him in the face and his teeth just come *flying* out of his mouth, and then I pick him up over my head and toss him into the path of an oncoming Sanitation truck, its driver casually looking the other way. And then I turn on my heel and walk home. My heart is pounding even as I imagine it."

"You have this fantasy often?"

"Often enough."

She cuts up some more sesame noodles. It is harshly lit in Ollie's but that does nothing except further dramatize Rebecca's astonishing and apple-cheeked beauty. Why would I tell her this story?

"Not like every day," I add.

She shrugs. "I have worse. A man in the hallway, faceless, forces me to, you know, eat him. I bite his thing off. For years now. Sweet little me." She eats a noodle. "Great table talk."

"It's not just us though. It must be endemic in New York now, in all cities."

"Fantasies of violence?"

"I'm sure it is. Do you talk to your girl friends about it?"

"Not really. I haven't described the fantasies. They say they're afraid to walk around at night and I say I have fantasies about the daytime and I wind up mutilating these men and they sort of smile at me and change the subject. Which doesn't mean they haven't had similar fantasies. It just means they don't feel close enough to me to talk about them."

"You don't have great friends here."

"The way I look is sort of an obstacle. This isn't, 'tell me how pretty I am . . .'"

"You're beyond pretty."

She waves me off. "It seems to get in the way of friendships; other women just instinctively mistrust me. It used to bother me a lot and then it became, 'screw em.' I mean, I'm not going to pour acid on my face just to make friends. It caused me enough heartache with my dad, my looks."

"You think it wouldn't have happened if you looked different?"

"I don't know. It's probably moot. All I know is I don't feel like apologizing for my appearance."

ONE hour later Rebecca moves slowly beneath me, her eyes closed, and it is just hard to fathom. That someone so exquisite should desire me. I hardly know who she is. She turns her head. "Okay," she whispers to herself. "Okay." I hang on, with the sense that we are, at least for now, two solitary travelers.

She stares at me afterwards, silently studying me, then begins slowly kissing my lips and, alternately, her own long fingers, an act of self-arousal that soon has me aching for her all over again.

After the second time, she lies with her head on my chest. I am not sure if I am actually inhabiting my own body. I am afraid to speak. Time passes; I turn and look at the clock on my night table. It is one-thirty in the morning.

"Rebecca?"

She is sleeping. I slip from beneath her and go to the bathroom. I shut the door and pee; I study myself in the mirror to see if there is a pronounced change in my features. There is not. At forty-five, I retain a look of longing, of embryonic incompleteness. I remain in a state of gestation. When I return from the bathroom, she is sleeping where I left her, a smooth naked comma in the center of my bed. The apartment is quiet except for the mechanical breathing of my refrigerator. The children are sleeping. I go back beneath the bed covers and stare out the window until dawn.

THERE is an empty lot next to our apartment house. It runs to weeds along the edges, but most of it is dirt. The neighborhood boys play stickball in this lot and dogs, stray and domesticated, use it to run and bark and shit. It is bordered by Ninety-seventh Street on one side and the backs of the retail stores that front Junction Boulevard on the other. It is a place, curiously, for reflection.

The lot is empty this afternoon, but for a skittish Irish wolfhound and her owner, a limping Italian woman named Luciano who lives in our building. The dog squats and defecates, looking as stripped of dignity as a human committing the same act in public view. When she is finished, the wolfhound frantically covers her load and races from the lot. Mrs. Luciano follows, with her rolling, impaired gait; she covers as much ground moving from side to side as she does going forward. The day is turning warmer and there are the first curiously sour breaths of spring in the air: defrosting dog droppings, the exhalations of new weeds. My shame seems likewise to thaw after a winter's repression. It is now nearly two years since my last encounter with my mother; almost a year and a half since my sister last graced my bed, yet my body seems to be permanently damaged. I wrote to Libby last month: "I feel this soreness from time to time." She wrote back and asked, with her usual precision, *"Where* do you feel this soreness? I'll bet I can guess." I don't know who to tell about my aching genitals: my parents are out of the question, as is the school nurse, Miss Del Greco. I reluctantly ask Dr. Halberstadt, our family physician, a burly refugee with a bald skull and brusque manner, renowned for his fastidious English tailoring. Under his white medical jacket he wears a blue-striped shirt, silk tie and wool slacks, all purchased at Turnbull and Asser. This Anglophile haberdashery is in no way at odds with his impeccable office in a Tudor house on Ninetieth Street in Elmhurst.

"What do you mean, 'sore,' " he asks me after a routine physical. I have eased my mother out of the examining room on the grounds of modesty.

"I feel this sort of pain."

He leans forward and adjusts his glasses, to get a better look at my genitals. He pulls on a rubber glove and turns my penis first to one side, then the other, as if deciding whether or not to make a purchase.

"No visible sores."

"I know that. I just feel this pain."

"Does that happen after . . ." He raises his eyebrows. I blush. "Boys do it. Is not to blush."

"No. It has nothing to do with my touching it."

"You have told your parents?"

"No. Please, don't tell her."

"Maybe you go to a urologist."

"It doesn't hurt all the time. Just once in a while."

"You feel this now as we are speaking?"

"No, I don't."

"The next time you feel it, you will call me on the phone and describe it, please?"

"Yes. I just don't want to talk about it in front of my mother."

"*Ich verstanden.*" He pulls off his rubber gloves. "I think maybe this is psychosomatic. Happens to boys through puberty. Their bodies change, they feel symptoms. The symptoms are usually only of shame, but they don't realize it. I could recommend you to someone. You could talk . . ."

There is a knock at the door.

"Is the secret examination over?" my mother asks.

"Dr. Breitbart, that is the name. He is in Manhattan, very competent man."

My mother knocks again.

"Hello, Dr. Halberstadt?"

"In a second." He drops his voice. "So?"

My mother opens the door "I was getting worried," she says to Dr. Halberstadt. "What should I know?"

"He's fine. A healthy boy with normal questions." Dr. Halberstadt smiles thinly at me. I don't believe that he thinks me either healthy or normal. Who would?

"Of course he is," says my mother. "Just a little bit of a worry wart, right, Robele? The worrier in the family."

I get up to leave. Dr. Halberstadt escorts my mother from the room. I follow. Over his shoulder, he murmurs to me, "Dr. Karl Breitbart, on the East Side, in the sixties. He's in the book."

MY mother and I walk home from the doctor's office. She puts her arm through mine.

"When I first came to this country I worked as a governess to very rich people who lived in Elmhurst. I would leave Carol with Oma. You wouldn't think rich people would live here, but they did. A big private house, three in help, their name was Solomon. Jewish, but old-time Jewish, not refugees, from the 1800s the family came here. A house also on Long Island, gorgeous, near the ocean. I was lucky to work for them. Walter Solomon. The wife was . . . Alice. Four beautiful children. For years they sent me cards on the holidays. For years and years. He was in the brewery business. I asked why they didn't live in Manhattan, on Park Avenue or Fifth Avenue; believe me they could have lived anywhere. He said, 'Liesl, Queens hits the spot for me.' That's how he said it. 'Hits the spot.' Such unpretentious people they were, with such beautiful manners. The way they did everything. When they had company, the table, the silver, the glassware . . ." She grips my arm harder and there is a dreamy look in her eyes. Overhead, the number seven train on the Flushing El begins its rhythmic roar, heading toward Manhattan. The ground vibrates.

"You were the housekeeper?" I ask, the handsome young consort with the psychosomatic pain in his dick.

"Governess. Just with the children. Someone else did the cleaning, someone else did the cooking. They had sixteen rooms in their house, sixteen rooms! Can you imagine? On Eighty-seventh Street. We all lived there." The Manhattan-bound train moves out of earshot. "How those children loved me. I think more than their own mother sometimes. But what I learned then, and I never forgot it, was having all the money isn't so important as long as everybody loves each other."

"They didn't love each other?"

"No, of course they did. What are you talking about? The Solomons. Of course. What do you think?"

"So what's the point? They had lots of money and lived in two great houses and they still loved each other."

My mother nods as if she is about to reveal the unutterable Sweet Mystery of Life.

"The point is, no matter what, you love your family. They were lucky, they had money. We'll never be wealthy, but look what we have. More than money what we have. But you won't realize this until you're older."

The express to Flushing now races overhead with the rivet-shaking speed of an Eastern European train barreling toward the border.

". . . than all the money," she is saying. She squeezes harder on my arm as the racket of the El gets louder. "All the money in the world."

DR. Karl Breitbart is listed in the Manhattan white pages at 301 E. 67th Street. I call three times: once I get an answering service, the other two times a man with an accent, presumably Dr. Breitbart, picks up. On each occasion, I hang up the telephone immediately and feel as if I have committed an obscene act. But I feel as if I have a secret ally, someone who doesn't even know my name. He *could* know my name; it wouldn't take much, just a completed phone call. But I draw back from the brink. It is like having the number of a house of prostitution and knowing that actual sex is there for the asking. I have such a number as well, at least I believe I do. That number is PEACHES. Dial P-E-A-C-H-E-S and the madam of a whorehouse will answer. So I have been told.

"Two kinds of shame," says Dr. Singer.

"That's a genius observation."

He has stuffed newspapers into the loose space between the upper and lower windows. A loose latch prevents a perfect seal and cold air has crossed his desk, causing his notes to fly around.

"I didn't know you still took notes on me." He has lost weight and it doesn't seem cold enough to justify a cardigan over a vest over a flannel shirt. A cup of tea sits steaming before him.

"Of course I do."

"I thought you just wrote 'ditto' three times a week." I turn around; Dr. Singer appears to be shivering. "I slept with this girl."

He blinks. "Really?"

"Yes." I turn back around and stare at the ceiling. " 'This girl.' *Rebecca.* Last Friday." This is Wednesday. Silence. Is he going to say it or am I? "I didn't say anything about it at the Monday session because I just didn't know what to say."

"But you were thinking of saying something."

"Oh, of course. For the entire session. Instead of chattering pointlessly about my mother's experiences as a housekeeper, like that was the important news of the day. Her fucking life and times."

"Well, maybe on Monday it was important."

"Please."

"You sleep with this woman you've been talking about since the autumn and you associate to your mother's experiences as a housekeeper to the wealthy, to a pain in your penis, to having, but not making use of, the telephone numbers of a therapist and a whorehouse."

"I'm not sure it actually was a whorehouse. There was P-E-A-C-H-E-S and there was also C-H-E-R-R-Y-S. Cherrys."

"Yes."

"I didn't call that one either. Out of fear. That's what you're saying. That I was ashamed to tell you I slept with this girl. So how come I told you today?"

He doesn't reply. I start to turn around but decide it's hardly worth the trouble. Just to see his blank, neutral gaze.

"I had just expressed surprise that you still made notes on me, feeling that there were no surprises. So maybe I told you this to surprise you."

"Did it surprise you?"

"Yes and no. I was surprised that she was so willing to sleep with hideous me, in the sense that we just went to a movie and then had some dinner and then we went to my apartment and made love, just like that. Like it was inevitable."

"From the way you had been talking about her, it did seem sort of inevitable. Unless you chose not to."

"Me?"

"Yes."

"I would have to agree with you." I sigh audibly and suddenly feel my mother's hand gripping my arm, beneath the El. ("More than all the money in the world.") "It was bound to happen and it was wonderful."

"You enjoyed it?"

"I did. During. Afterwards I couldn't sleep. I felt maybe she was too young. That I took advantage of her."

"Took advantage of a child?"

"Yes. I know it's not true. It's not equivalent to what happened to me, it's not something I forced upon her in any way. Not at all. But she's twenty-four and I'm forty-five"

"And that's why you couldn't sleep."

"I felt a familiar, physical sadness. A sadness of my body as much as of my mind. A sense of defeat."

"Defeat?"

"Is that an odd word?"

"Odd, no. I'm not exactly sure what you mean, though."

I GET up again at six-thirty and go to the bathroom, where I throw up as quietly as is humanly possible. Then I wash up, brush my teeth and go back to bed. Rebecca remains asleep, her left arm thrust beneath the pillow, her right hand spread cautiously before her face. At ten past seven the sun hits her in the eyes and she awakens. She squints at me, looking—my imagination?—faintly surprised, then scurries out of bed, hunched over but still magnificent, a Manet, and disappears into the john. She emerges five minutes later, wrapped in a bath towel.

"It's all the sunlight. I'm not ready to be *that* naked yet." She sits down on the side of the bed and smiles, unembarrassed, looking as much eighteen now as twenty-four. This is absurd.

"How do you feel? Weird to be here?"

"Not *weird*. I mean, it's not home sweet home, obviously."

"Obviously."

She stares at the digital clock: 7:17. "It's very early to be up, isn't it, for a Saturday. You have plans?" Our life together begins.

"I was going to go to the library for a while, do some Capone work." I am researching popular views of Capone during the Depression. "You?"

"I'm supposed to meet my mom for lunch at the Museum of Modern Art."

"She's coming down from Katonah?"

"Apartment-hunting. Now that my brother Doug's at Amherst, she's been talking about moving."

"I'm surprised that she stayed there after . . ."

"Oh, that was a different house. When he killed himself. That was Pound Ridge." She yawns, pushes hair from her eyes. "We moved to Katonah the next year." The towel begins to slip; she grabs on to it, holds it over her bosom with both hands.

"Would you like a pair of my pajamas?"

"That would be great."

I go to my chest of drawers.

"It's not coyness, believe me, I'm not looking to saunter around here looking like a Van Heusen shirt ad or something . . ." In the bottom drawer, I find suitable pajamas.

"Blue plaid." I hold them out in my hand. She gets up and takes them, letting the towel drop to the floor, then scoots back into the bathroom.

"I'll make coffee," I tell my mirrored image on the back of the bathroom door. My image is smiling in a curious fashion.

"We only stayed in Pound Ridge six months after he killed himself. It was just . . ."

"I can imagine . . ."

"Every time you walked past that bathroom, I mean, he might as well have still been in it. It was just impossible. We all wanted to get out. This is fabulous coffee."

She is in my kitchen, in my pajamas, the sleep still in her eyes on a Saturday morning that is already turning gray over Morningside Park. For this moment she seems to be mine. In this quiet morning, the steam rising from the coffee mugs, the radio playing softly in the background. Scarlatti? I barely know what to say, so afraid am I of breaking the spell, uttering the forbidden word. We have this moment together and it seems very comfortable. We have slept together and I feel, for at least this morning hour, that I have my bearings. True, I vomited, but Rome wasn't built in a day.

"What are you thinking about?" Rebecca asks. "You were off somewhere."

"I'm thinking that I feel very happy."

"Which is not a run-of-the-mill feeling."

"No. Not at all."

She nods. The warm coffee brings a roseate glow back to her cheeks. I see Libby falling away from me, can still hear the pages in the hall ("Dr. Katz, Dr. Katz," "Dr. Greco, Dr. Greco" over and over as she died), and then I banish the thought.

"Yes?" she asks.

"What?"

"You were off again. Just like that."
"I'm back."

WE shower together. She is mine. I cannot destroy this. Please God give me the power not to destroy this.

1986 / (1990)

S HE dies in her sleep at the age of seventy-four on April 10. I
receive a call in my office from her sister Hilde.

"She felt nothing," Hilde says over and over. "The *butz-
frau*," the cleaning woman, "found her in bed. She looked content.
That's the important thing."

"And then the cleaning woman called you."

"What a shock, Robele. I passed out for a few seconds. Right on
the phone."

I do not understand why the cleaning woman called Aunt Hilde,
rather than me, but I suppose it is moot. At the moment, however, it
doesn't feel quite moot; it feels like a slight, like the denial of a son's
inalienable right to be the first to know.

"You have to make the funeral, Robele. You have to make the
arrangements. You do it out here," meaning Queens, "like your
dad. And the cemetery, Fern Cliff. You do that. What a shock. You
can imagine what it is for me. I still have *herzklopfen*. Never in a
million years did I expect this. Only two left now, me and your
uncle Max. You want to call him in Atlanta?"

"I'm going to have a lot to do."

"You have his number? Hold on. *Gott:* My heart. I never thought
I see this day, that it happens to your mother. The best person.
Here: 404-555-1332. That's the store. He'll be there." My head is
spinning. There's the shock, there's the vast yawning chasm of

seemingly unfillable tasks, and there's the knowledge—as sudden and instinctive as an infant's need for milk—that there is now no one left who cares if I live or die. "You'll call me later, Robele."

"Hilde?"

"What?"

"Do you feel for me at all?"

"Please: how can you say such a thing today?"

I swivel my desk chair toward the window and look out over the campus, vivid in the April sunlight. Students follow their morning shadows up the steps to Low Library and out through the gates onto Broadway. I am in Manhattan, but it could be Madrid, London, anywhere. I am a Jew in an office, alone with his books and his papers. A Jew without a family. A Jew without his mother, suddenly as vulnerable as a baby chick.

I place a call to my sister, who now lives in the Brentwood area of Los Angeles with Sidney Mann the talent agent. Although they maintain their apartment on Central Park West, it is in use only six or so weeks of the year. With both her children in college, Carol devotes much time to the Children's Hunger Foundation and has traveled within the past few years to India, the Sudan, and Burma, in the company of other important entertainment industry wives. Her marriage, she told me last year, "is serviceable," which I took to mean that she is still sampling the world's many pleasures.

I reach my sister's housekeeper Estrella, who informs me that Carol is en route to the gym and transfers me to the car phone, thus enabling my sister to learn of her mother's death while motoring down San Vincente Boulevard.

"Oh, God," she says, through a blizzard of static. "I have to pull over." She stops the car and then we are cut off. I stare dumbly at my phone, which is as dead as my mother, and then hang up. I call her house again and this time Estrella can't forward me.

"She must be turn off the car," she informs me. I hang up and begin to cry. It is very short, just a gust of grief really, and then my phone rings. It is Hilde, with more phone numbers.

"Cousin Martl in Belgium, you should call her. Ernst in San Diego, he'll want to know."

"I never heard of Ernst."

"Come on, what are you talking about, of course you know him,

Cousin Ernst from Mannheim. The Funke sisters, Lotte and her sister Anne-Marie; they're still up in Washington Heights . . ."

"Could you maybe call them?"

"LORRAINE 5-3060." My aunt insists on the proper names of local phone exchanges. "Hanna and Fritz Ehrlich, they're in Jersey. Teaneck. That's MAPLE 4-2890."

"Hilde, I'm waiting for my sister to call back." My aunt hangs up abruptly. My sister is still big news in the family.

When Carol calls, she is in the gym and she is crying. "Jesus, Rob, I spoke to her Sunday, she sounded okay. I mean nutty, but okay. Oh, God. And the cleaning lady found her? Is there going to be an autopsy or something?"

"What for?"

"Just to know for sure."

"I assume it was her heart. She had a physical six months ago, she was okay. An autopsy, you're talking about . . ." About sawing the top of her head off, about scooping vital organs out of her body like so much dog food.

"I know. All right, I have to make arrangements so I can get out of here this afternoon. We have a lot to talk about, don't we. Oh, Jesus, this is like Stalin died or something. I can't describe what I feel. It's not sadness."

"I know."

"It's not even shock. No, it is shock, what the fuck am I talking about? Of course it's shock, but it's beyond that. I didn't feel this when Dad died."

"No."

"Do you have a girl friend?"

"No. Not now."

"God. I feel like a war criminal. Everything that happened when we were kids. You know, under totalitarian conditions, things occur and then when the conditions no longer exist . . . Jesus . . ."

"I know."

"I can't talk about this over the phone. Poor woman. But still, she drove me crazy. And with us . . ."

"We'll talk in person."

"You have no one?"

"Not at the present time. My shrink, he's the closest."

"I'll take a three-thirty flight, so I'll be in around midnight. I'll be at the Carlyle. You want to meet me there for a drink? Are you up for that? It'll be at a ridiculous hour, one or something."

"Probably. It'll be good to see you."

"Yes." She starts crying again. "Oh, Robby, what a fucking mess."

I TAKE the train out to Queens and walk down the steps from the elevated platform at Junction Boulevard like a man descending a gallows. Ninety-seventh Street is nearly deserted; a Latino mother pushes a solitary toddler up the street and smiles at me. The temperature is in the mid-fifties, yet the child is bundled up for winter, in a down vest and wool cap. The mother is in her mid-twenties, yet her smile is filled with gold. She is headed for the supermarket, like thousands before her on this block. Queens is a land of domesticity; everyone—Jew and Colombian, Italian and Greek—walks, and has always walked, with the gait of middle-age: slightly stooped, a little lost, abstracted by the gap between the *is* and the *ought*, the expectation and the reality.

I reach my mother's building and stop. Here it stands: my past entombed in red brick. A six-story sarcophagus of sin. I sit down on the stone ledge by the iron fence which once bordered shrubbery and now bounds only dirt, like a vacant cage in the zoo. A Latin teenager carrying a baseball glove runs out through the front door and passes me without so much as a glance; I am as invisible as the Stage Manager in *Our Town*. I watch his speedy progress up the block. Birds call to one another; the same birds who once sang to me and my neighbors now democratically serenade Latins and Pakistanis. How expendable we are. I turn and retch into the dirt, then look up and see our darkened living room windows. I take the keys to her apartment from my pocket and walk slowly and woozily into the lobby.

The fluorescent light in the elevator is buzzing. There are a few names scratched into the walls: Julio, Macho Man, Dust. I imagine her standing here with her shopping cart, staring at the passing floors, and wonder how she managed to live as long as she did. How alone she must have been; how alone I left her. Seventy-four years old, shoulders slightly hunched, her bags of groceries stacked in the cart: milk for coffee, juice, Golden Delicious apples, Wild's Bauen-brot, a half salami, a cut-up chicken, greens for salad. I know the list by heart.

The elevator stops; I get out and walk those twenty paces to 4C, my Via Dolorosa. Game show applause swells from 4D ("Patel") as I turn the key to her apartment and push the door open. I pause outside for a moment and then enter as quietly as a late arrival to a party.

For what seems like ten minutes I stand in the foyer with my coat on. I finally take it off, draping it carefully over a chair, and begin to walk from room to room with the benumbed deliberation of a homicide detective who finds murder in his own home. In the kitchen I find a damp Lipton's tea bag on a saucer, toast crumbs on the counter; the final physical evidences of her life. Water is dripping in the bathroom sink; water that she turned on to wash her face and hands for the last time.

I go to her bedroom. The bed is unmade but in no disarray. She must have died like a princess in a fairy tale, on her back, hands folded. There are no signs of distress anywhere; only that the bed is not made. I almost never saw this bed unmade unless she was in it. The first thing she did upon arising, even before the brewing of coffee, was to unfold the bedspread, walk from side to side and straighten it, toss the five pillows upon it, and then take a final martial walk of inspection around its three sides, tugging, pulling and straightening.

I sit down on the side of the bed and put my hand on her pillow, hoping/not hoping for a touch of residual warmth from her cheek, for a last transmission of body heat.

The pillow is cool. She is gone.

Her phone rings and I answer. It is a solicitation for a travel magazine. I inform the solicitor that Mrs. Weisglass will not be home until evening. The mouthpiece of the phone smells slightly of Life-Savers. I inhale deeply, savoring traces of her final minty breaths, remembering the mothball smell of her coat, the leather and peppermint aroma of her handbag. An olfactory biography. I hang up the phone, then turn and see a hair beside her pillow. I pick it up with slow careful fingers; it is gray and dull and sits in my palm like an oily whisper. The suggestion of a tickle. Perhaps she had her hair in a bun and let it out before she fell asleep and died. Hair cascading over her bare freckled shoulders before she lay down for her concluding dreams. And what where those dreams? A cobbled German street at evening, her mother shouting from a window, someone passing on a bicycle; figures in a doorway, kneeling in a strange way. Are they wearing uniforms? Steamships crossing the Atlantic; is that my father passing her on the deck? Is that him leaping into the water and beckoning her to join him? Corona: he walks home from the elevated line, a strange woman on his arm, laughing, smoothing her summer dress. No, it is not a strange woman, it is her younger self. No, it is not Herbert, it is Robele, and they are walking together toward the house arm in arm and the summer sun is setting and there is an enormous sound, like the beginning of an earthquake. It rattles windows and causes dogs to bark and birds to fly from trees and telephone lines in one single black flapping mass. Rob and Liesl walk into the building as it begins to collapse. Bricks and masonry and light fixtures topple as if in slow motion, dust rising like an atomic cloud, but they walk resolutely toward the elevator, arm in arm, her right breast pressing against his left hand. He looks very pale but he is smiling, that smile she loved, the smile that showed he felt safe and strong in her company. The elevator door closes and she can see her neighbors fleeing into the lobby but she is safe with her son. The elevator moves upwards and they are in Bloomingdale's and people are frantic, pushing toward escalators and exits, and they go up past linens and women's sportswear and now they are back in Corona, just for an instant, but they are going past the fourth floor. She pushes the button to no avail; the elevator ascends through the debris and the collapsing walls and merchandise of Bloomingdale's, past toys and pets and housewares, past the wrapping desk, past the Christmas department where Kurt's wife Grete worked during the holiday season of 1952, selling fruitcakes, and up through the roof into a still clear absolute darkness where the only sound is of her lips as she kisses her son. Kisses him again and again. There is no elevator. Just them on the roof; and then there is no roof. Lights become visible in the distance: the steamship. It does not move toward them and then, without warning, it produces an enormous beacon of light, then becomes the very light itself. And then, just as abruptly, it sinks from sight, and there is utter darkness.

When I emerge from this thought, I am seated on the floor beside my mother's bed. I get up and lie down on her bed for a few minutes, studying her ceiling. There is a water stain from a decade-old bathroom flood in 5C, there are the cracks that resemble the profile of Smilin' Jack, the fearless airplane pilot from the *Daily News* comics page. Here she lay for forty-five years, my father beside her for thirty-six of them. Two people divided by a forest of secrets. I imagine my father's thoughts, attempting to fathom her silences, waking up one night and finding her absent. A noise from the next room. Eyes open, listening. Worse: arising and going to the hall, standing breathless outside my room, hearing, denying the brutal evidence of the senses, then racing back, falling into bed, feigning sleep as she slips back into the room, hair loosened and cheeks reddened.

It couldn't have happened. He could not have lived through that, could not have arisen the next morning, whistling, shaving, sipping his coffee. It was our little secret. And now it's my secret exclusively, mine and Dr. Singer's.

I turn on my side, knees pulled up. A toilet flushes from a neighboring apartment, perhaps one of the Patels vanquishing a curried feces into the United Nations of New York's sewers. A musical soft-ice-cream truck rolls up the street, its tune repeated on a loop. My eyelids feel heavy. Thoughts trail off, or bang randomly into other thoughts.

A ringing phone awakes me. The pillow is soaked with perspiration; I feel droplets in my hair. I check my watch; only a half-hour has passed. Disoriented, I reach for the phone and knock it to the floor. I crawl to it, answer on my knees.

"Hello?"

"I knew I find you there." Again, it is Aunt Hilde. "You know who I forgot? Leo Leprecht in St. Louis: 314-555-8657."

"Could you please call him?"

"I have so many calls."

"Please."

"When I think that she died alone, Robele. That's what gets me."

"I know."

"You sound tired."

"I was actually taking a nap."

"Also you should call Karl and Lotte Strauss in New Paltz. That's MOHICAN 5-2341. You remember them from Fleischmanns."

"Vaguely. Did he have a stutter?

"Terrible stutter, then it got better. Wait a minute, they moved to Florida. Orlando."

"I'm not going to call them.

"The funeral, Robele, that's going to be Schwartz?"

"At two o'clock."

"They can't do it earlier?"

"No."

"Who did you talk to?"

"Why, do you have connections there?"

"I knew a Mr. Heilbrunner."

"This was Mr. Samuels. What difference does it make what time?"

"And afterwards, what?"

"Afterwards? After the cemetery?"

"Sure. People want to be together."

"I think it would be ghoulish to come back here. Carol is going to be at the Carlyle."

"Everybody has to go to the city? They can come here to Kew Gardens."

"Hilde, this is my mother."

"She wasn't my sister?"

"I think it's more appropriate . . ."

"I'm just trying to make it easier for you. Carol is going to be exhausted . . ."

"I'm sure she'll want to host it. She's the eldest child."

"I call her."

"She's on an airplane."

"The Carlyle you said."

"Yes." I slide down to the floor.

"I call her. We'll talk."

"Fine. Listen, I have to go to Schwartz."

"Now?"

"Yes."

"I'll meet you there."

"It's really not . . ."

"I need to keep occupied. You don't know what this is, losing a sister."

A BLOCK from the Schwartz Funeral Home I spot Hilde already there, leaning on a cane, wearing a belted leather coat. She waves, then limps forward and throws her arms around me.

"Bubele."

I well up in her arms, even though we have never been terribly close. My mother had always installed warning signs and sawhorses around relatives she thought might compete with her for my affection, so Hilde had always been targeted in the family as "selfish," principally due to her decision not to have children. "Bad hip or not," my mother would say, "you have to make sacrifices. That's what children are. Sacrifices. She was just too selfish." Hilde had never struck me as being inordinately selfish, just self-involved, like everyone else in the family.

"I did you a big favor," she tells me. "I called the Strausses in Florida. You can imagine the shock."

"Sure."

"I don't think he gets everything anymore, you know? But Lotte was very upset."

"I'm sure . . ."

"I could tell. Karl didn't say much . . ."

"Well, the stutter . . ."

"I don't think it was the stutter. I'd heard he was getting a little slow, Henny Koenig told me, but Lotte, to her it was a tremendous shock. You know your mother, many people loved her, Robele."

"I know."

"She wasn't always the easiest person, but her life, what she went through."

"Of course." I am reduced, as always, to monosyllables.

"With Opa in the accident and Oma going crazy, she didn't let it show, but I know what it was for her."

"I remember she'd just have toast and tea when my father and I visited Oma in the loony bin. She wouldn't even go in."

"She was too strong."

What can I say? Do these people actually believe this shit? "Too strong," "too good."

"No life is perfect," I tell Aunt Hilde.

"We went through a lot, Robele. You don't even know how much. We spared you children. Maybe too much."

Mr. Samuels of the funeral home sells me a mahogany coffin with brass handles. Carol and I had worked this out over the phone. The funeral will cost about five thousand dollars. This includes the hearse, four limos, all embalming and cosmetics, plus rental of the room.

Aunt Hilde is impressed with the coffin.

"Very tasteful. Like her, Robele."

I am in what can only be described as a daze as Mr. Samuels walks me through the steps of the funeral, shows me the chapel, the room where the family will greet visitors, the book in which guests will sign their names. We discuss flowers, rabbis, music. Hilde trails behind me like Sancho Panza, until Mr. Samuels walks us outside, shakes our proffered hands, then walks back inside to answer a telephone page.

"A *shvule*," she says.

"Excuse me?"

"Mr. Samuels. A *shvule bruder*."

"You think he's gay?"

"It makes no difference. The place is spotless. The way they keep it up. Beautiful." Busses roar by on Queens Boulevard. Children are racing home from school, bopping each other on the head. Aunt Hilde begins to cry. "The world will never be the same."

CAROL rises from her table in the bar of the Carlyle. Her eyes are reddened, from grief and fatigue.

"Oh, baby." She kisses me on the mouth, holds me tight. The bar is empty but for two young Africans, diplomats in Savile Row suits, who sit chewing peanuts and drinking sherry.

I hold her, arching my body to keep full contact at a minimum. One of the Africans begins to write something down on a bar napkin.

"What a day," I tell her. "It's like ten days. Ten bad days."

"I know. The flight took *forever*. I didn't know whether to drink or not. I decided to wait till I got here . . . God." She stands back, dabs at her eyes. "You went out to Queens?"

"Sure."

"I haven't been in the apartment in five years. I always had her meet me here, or wherever. The Sherry. The Pierre. We'd meet, we'd have lunch. Sit; why are we standing like ninnies." She sits down and I join her. "Once in a while I'd take her shopping with me, but that was always a disaster." Carol blows her nose, then sips at a scotch and soda. She's wearing a rust-colored suit, a silk blouse and two strands of pearls. Diamonds adorn her ears. At fifty she is more beautiful than at forty: more settled. She always seemed sure of herself; now she seems sure of everyone else as well.

A waiter leans toward me and says nothing. He simply raises his eyebrows and I ask for a Rémy Martin. He steals away as silently as he arrived.

"How's the apartment?" Carol asks.

"As ever. There's some stuff we should talk about splitting up, of a sentimental nature, things that might mean something to your kids one day. Dad's old fountain pens, that velvet smoking jacket he brought over from Germany."

Carol just waves her hand.

"That's yours."

"I wouldn't wear it in a million years. Maybe Jeffrey, as a goof, to a party."

"Jeffrey's six foot two. It would never fit him."

"Sidney?"

She smiles.

"Not in velvet, thank you. He's put on about twenty-five pounds." She sighs, looks around the room. Her eyes tear up again. "I'm a fucking orphan."

"Yeah."

"You know why this makes me so crazy." The tears are more copious now. "Shit." She wipes at her eyes. The one African is scribbling on yet another napkin while the other signals for two more sherries. "It makes me crazy because I tell myself I'm an orphan and it doesn't feel any different than before. It's like they were never there."

"Well, Dad's gone nine years already . . ."

She shakes her head.

"That's not it. It's not about time healing . . . It's about that I feel no *sadness*. Emptiness? That I feel, but I've felt it since I was a teenager. That's the hideous part. Mom dies and I don't feel any different than when she was alive."

"There has to be a certain measure of shock operating here."

"Yes. I agree." The waiter brings me my Rémy and a small dish of nuts. He nods at me as though we were old allies, linked together through decades of cognacs and cashews. No wonder people love these hotels.

"I find myself principally feeling guilty," I tell my sister.

"What do you *possibly* have to feel guilty about?"

"I could have been nicer to her in the last few years. I could have visited her more."

"To what end?" She sips none-too-delicately at her scotch.

"Listen, if you're feeling rotten about hardly seeing her, there's no reason . . ."

"No, it's not about that. I think I was really very decent to her, considering that she couldn't ever stand me, I mean like from the day I was born. Well, maybe when I was *born*, the early years *possibly*. But starting at like seven, when it was clear that I was going to be seriously good-looking, forget it. So I basically said, fine, we'll both forget it. Which is why at age twelve I became this little sex machine."

"Not twelve."

"I vas dere, Charlie."

"Twelve?"

"Johnny Ferraro," she states simply, as if saying "Paris" or "Rome."

"Johnny Ferraro what?"

"Do you remember him?"

"From Thirty-eighth Avenue. He wound up in jail, I think."

"That was his brother Vincent. Johnny became an engineer, for Grumman out on the island. His parents both worked. He was fourteen, I was twelve; this is early 1948 we're talking about. Winter, a ton of snow still on the ground, post-blizzard of '47."

"So I'm like three."

"You're three and home with Mom, who has neither a clue nor a care as to what I'm doing. The moment my boobs emerged, she saw me *solely* as a threat, like a sexy boarder from a James Cain novel. Dad, of course, was out to lunch completely. So I was on the loose, basically, and one afternoon Johnny Ferraro tells me that both his parents work and there's something he wants to show me. We walk to his place and I remember the ground was icy, so I kept holding onto his arm to keep from sliding and, of course, just to hold onto him. When we get to the apartment, it's like Crucifix City: the Blessed Virgin everywhere and portraits of Jesus, the couches and chairs wrapped in plastic covers, and this strong cheese smell in the air. I sit down and ask him what he wants to show me. 'This,' he says, and pulls out his pecker, which I'm really very happy to see."

"Just like that."

"Just like that. It was that simple. And for like, I don't know, four months, I would go there nearly every afternoon and we would play. He was really very discreet for a fourteen-year-old guy; he didn't tell his pals, didn't brag. I was his private stock, his little sex pet."

"Twelve."

"It's something, isn't it? And all I really wanted was to be held. He was a sweet guy, Johnny, very cute and considerate." She picks up her scotch and soda. "What I learned from those afternoons was that sex was better than anything else in my miserable little life."

"You felt no shame?"

"No." She finishes her drink, glances toward the waiter and taps her glass.

"In 1948."

"I wouldn't have felt any shame in 1848. It was just my nature. Maybe if Dad had hugged me like once in my life, which is to say if he hadn't been Dad, and if Mom hadn't been Mom, then I wouldn't have been me, right? But they were, and I was. End of story."

"Twelve."

"You can't get over it."

"I feel a little betrayed. Like you were cheating on me."

"You were three."

"All the worse."

She leans over and takes my hand. Those familiar fingers, that familiar pressure. "I had no choice, Robby, I swear. My entire identity was sex. That was it. Mom could never touch me in that department. The way I dressed, the whole deal, it just put miles and miles between me and her. And that was fine with both of us, that distance. Particularly her. For me, I could either feel rejected by her or go out and screw my brains out, figuring that the best defense was a good offense. So that was that. From Johnny Ferraro on, I was on the make."

"And me?"

"You?"

"Us. Those nights in the room."

She squeezes my hand, then lets go. "You know what's so bizarre? Sick as it was, it still doesn't *seem* sick to me. The atmosphere in that apartment was so weird that having played with you seems absolutely normal. I don't have any real qualms about it, that's the amazing part. I talked to my current shrink, Alan, about what happened, obviously; you know what he said? First shrink that *ever* mentioned it."

I know what she's going to say.

"What?" I croak.

"He said he wouldn't be surprised if Mom had made a move on you. I don't even remember what we were talking about, but he just mentioned it, as an aside. Needless to say, it didn't *remain* an aside."

"I can imagine."

"First I just said, like, 'holy shit,' but when I thought about it a little . . ."

I sip at my Rémy Martin.

"You don't have to answer this, Robby."

"I know." I shake my head from side to side.

"Why are you shaking your head?"

"It was a crazy house."

Carol recoils slightly in her chair, grips its arm.

"So she did?"

"Sort of."

"*Sort of?*"

"Sort of."

"Like she acted seductive? I saw that. But beyond that, anything overt?"

"No. Not . . ."

"Not overt."

"No. Just like an ambiguous attitude, I would say."

She is a woman, so Carol knows that I am probably lying. But she is also my sister, the daughter of our shared and demented mother, and there is undoubtedly a limit, particularly on this day of death, to what she wants to know.

"Did she ever *say* anything?" Carol asks a little wildly.

"Mom?"

"Yes."

"You mean sexual?"

"I guess. I don't know what the hell I'm talking about." She tears up again. "Jesus Christ. I was thinking, on the flight in, about the night before your bar mitzvah, you know . . ."

"Yeah . . ." My mouth turns to sand.

". . . when you buggered me. Jesus, to think we even had the *imagination* for it."

"We broke a lot of commandments that night." I am having trouble taking a deep breath.

"All of them, I'm sure. Commandments with asterisks we broke, unlisted ones." She laughs a little, dabs at her eyes with a richly scented handkerchief . . . "God. That little apartment. I've been everywhere, I've done everything with everybody, but nothing has ever been stranger than what went on in those four rooms."

"I try to think about what Mom and Dad went through, but then . . ."

Carol shakes her head.

"Then you run into reality, then you run into *the actual facts of our life*. If you focus on what they went through, then you make yourself responsible for everything. They went through plenty, granted, but also they were *nuts*. There's no accounting for it otherwise. Oma Hedwig up there in that home in Nyack eating newspapers, cracking up because Opa died in that crash—*come on, that's to be expected?* It isn't. What you and I did in our room, Mom coming on to you, if that's all she did, if you haven't blocked the rest—what are we talking about, a response to the Holocaust? We're talking about fucking *pathology*. That's all it was. Here you are, forty-one, right? A cute, bright guy and you haven't come *close* to getting married since that sweet girl died and *that*, if I may say, seemed like a neurotic kind of relationship, a little brother-sisterly, may I say?"

"I loved her."

"I know you did. But how come she was the only one? How come?"

"I don't know."

Her scotch and soda arrives. "Frank, sweetheart," she tells the waiter, "could you get me like a club sandwich, no cheese, whole wheat? I'm starving."

"Of course, Mrs. Mann," says the waiter.

Carol looks to me. "You hungry?"

"No."

"You're sure?"

I hesitate. I realize that I am starving.

"Have a club sandwich. They're very good here. And bring us some fries, Frank. Fuck the diet."

The waiter nods and walks away.

"What I meant to say was 'fuck the diet, my mother just died' but that would have sounded coarse, don't you think?" Carol sits up straighter and her breasts push against her blouse. "You still seeing the same shrink?"

"Yes."

"And what does he say about Libby?"

"It's complicated . . ."

"I think you bonded with Libby for some special reason and then, when she died, something went flooey for you. I'm just guessing here, but I've never figured out why someone as attractive as you would never have gotten seriously involved in all this time. It's a mystery to me."

I go into neutral.

"Yes."

Carol studies me. Tears again spring to her eyes.

"Did I ruin you? Was that it?"

"No."

"Not at all? It had to have some effect. You were such a baby." She begins to weep. "God, I was so fucking crazy. What was I thinking?" The two Africans turn and observe us. "That I was going to save you from her or something? You were *twelve*. And I'm asking why you've never had a serious relationship since Libby. It's a miracle you had one with her. It's a miracle you're not a fag."

* * *

A COLD, driving rain beats down on the cemetery. There are maybe twenty of us standing beneath umbrellas as my mother's body is delivered unto the ancient earth of Ardsley, Westchester County. Aunt Hilde is weeping openly, a plastic rain bonnet wrapped around her head. My uncle Kurt, bronzed from a winter in Palm Beach, stands with his second wife Gail, his hands folded before him, thick gray hair slicked straight back, disdaining an umbrella. He catches my eye and nods. I nod back numbly. I feel physical sensations—a certain looseness in the bowels, the beginnings of a headache, but I cannot or will not connect this box containing my mother with any memory that I can convert into an appropriate emotion.

Rabbi Eckstein recites the mourner's kaddish and there is a creaky echoing chorus of "Yis'g'dal's" from my secular family. Rain begins to drip off Rabbi Eckstein's nose as steadily as if he were a garden fixture. The dirt around my mother's grave turns to mud. The coffin descends, aided by gravediggers wearing hooded slickers with "Fern Cliff" stenciled on the back. The rabbi hands me a shovel; I dig out some mud and dump it on the coffin, then hand the shovel to Carol. She digs in, begins to lose her footing, slips out of her heels, wobbles at the precipice. I reach for her, pull her back. She puts the shovel down on the ground, picks up some mud with her bare hands and drops it into the excavation. Then she puts her arms around me, lays her head on my shoulder and begins to sob. Uncontrollably. She is saying something into my ear. "I'm sorry" is what she says, and then, "I love you."

CAROL has changed and pulled herself together for the family gathering that occurs later in her suite at the Carlyle. Except for Kurt and his wife, nobody looks terribly comfortable in these ornate rooms. Hilde sits in a corner and sips vermouth, Uncle Max and Tante Frieda stand at the living room window and discuss the view of Madison Avenue, while the Funke sisters reminisce with my sister about Queens in the 1940s. Hanna and Fritz Ehrlich from Teaneck, he nearly blind, are welded to the couch like figures in a George Segal sculpture. There is a feeling of vacancy to the entire afternoon and people leave fairly quickly; there is a sense that not only has this group gathered for the last time, but that it is just as well. Only Kurt and Gail remain for a final cup of coffee. Kurt takes out a cigar and holds it up in a questioning manner.

"No problem," my sister tells him.

"You have to ask everywhere these days," Gail says. Her voice is husky, and her jaw as squared-off as that of a British prizefighter.

"Rob?" Kurt points to the breast pocket of his jacket. "How about a Havana? Live a little."

"No, thank you."

Kurt lights the short but stout cigar slowly and with great tenderness, almost totally obscured by blue smoke. "One of life's great remaining pleasures," he says between puffs.

"You were always the hedonist in the family," my sister tells him. Kurt appears pleased.

"There was not a great competition for the post," he says.

"My mother was a secret hedonist," Carol says. "But very secret."

"I don't think 'hedonist' is the correct word for her," I say, feeling suddenly protective. But of whom?

"I agree," says Kurt. "She was a pissed-off person."

"Kurt," his wife murmurs decorously.

"Hey, we're *mischpocha* here, right? There's no secrets with us. My sister-in-law was a difficult person. We all went through a lot."

"You didn't all wind up the same," Carol says.

"No, but we all have our *mishugas*, our craziness. Hers took the form of being a more or less negative person. I had the advantage of being the youngest, I could be a *momser* for my whole life. It was expected of me."

My sister smiles. "You're still a *momser*, Kurt," she says, and there is a palpable moment between them, a conspiratorial moment strong enough to prompt Gail Weisglass to clutch Kurt's hand and put it in her lap. One hand clutching his cigar, the other held captive by his second wife, Kurt can only stare helplessly at my sister and smile. Is it possible that the incest extended to them as well? Did my entire family live outside the bounds of civilized society, like a group of Tennessee hill people? These are German Jews I'm talking about; Freud, Marx, Einstein—the intellectual behemoths of the modern era—were my compatriots, my *landsmen*. So what was with my family? Did we represent some mutant strain of German Jewry, some morally diseased stock?

"You're still a beauty," I hear my uncle Kurt say. "Still ravishing." His wife is biting her lip. She looks to me but I look away. My sister smiles at Kurt, crosses her legs, and lights a cigarette.

''What did she say?" They wind is rattling the venetian blinds on Dr. Singer's window.

"She denied it."

"Completely?" he asks.

"She said they never had sex. She mentioned that he used to hug her tightly enough so that she could feel his erection."

"His erection."

"Yes. E-r-e-c . . ."

"I just mean that he was excited when he hugged her."

"Apparently."

"But you suspected that something else had gone on."

"Yes, and I still do, and I'm still talking about it, four years after my mother's funeral. It still feels like a betrayal."

"You don't think she would have admitted it if it had actually happened?"

"I saw this look between them."

"It was a lustful look?"

"Conspiratorial."

"Well, it could have been conspiratorial without necessarily being lustful." Singer begins to cough. I turn around and his face is very red and his mouth is buried in his handkerchief. He does not see that I am watching. Finally, I turn back and fold my hands across my stomach, like someone who has just eaten. I wait for Singer to stop his coughing.

"What I mean," his voice is sounding very tired, "is that, given your family, it's probable that some sort of conspiracy did exist between them. He was the only person she could turn to, he was the only, what should we say, 'hip one' in the family. There is that kind of conspiracy."

"So why is it still on my mind four years later?"

"Because you're hanging on to it. Let it go. I'm telling you, Rob, let it go."

I BELIEVE it is the only time he has ever called me by name.

1951–1952 / (1991)

PUBLIC School 19 is an enormous red brick building with white masonry bordering its windows and steel doors; its vast schoolyard is surrounded by a chain-link fence with numerous lacunae for easy access. Like all New York City schools built in the first two decades of the twentieth century, it is an imposing and authoritarian structure, with more than a whiff of the penitentiary about it. Seen from afar, rising above the elevated tracks on Roosevelt Avenue, it does not radiate welcome. In fact, it scares me to death, each and every day that I go there. I deal with this fright, at age seven, by vomiting at regular intervals.

"He has a nervous stomach," my mother says. "That's just the way he is." I can smell the coffee burning, hear the water running as my sister takes her lengthy diurnal shower.

"I don't understand," my father replies. "He doesn't like school, is that it?" From seven in the morning on, he is seated in the kitchen, clad in his suit pants and an undershirt, reading the New York *Times*, which he purchases the night before on Junction Boulevard and then puts aside because he likes it "fresh" upon awakening. He doesn't so much as steal a peek at it, just folds it into quarters and leaves it at his place on the kitchen table. No, before retiring, he will read the *Daily News*, "just for a quick once-over," so that he will be properly armed for the serious work of the *Times* when he arises. My father has his greatest presence in the morning, before the subway travel and the cheap lunch and deadlines at the office wear him down to the pale, largely mute person who returns to our lives each evening. He is more sentient in the morning. I am the basket case, holding a hot water bottle to my stomach as dawn lightens Corona.

"It's just a nervous stomach," my mother repeats.

"He has the runs or he throws up once, twice a week . . ."

"He takes things too hard. He's so much like me. Something happens, he gets very excited. He worries about it."

"I don't know," my father says. "To be seven years old and have a stomach like this."

"I spoke to Dr. Halberstadt," my mother assures him. "He said the last checkup, everything was perfect. He told me, 'Maybe you're too good to him.' That could be it. At school . . ."

"Not everybody caters to him . . ."

"He's on his own, more. So he gets nervous."

Nervous is not how I would describe it. It is a kind of terror. In the autumn of 1951, the thought of leaving my apartment, the only place on earth that has even been defined for me as safe, for the Leavenworth, the—dare I say it—the Auschwitz of P.S. 19, with its steel fencing, its vast, dim, sinister basement, its thundering furnace and steadily spewing smokestack. This fear pins me to my bed each dawn. Each dawn I die.

"I have breakfast for you." She stands at the door, an apron tied around her waist, her hair in a neat bun, looking like a refugee Betty Crocker.

"I'm not hungry."

"Rice Krispies and that cinnamon toast you love."

"Not hungry."

"It's cool out today. After you eat you put on something warm."

Sometimes I throw up at home, sometimes at school; sometimes I make it to the boys' room; sometimes I don't. My dim, softhearted teacher, the tiny and olive-skinned Mrs. Sirota, is at a total loss.

"You're a good boy," she tells me one January morning. I have thrown up on my desk and my classmates have temporarily evacuated the room. Mr. Williams the janitor slowly mops up the mess, glaring at me all the while. "You're a smart boy, the other children like you. What are you so nervous about, Robby? Can you tell me?"

I shake my head.

"Is there something at home? I've met your parents and they're wonderful people. They love you very much and I know they want you to be happy in school. We all do: me, Miss Tetzlager"—P.S. 19's principal, a brutish Teuton with enormous freckled breasts and a raisin-sized wart on her nose—"that's all that we want for you." Mrs. Sirota wipes my damp forehead with a cool hand. "If there's anything bothering you that you want to tell me, please, don't be shy."

I mumble "no" as Mr. Williams pours disinfectant on my desk and wipes at it with a rough cloth. The classroom begins to smell like the asylum that houses Oma Hedwig.

"I'm going to bring the class back in, okay, Robby?"

"Sure," I tell her.

Mrs. Sirota takes my hand. "This is happening too much, Robby. I want you to be happy here."

"Yes" is all I can say.

ONE November evening, shortly after dinner, a chestnut-haired woman from the Bureau of Child Guidance appears at our door. She is very tall and carries a briefcase. It is quite unusual in 1951 to see a briefcase in the hand of a woman. She introduces herself as Miss Warren. My parents stare at her with some trepidation and then ask me to retire to my room.

My sister is seated on the chest of drawers, painting her toenails red. An unlit cigarette dangles from her lip.

"They sent someone from the Board of Ed about your puking?"

"I don't know." I lie down on my bed and curl up.

"That's what it's got to be about, the puking. Don't you think?"

"I guess. She's from the Child Guidance she said."

"Then it's definitely the puking. They're going to want you to see a psychiatrist."

"No they won't."

"It might be a good idea. You don't want to puke forever, do you? I mean, for as long as you go to school? Junior high school, high school, college?"

"It'll stop one day."

"All by itself?"

"Yes."

"They never sent the psychiatrist for me."

"Who said she was a psychiatrist?"

"That's what Child Guidance is, dope."

"They think I'm crazy?"

My sister works on the small toe of her right foot. Her tongue is pressed between her lips, as she concentrates on this utterly feminine small motor skill.

"I didn't say crazy. You did. Disturbed, maybe. That's not crazy. Just a little disturbed."

"So what does that mean? They put me in the Disturbed Class?"

"Maybe."

"I'd quit school first."

"You can't quit school. They'd arrest you." (Years later, my sister denied she ever said any of this.) "Or maybe they'd just arrest Mom and Dad."

"I can't be in the Disturbed Class."

The Disturbed Class in P.S. 19 occupies one of the four basement classrooms which ominously border the school's furnace, silently tended by the massive and bald-headed Mr. Torvald. The basement classrooms are occupied by the Disturbed Class, the Retarded Class, the Mongoloid Class and the Crippled Class. These students arrive each day by bus from all over the borough, shepherded toward the basement doors like maimed dumb beasts. They grunt and moan, they drag their twisted, paralyzed limbs toward the double doors, some break wild and run back toward the street, only to be quickly recaptured by the teachers and assistant teachers. It takes over a half-hour to funnel these broken, wild-eyed children into the school, before the basement doors are slammed shut behind them and the fleet of Special Busses pulls away from the curb, only to return at three, when the ritual is reversed, only the children are both wilder and more exhausted and the process can often exceed one hour in length.

When sent to the basement on errands—to clean erasers, to deliver sealed envelopes to the school nurse—I race breathless down the hall, fearful of even looking into the special classrooms for what outrages, what carnage, what physical wreckage I might spot.

"Were you running?" the nurse asks.

"No," I tell her.

She tears open the sealed envelope and scans the daily report from Mrs. Sirota with the nonchalance of a career diplomat. Then she looks up at me.

"And how are you feeling today?"

"Fine."

"You're having a good day?"

"Yes, I am."

"And how are your parents?"

"They're fine."

"They're very special people," the nurse tells me. "Very refined. Many parents here are not that refined, do you know that?"

"No, I don't."

"They're very fine people, so that's why you may be a little high-strung, Rob. It may be in the breeding." I feel like a collie. "The European breeding. Just don't be nervous, Rob, because we all like you so very much."

I nod at the nurse. She smiles at me; her uniform is a blinding, soap-powder white. I think that she is actually quite beautiful.

"You can go back to your room now."

MISS Warren of Child Guidance is seated on our couch, her briefcase resting against her leg, her knees welded together. My mother has made her a cup of tea, which Miss Warren holds delicately between thumb and forefinger as she sips. I have been summoned into the living room after approximately a half-hour of what has seemed, at least from the perspective of my bedroom, to be a monologue by Miss Warren punctuated by random exclamations from my mother.

Seen up close, Miss Warren is a little older than I had originally thought, closer to forty than thirty. She is very pale and her nose is pushed in too closely to her face, like a cartoon nose. She smiles at me. My father fills his pipe and coughs; my mother is kneading a salmon-colored handkerchief in her hands.

"So this is the boy who doesn't like school so very much," Miss Warren begins.

I look at the floor and shrug. Suddenly I feel slightly dizzy.

"He likes school," my mother interjects. "He just gets nervous sometimes."

"Is that true?" Miss Warren asks. "You just get a little nervous sometimes?"

"Sometimes."

"And what does that feel like?"

"I feel nauseous."

"In your stomach?"

"Yes."

"And what are you thinking about when you're nauseous?"

I look around the room, like a stumped contestant on a quiz show. "Thinking?"

"Any thoughts you might have." Miss Warren nods encouragingly, sips at her tea.

"If you want more tea . . ." My mother gets up from her chair, lunges toward Miss Warren.

"I'm fine. Thank you so much." Miss Warren smiles at me. "You certainly have a wonderful family." My mother retreats to her chair, reflexively runs her hand across her ass before she sits down.

"Of course he does," my mother says. "Everybody loves him."

"And that's a wonderful thing," Miss Warren adds. I nod obediently. "So when you're nauseous, Rob," she continues, "what exactly is going through your mind? Can you think about that for me?"

I search for an answer. "Sometimes, at the start of the year, it's the smell of the paint."

"The fresh paint?"

"Yes."

"That's not a very good smell, is it?"

"No. That makes me a little sick. And the other times . . ." I bite my thumbnail; images of burning bodies light up my mind. "I just get scared."

"Of what?"

"There's nothing to be scared about," says my mother. "What should you be scared about?" Miss Warren smiles weakly at her; it's pretty clear she'd be happier without my mother's intervention.

"You get scared of what, Rob?"

"Just things."

"Different kinds of things? Or the same thing every time?"

I take a deep breath.

"Like something is going to happen to me."

"You'll be hurt or injured in some way?"

"Yes."

Tears come to my mother's eyes. "Where he gets this I don't know. Herbert?" She looks to my father, but he is staring off into the middle distance.

Miss Warren puts her teacup down on the coffee table, then leans forward.

"Do you think the teacher might hurt you?"

"No."

"Your schoolmates?"

"Sometimes."

"Has that happened?"

"No."

"But you feel threatened."

"Sometimes."

"Anybody specific?"

"No."

"Just in general, a kind of a feeling?"

"Yes."

Miss Warren settles back on the couch and folds her hands before her.

"How would you feel, Rob, about talking to me once in a while, about things that were bothering you?"

I shrug my shoulders. My mother looks stricken; her hand is actually clutching her left breast.

"I would come by the school and we could talk, say for twenty minutes or so. Maybe once a week. I use the nurse's office. Do you know where that is?"

My stomach turns over. "In the basement?"

"Yes."

"Do I have to be in a special class?"

"No. Of course not. We could meet say, Tuesdays, during the lunch period. I'll tell Mrs. Sirota."

My mother clears her throat. "He comes home for lunch."

"Each day?"

"Of course."

"Well, maybe just on Tuesdays . . ."

"*Liebe Gott.*" My mother is now clasping her entire chest.

"It would just be Tuesdays . . ."

"What does he do for lunch, then?"

"He could eat a school lunch, perhaps . . ."

"No!" My mother almost shouts her reply. "I make him a lunch, a sandwich."

Miss Warren's mouth purses, then opens and shuts silently, as if the sound has gone dead. Finally she says, "Well, you could certainly do that. Make him a sandwich. Right, Rob? That wouldn't be so bad. You could eat with your friends and then come to see me, or you could even eat in the nurse's office, as long as we didn't make a mess."

Tears stream down my mother's cheeks. Miss Warren doesn't acknowledge them. My mother wipes them away with the flat of her right hand, her handkerchief clutched in her left.

My father finally speaks.

"Nothing wrong with a sandwich," he says.

OUR Tuesday sessions last for about six weeks. I race past the special classes at lunch time, just as the retarded students are getting particularly restive, bellowing, kicking, slamming their hands on the wooden desks. The classes of polio victims, their legs encased in braces, are swinging themselves on crutches toward the lunchroom, step by pitiable step. I slip into the nurse's office and slam the door behind me, my heart pounding. Miss Warren invariably greets me in an effusive manner, then lowers the shade on the window of the door, "so we won't be interrupted."

We usually discuss how my day is progressing. She never asks me about my family in a direct manner, except to inquire as to their general state of health and happiness. She sticks to the party line about their level of culture and refinement, which I encourage by referring to their manner of coming to the United States, fleeing across stormy, editorial-cartoon seas, with an infuriated Hitler shaking his fist at them from the borders of the Third Reich. Miss Warren clucks her tongue at any mention of the Nazis, as if they were a particularly unruly child. She is simpleminded in the best sense, kindhearted and filled with good will. I have never met a less complicated person than she, my very first shrink, and the result is that on Tuesday mornings I arise from bed conspicuously lighter of heart.

"You're seeing that woman?" my mother unfailingly asks. "If you are I make a sandwich."

"Yes, it's Tuesday."

"It's every Tuesday, right?" my father asks from the breakfast table.

"Yes."

He turns to my mother. "So why do you ask like maybe he doesn't see her."

My mother takes a loaf of pumpernickel and a salami from the refrigerator. "I just want to know before I make the sandwich, that's all." But there is disappointment in her voice, that special regret which only I understand, like a dog responding to a high-frequency whistle. On Tuesdays she does not kiss me before my father silently walks me to school, always finding a rationale—the onset of a cold, a last-minute rush to the bathroom. This is something which I never tell Miss Warren; it is much too personal.

What I do finally tell her one Tuesday is of my fear of extermination in the basement of P.S. 19.

"My parents talk about the concentration camps a lot, even though they weren't in them themselves. And people, you know, were burned there. Burned alive sometimes. Put in ovens even though they weren't really dead yet. Really sick and weak, but not dead. I've seen pictures of the buildings and they had these big smokestacks like we have here . . ." Miss Warren listens raptly, her eyes as wide as if watching atrocity footage in a newsreel.

"So the building scares you."

"Yes."

"Who can blame you?" *Who can blame me?* This is not a crazy thought?

"So you know what I'm talking about?"

"The school reminds you of a Nazi camp."

"Not the teachers, not Mrs. Sirota."

"No, I understand. The actual building. The smokestacks, the furnace . . ." She is writing notes down in a spiral notebook.

"Well, here's the thing you should know, Robby. We all love you here and no one wants to hurt you. It's just a building and the furnace is so we can keep warm in the wintertime and the smokestack is to let all the soot out. Okay?"

"Yes." I would like to cry, but it seems like a shameful thing to want to do.

"People like your neighbors built this building sixty years ago. Not Nazis, regular Americans, all right?"

"Yes."

"And I know that Mr. Torvald who runs the furnace is a little bit scary-looking because he shaves his head, but he's really a very nice man who just wants all the students to be comfortable. So when you see the school, Rob, and when you think of the school, just try to imagine a happy place and try not to think of the Nazis and maybe I'll talk to your parents and tell them that these stories about Germany might be a little too much for you to handle right now. What do you think?"

I don't know what to say. I have never encountered such rationality before; never had a dialogue in which guilt and shame were not the governing passions.

"I guess so."

She smiles. "I think it's a good idea. I'm going to call your mom this afternoon."

THAT evening after supper I am lying on the floor of the living room reading a Little Lulu comic, while my sister does the dishes. My father is planted in his chair, listening to *The Flying Dutchman* on the radio and scanning the *World-Telegram*. My mother enters the room and seats herself on the couch, then begins to darn socks, using a wooden egg.

"So we scare you too much," she announces as if giving the final score of a ball game.

I look up from my comic book. My father turns to the next page of the *Telegram*, folding and refolding the paper.

"She says all the stories are too much. What we went through to get here." I just look at her. I am seven years old and I have no arguments to counter with. I don't actually know what an "argument" is. "That it's too much for a boy to handle, what we all went through." She says all this to an argyle sock. "I said, of course, I didn't realize that, or else I wouldn't have said anything. I'm not a psychologist, just a mother, just a person who lost half her family to the Nazis. I try to do better next time, I told her, I try not to frighten you. You can tell me about these things, you know, not just her."

"It came out when we were talking."

"I'm a person also you can talk to. I'm your mother."

"Yes."

"What does she know about the Nazis, what we went through. An *Amerikanner*. You think she lost family?"

"No."

"So she can't know this. I'm sure she's a very decent person, but how can she talk to you about this? Herbert."

My father is refilling his pipe. "They just talk about all kinds of things." He looks at me. "Is that right, Rob? You sit in a room and talk?"

"Yeah. All kinds of things."

"So," he says, lighting his pipe and returning to his newspaper.

My mother finishes the first of many socks. "I tell her I do what I can. I try to be better."

When I see Miss Warren the next time, I ask her if she spoke with my mother.

"Didn't she say anything?" she asks.

I hesitate. I suddenly don't know why I have lied about this, or why I brought it up at all.

"Yes."

"What did she say?"

"I don't remember."

"You don't?"

"Not really."

"Did she seem like she thought it was a good talk, or did she seem upset about it?"

"No."

"No, not upset?"

"I don't remember."

Miss Warren smiles, runs a hand through her hair.

"All right . . . Well, I thought we had a nice talk. She certainly sounds as if she's led a difficult life and we have to take that into account, how hard it's been. You certainly have to admire people who overcome so much adversity and still manage to raise their children and live a normal life."

I just nod, beginning to feel a little nauseous. The salami is turning foul in my stomach. I sense that I have been abandoned, that my mother has somehow managed to regain control.

Miss Warren folds her hands before her. "Is there something you want to tell me, Rob?" Yes, I want to tell her to stay on my side, to tell me again and again that the teachers love me and that my fears are imaginary and that this building, this school, is a place that I belong to, an American place that is as much mine as anybody else's. I do not know how to put these feelings into words. All I can do is shrug.

"You look disappointed. Tell me what's on your mind."

The churning in my stomach grows more ominous. It is a sensation I know as well as the onset of a sneeze. I point to my mouth, get up from the chair and run from the room. The hall is now crowded with mongoloids being herded back into class, bellowing like cattle. Sick and terrified, I run past them into the boys' room, where I vomit copiously into the sink. My head is spinning. I drop to my knees beside the sink and spot Mr. Torvald turning from the long stone trough that serves as a urinal, zipping the fly of his work pants. His bald head is lustrous beneath the ceiling fixture as he gazes toward the odious sink.

"Whassa matter?" he mutters in barely decipherable English. "Too fancy usa toilet?" As brutish as Frank Norris's homicidal dentist McTeague, he lumbers toward me. "Li'l kike," I believe he says as I scoot, still dizzy and sweating, back into the hall. Miss Warren is walking toward me, her arms outstretched. I run toward her and she picks me up in one easy motion. I begin to cry as if my life were about to end.

"That's okay," she whispers. "You'll get over this. I promise."

TWO weeks later, the Board of Ed transfers Miss Warren to Staten Island and I never see her again.

* * *

Rebecca Rosengarten and I are married on April 6, 1991. The ceremony is held at the Carlyle Hotel before approximately fifty guests, most of them from Rebecca's side: her mother Betty, her younger sister Ellen, various aunts and uncles, all of them prosperous and well-groomed people. My sister and her husband Sidney fly in from the coast for the affair, Uncle Kurt and his wife Gail have come up from Palm Beach and my aunt Hilde treats herself to a cab in from Queens. I have invited Harvey Rosen from the history department, as well as Dr. Singer, with whom I have terminated my treatment two weeks before. Among my reasons for terminating is that I wish him to be at my wedding and he feels he cannot attend if he is still treating me.

"I feel ready to end this anyhow," I tell him on a wet January morning.

"Yes."

"I'm forty-six years old. Enough is enough."

"Enough is a relative term."

"I want to terminate before you do. I don't want be abandoned."

"Like Miss Warren from Child Guidance abandoned you."

"That's right."

"I won't be transferred to Staten Island."

"You might die on me. You're not getting any younger. You look lousy. Of course, you've always looked lousy."

"I can't argue with that." Such jocularity. We must be getting close to the end.

"So you'll come?"

"If we've terminated. I don't feel it's appropriate if the treatment is continuing."

"But you feel termination is possible?"

"Yes."

For the remaining twenty-five minutes of the session, I lie mute on his couch. The prospect of ending a dialogue that has sustained me for over twenty years is so daunting it cannot be articulated, only felt as a kind of ache, a kind of homesickness.

I am unable to sleep that night. Rebecca stays up with me.

"It's absolutely for the best, Rob."

"I'm sure it is, but am I trading one dependency for another?"

"You mean getting married?"

"Yeah."

"It's interdependency, if it's any good. At least, that's the hope, right?"

All I can do is sigh. She wraps her slender arm around my chest.

"Getting married is a good idea," she says. "Stopping treatment is a good idea. Better than good, healthy. Onward. I stopped. I got what I could from it and then I stopped."

"And you survived."

"Here I am." She snuggles closer. "I feel great. You don't need it anymore, I'm telling you."

"Five days a week for twenty years."

"You'll have me seven days a week."

"You're not a shrink."

"You want me to be?"

"No."

"So there we are. You don't need it. Take off the training wheels."

"I'm forty-six."

"So what."

"What do you want with a forty-six-year-old infant?"

"You're not an infant. You know you're not an infant."

"I'm carrying on. You know I like to carry on."

"You want reassurance. I'm giving it to you. You're fine. You're great."

"I'm not great."

"Okay. You're as close to great as one can be without actually being great."

"Okay."

"You'll accept that?"

"For now."

There is the sound of tires stopping short and then a bang of colliding metal and the smash of glass.

"Bingo. The nightly mishap." Doors are opened, angry Spanish words are shouted. Rebecca runs her finger across my lips, gently kisses my eyes, then pulls me toward her. "Stop thinking. Live a little."

At four in the morning I am still awake. Rebecca is unconscious beside me, framed by hair and blanket, precisely and gravely beautiful in sleep. She does not seem to be an inanimate stranger, lost to me until morning. No, she is mine, intensely familiar, a friend to my heart. My wife.

M Y last session with Dr. Singer is a curious and anticlimactic affair; it has the feeling of an unsuccessful retirement party. Is it possible that we have run out of things to say?

"I would have thought that at least you'd spring for a bottle of champagne, considering the fortune I've dropped here."

"We'll have the champagne at your wedding."

"That's pretty lame."

Silence.

"At the final session, I expect a steady line of chatter from you, doc. Continual and relevant observations." Of course, he says nothing. I stare at at my hands, folded across my stomach. "Did I ever talk about my father's retirement party? I can't remember if I ever did."

"You never brought it up."

"You can remember twenty years of these half-assed stories?"

"Yes."

"All of them?"

"I take notes"

"And I never told you about my father's retirement party?"

"No."

"What if I get to the middle of it and we run out of time?"

"Is it a very long story?"

"I don't know yet." I check my watch. "I do have thirty-sixty minutes left."

"So there'll probably be enough time."

"Is there somebody coming in after me? What if I run a couple of minutes over?"

"There is someone at four."

"The Chinese girl? Didn't she have the baby yet? Maybe she went into labor today. You'd have more time."

Silence.

"Don't go silent on me. Come on. Promise me you'll give me an extra minute."

Nothing.

"I don't want this to end, do I? That's a staggering insight. Holy shit."

Dr. Singer clears his throat. "Worse comes to worse, we could schedule one more session."

" 'Worse comes to worse'? What the fuck does that mean, 'worse comes to worse'? If I run out of time with one remaining epiphany left undelivered?"

"It just means that conceivably an additional session could be scheduled."

He starts coughing.

Enough.

Enough. Enough with this office, with these dull, second-rate woodcuts and photographs, the threadbare couch, the pawed-over Smithsonian magazines in the dingy waiting area. Enough already.

"No. This is it. I schedule one more session, I'll want twelve more. You're like a fucking crack dealer. You're insidious."

"Yes," Dr. Singer says. "This is the last session. The last."

I sigh, hugely. Tons of air escape from my lungs. I rest, close my eyes.

"Okay. His retirement party was sort of like this session: a major non-event. It was at his office, at Chronicle, on Madison Avenue and Fifty-sixth Street, and we talked about it at home for weeks and weeks, talked about it in such terms that you would have thought he was being knighted by the Queen of England: the honors that would be bestowed upon him, the speeches, the delicacies that all the hotels he'd written up were going to contribute. The expectations were enormous, like my expectations about this session." I breathe deeply, run my hands, simianlike, across my face.

"So I put on my best suit—this is 1973, and I'm already at Columbia, an assistant professor. My sister is in the last throes of her divorce from Stanley Warshauer and has taken the kids to California to be with Sidney the agent, so she's a no-show. My father's a little hurt by that, I think. My mother is relieved because when my sister's around, no one looks at anything else, and Chronicle, except for the secretaries, is an all-male enterprise. I meet my parents in the Oak Room of the Plaza for a drink before the party—my idea, my treat—and my father is *extremely* nervous. They've never been in the Oak Room and they're very impressed, although my mother is concerned with the expense, and the bill for three drinks, even then, is like twenty dollars. My father can't make anything resembling eye contact; he looks like someone on Death Row and even a scotch and water doesn't help. We sit around checking our watches for about a half-hour, then decide it's the appropriate time to make our entrance at the party. He's usually a little frantic about time, my father, but this evening it seems irrelevant to him."

"He didn't really want to go."

"Perhaps. Perhaps he knew what was coming, or what wasn't coming.

"He was afraid it wouldn't be what you had all talked about."

"Whatever. So we leave the Plaza and walk slowly over to Chronicle, three blocks away, and I don't know what I expected would happen when we walked through the door, but I thought it would be something much more momentous . . ."

"More celebratory?"

"I thought there would be an explosion of sound when my father entered the room."

"And there wasn't."

"There wasn't. There were a couple of dozen men and women standing around, looking like they were anxious to get home, because to them this was just another working day. There was a table laid out with cold cuts and bottles of liquor and some sort of generic champagne. We walked in and he was greeted, you know, warmly, by the old hands, Bob Larsen and Tom Harris and Jerry Zeitlin, and Mr. Stein kissed my mother and shook my hand and said this was a sad day, an inevitable day but still a sad one. Then the younger blood in the company, these guys who looked so incredibly bland and yet somehow *evil* to me—Jack Murphy, Dan Cohn, Phil Abrams—they sort of sidled up to my father and congratulated him. My mother looked at these younger men as if they were members of a different species. My father introduced them to her, but she didn't seem to comprehend who they were. A few of them struck up conversations with me, but their eyes turned glassy when I told them I taught history at Columbia. I felt totally out of place. There was about a half-hour of milling about and chitchat, reminiscences about past deadlines and disasters—my father getting lost on his way to the Loch Sheldrake Arms back in 1950, Bob Larsen mistaking Paul Grossinger for some caterer—none of them terribly hilarious or dramatic. Finally Mr. Charles Stein tapped his champagne glass and gave his tribute to my father."

"What did he say?"

"He spoke about my father's reliability, how you could set your watch by his arrival and departure each day; he spoke of my father's heroism in leaving Germany and starting a new life here during the Depression, how difficult it must have been. I noticed some of the younger guys eyeing their watches and shifting their feet. One of the secretaries actually left. My mother started biting her nails, which she only did when highly stressed. Mr. Stein said how much he was going to miss 'Herb,' how Chronicle would never seem the same without 'Herb's grace and civility,' those were the exact words, I remember. Then he opened this box and handed my father an Omega watch with his name inscribed on the back and the words 'Chronicle Publications, 1948–1973.' Then there was some applause that sort of swelled and then abruptly ended, and that was that. That was the whole thing. People started leaving. They shook my father's hand, got their coats and began streaming out of the office."

"Your father said nothing?"

"Not much. He thanked everybody, thanked Mr. Stein, said how glad he was that his family could be there, said that Chronicle had always been a 'dignified operation,' I think those were his words, and said how he would always miss the whole gang of them, and then he said he would come by from time to time just to make sure that the writers were using 'fewer' instead of 'less.' That was his pet editorial peeve, that people were always screwing that up. Then we went home. I don't think the whole affair lasted an hour. Maybe fifty minutes. Just like this session."

"Interesting symmetry."

"Isn't it. Twenty-five years he'd been there and you just had such a sense of his utter dispensability, how the next day it would seem that he'd never been there."

"Are you afraid that's how your treatment will seem to me? That starting tomorrow, it'll be as if you'd never been here?"

I turn around and face him. Dr. Singer is seated, as ever, behind his bare desk, with that dopey Bon Marché lamp screwed onto the side. He has what I take to be a melancholy smile on his face and I am overcome with the thought that he'll miss me terribly. We just stare at each other for a long moment; we have gone through so much together, so much of my daily life has been entrusted to him. My life over the past decades is literally unimaginable without him and I realize that his life is likewise entwined with mine. I am past all words. I get up off the couch and throw my arms around him and just cling to him for my remaining six and one-half minutes of allotted time. My head is on his shoulder and tears are coursing down my cheeks. Finally I hear that mellow baritone say, "Well, we're out of time today," and when I pull away I observe that his blue eyes are gleaming and his lower lip is quivering.

1992 / (1949)

Hᴵˢ name is Richard Herbert Weisglass and he is born on November 11, 1992. Armistice Day. He is seven pounds two ounces in weight and twenty inches in length and his arrival occurs after approximately twelve hours of labor at Roosevelt Hospital. I have not been inside a hospital since Libby's death, but I feel no dread walking through Roosevelt's ancient, grimy corridors, only the harmonious glow of creation. My wife produces our son with the proud, soft force of someone born to do this very thing; she has never looked more beautiful then in the moments just after birth, when Richard has been cleaned off and placed in her arms. Even our obstetrician, the dour and sallow Dr. Hirsch, can't help but stare at my lovely wife.

"He looks like a cantaloupe," Rebecca says with some finality.

I dry my teary eyes on the green surgical robe Roosevelt has furnished me. I look nothing like a doctor.

"But he's our cantaloupe," she concludes.

I take many photographs and Rebecca never once looks at the camera. She cannot take her eyes off Richard.

"Look at these eyelashes. What a killer. Hi, sweetie," she coos to him. "Enjoy the trip? You're in Roosevelt Hospital on beautiful Ninth Avenue and your father is taking pictures and that man over there is Dr. Hirsch, who delivered you. Can you remember that? Hirsch? H-i-r-s-c-h."

"He's a gorgeous baby," says Dr. Hirsch.

"You must say that to everybody," Rebecca tells him.

"I do. But this one is really gorgeous. Could be a C-section, that's how lovely he came out. You did a fantastic job, Rebecca."

"He says I did a fantastic job," she tells Richard, kissing his tiny, smooth, sweet-smelling forehead. "So one day when you're really pissed at me I hope you'll remember that." She nuzzles him. "What a great kid you are. I can tell already. You're good-natured, you have a great sense of humor, you're a good dancer."

I finally put my camera down and sit gingerly down on the edge of the bed.

"Here," Rebecca says and hands me my son. Finally. Seven pounds of fate. His eyes are shut tight and his fingers are balled together. He has my father's firm chin and everything else looks to be pure Rebecca. God only knows what first impressions are being recorded in that tiny brain, what colors, what sounds, what degrees of light and dark. The tape is rolling; it is all beginning. Seven pounds of pure feeling.

"RichardRichardRichard." I kiss his lips. "I will protect you forever." His fragrance is overwhelming, the sweet dank musk of birth. I started out like this; it is true but does not seem possible. Did my parents feel these same emotions? And if they did, how could they have caused such chaos, how could they have stormed over my person as if I were some barren field? There is a sudden rage in my gut. I gently sink my face into the folds of his smooth wet neck—odors of the birth canal, the tidal pool of our ancestors. He is mine; bury the past. Impossible? Richard; RichardRichardRichard.

"Rob?"

I look up.

"We're us. It'll be different. Screw the past."

She holds out her arms. I hand her the baby and then myself. I lie down beside them. Them. In an instant, we are a family. My arms around Rebecca, her arms around Richard.

"We'll protect each other," one of us says.

WHEN I leave the hospital, it is raining. I cannot feel the rain, although I know I am getting wet. By the time I reach my apartment building, I am soaking wet. The doorman gives me a baffled, slightly alarmed look, but when I tell him that I have become a father, he embraces me with considerable feeling. He disappears behind a door and then follows me to the elevator, holding a bottle of overproof rum and two paper cups. One sip of the rum and my legs wobble. The doorman smiles, waves, blows a somewhat drunken kiss as the doors close.

My apartment seems to almost ache with expectation. Finally, an actual family to replace the ghosts who have roamed its four and a half rooms for the past decade. I sit in a chair and stare at the London Economist. My mind spins and then I fall asleep. I dream the following:

Rockaway Beach, April 1949. A bright and windy Sunday morning, with early spring suggestions of heat. My mother, Aunt Bertha and Carol are off in the distance gathering shells; my father is alone with me. A fishing boat bobs a half-mile out to sea. We stop, my father and I, to watch the boat.

"Pick me up," I ask him.

He reaches down and lifts me in the air, nuzzles my face against his. His cheek is cool and scratchy, the wind lifts his hair. He begins to kiss me, again and again.

"My boy," he whispers to my enchanted ear, "my boy."